Dirt

Other Large Print Books
by Stuart Woods

Choke
Imperfect Strangers

Stuart Woods

DIRT

WHEELER
PUBLISHING, INC.
ROCKLAND, MA

★ AN AMERICAN COMPANY ★

Published in Large Print by arrangement with
HarperCollins Publishers, Inc.
in the United States and Canada.

Wheeler Large Print Book Series.

Set in 16 pt. Plantin.

Library of Congress Cataloging-in-Publication Data

Woods, Stuart
    Dirt / Stuart Woods
        p. (large print) cm. — (Wheeler large print book series)
    ISBN 1-56895-398-4 (hardcover)
    1. Private investigators—New York (State)—New York—Fiction.
2. Gossip columnists—Fiction. 3. New York (State)—New York—Fiction
4. Large type books. I. Title. II. Series
[PS3573.O642D57 1996b]
813'.54—dc21   96-50224
                                                                      CIP

This book is for David and Lynn Kaufelt

Acknowledgements

I would like to express my gratitude to every gossip columnist in the business, for giving me such good material.

I am also grateful to my editor, HarperCollins Vice President and Associate Publisher Justin Carr, and her staff, for all their hard work; and to my agent, Morton Janklow, his principal associate, Anne Sibbald, and all the people and Janklow and Nesbit for their careful attention to my career over the years.

Chapter 1

Dinner had been wonderful—twelve around a gleaming oval table of burled walnut in a dining room a dozen stories above the light-flecked carpet of Central Park, the cooking by the chef of a famous restaurant a few blocks away, the wines from the host's superb cellar, and the company carefully chosen by a couple who could cast a wide net. Amanda Dart felt quite at home among them.

As they moved from the table into the library next door for coffee and brandy, Amanda reflected that her presence there was as much a tribute to her position as to her personality, though she could certainly hold her own in any company. Of those present—a movie star and his gorgeous companion, a captain of industry and his dowdy wife, and a former British prime minister, her dinner partner, among them—Amanda alone possessed the power to tell the world just who her hosts had attracted to their table, something the couple wanted very badly for the world to know. It was vulgar to drop names; Amanda Dart, queen of gossip columnists, would do the dropping for them.

Lord Wight, the former prime minister, was taking a keen interest in Amanda, attention that, on another night, would have been a great deal more interesting for her. Tonight, however, she had other plans, other company in mind, and the thought made for a weak feeling in her crotch.

1

"I chose my title from the island of my birth," Lord Wight was saying.

"Oh, yes, the Isle of Wight," Amanda said, returning his serve. "I believe the town of Cowes there is the capital of British yachting." Point made.

"The capital of *European* yachting," his lordship replied.

"And that's where you sail your little yacht?"

"Actually, it's quite a large yacht," Wight replied testily. "And I don't just sail it, I *race* it."

"Tell me, Lord Wight," Amanda asked innocently, "just how does someone amass enough of a fortune to buy a *large* yacht during a lifetime of public service?"

"Fortunately, my dear lady," Wight said, smiling softly, "in my country the amassing of a fortune is not incompatible with a life in politics. One acquires knowledgeable friends who advise one on how to invest one's money."

Amanda winked at him. "One understands," she said.

Her hostess joined them. "Amanda, dear," she said, "you made me promise to tell you when it was midnight, and it is. You're catching a plane?"

"To St. Bart's," Amanda said, moving forward in her seat in preparation for standing.

"Surely there's no plane out of Kennedy at this hour," Wight said, consulting a gold watch from his waistcoat pocket. "They do have noise regulations, don't they?"

"Not at Teterboro," Amanda replied. "One is fortunate enough to have friends with jets." She stood up, bringing Lord Wight with her.

"My dear," he was saying, "I do hope I can see you when I'm next in New York."

"Of course, Lord Wight," Amanda replied, fishing in her little clutch purse for a card. "I would be delighted to hear from you." *Any night but tonight,* she thought.

She made her goodbyes, collected her coat from the butler, and slipped out of the huge apartment.

Downstairs, her trusty driver, Paul, and her elderly Cadillac were waiting. Amanda slipped into the back seat, and in a moment they were moving. "The Trent, Paul," she said.

"Yes, ma'am," Paul replied.

It was Amanda's fiftieth birthday, though no one knew it; she was in spectacular shape, her firm body the product of a regular program with a trainer in her own little gym. Amanda allowed no other person to see her perspire. She placed two fingers on her carotid artery and glanced at her watch. Her resting pulse was normally forty-five; tonight, it was seventy.

Amanda lived her life in very public view, and she took great care in how she presented herself to her world. Although of a deeply sensual nature, she was known as something of an ice queen, and she was quite happy to keep it that way. Her sexual alliances were few, but athletically maintained, with men who were always wealthy, off her beaten track, very discreet, and usually younger than she. Tonight and for the weekend, she would see her very favorite, a real estate developer from Atlanta named Henry Bell, who made it to New York no more than once every eight or nine months. Perfect for Amanda.

Henry was a pillar of Atlanta society, the husband of a retired opera singer and the father of two daughters whose social ambitions were relentless. Amanda had helped them meet tout Gotham while, unbeknownst to them or anyone else, she had established a highly erotic relationship with their father, who was a youthful forty-five. This weekend he was in New York, ostensibly for a board meeting, and he was waiting for her at the Trent, a small, elegant hotel in the East Sixties. They planned to be together until early Monday morning.

The car glided to a halt at the Trent's discreet entrance. Amanda looked up and down the block before she got out; she had no wish to run into anyone she knew. "No need to get the door, Paul. Please meet me here after midnight on Sunday—say, two a.m."

"Two o'clock Monday morning," Paul said.

Satisfied that the block was empty of pedestrians, she slid out of the car and ran across the sidewalk, slipping on a pair of dark glasses. She paused for a moment in the foyer of the hotel and glanced across the little lobby at the front desk, where a man in a tailcoat was working. She waited until he turned away, then scooted across the lobby, unspotted, to the alcove where the elevator was. She pressed "P" for penthouse and waited while the car traveled upward for fifteen floors. When the door opened, she popped her head out to check that the hallway was empty, then walked out of the elevator and to the end of the hall, stopping before double doors.

Glancing around once more to be sure she was

alone, she stepped out of her shoes, then slipped off her panties. She was not wearing a bra under the little black dress. She took off her coat and unzipped her dress. Then, holding her coat, shoes, and panties in her hand, she rang the bell. Seconds later the door opened, and she stepped inside.

Henry Bell stepped back to allow her to enter. He was wearing a silk dressing gown. He said nothing, but untied the belt and whipped it off, presenting a trim physique and a throbbing erection. Amanda dropped her belongings on the floor, wiggled her shoulders, and let the little dress fall off, revealing full breasts and a finely crafted body. She kicked the dress out of the way and stood there, wearing only black stockings and a black garter belt.

"Hello, sailor," she said, and went to him.

Late Sunday evening, they sat propped up in bed, naked, next to the remains of a room service dinner on a tray. Henry dozed lightly while Amanda watched yet another of his endless collection of erotic Scandinavian videotapes. Henry had a little man in Stockholm who sent them to the Trent whenever he was in New York. Amanda loved them.

This one was particularly intriguing, she thought, glancing at Henry. Poor baby, she had given him a real workout for the whole weekend. He deserved his rest; still....She reached for his penis and began kneading it gently. A small smile appeared on his sleeping face.

"We've just time for one more round, sweetie," she said.

Henry didn't open his eyes. "If I can," he whimpered.

Amanda rearranged herself slightly, then bent over and took his penis into her mouth. Henry gave a little groan and began to respond.

At that moment, the doors to the suite's bedroom burst open with a bang, and the room was filled with light.

"Over here, Amanda!" a man's voice shouted as a flashbulb went off.

Amanda sat straight up in bed, her mouth open, her eyes wide. Her left hand still rested on Henry's penis. "What?!" she screamed. There were all sorts of lights, those that flashed and those that burned steadily.

"Get out!" Amanda screamed, shaking a fist at the lights.

Henry sat frozen, dumbfounded.

"Just one more, Amanda!" the man's voice shouted.

Amanda picked up a heavy clock from the bedside table and threw it at the light as Henry suddenly came to life. He started toward the intruders, but the bedroom doors were slammed in his face. He threw his shoulder against them, then howled in pain.

Amanda did what she most wanted to do in the world: she screamed.

An hour later, fully dressed but still trembling, Amanda fled the hotel, got into the back of the Cadillac, and was driven home. She looked over her shoulder but saw no witness to her leaving. She was in control again, and she had begun to assess the damage. It promised to be considerable.

Chapter 2

Amanda walked into the office suite of her penthouse, dressed in her standard uniform of Chanel suit, Ferragamo shoes, plain gold jewelry, and a gold Cartier Panther wristwatch and bracelet.

Her staff of three, at their desks five minutes before her always precise nine o'clock arrival, leapt to their feet as one, welcoming her back and complimenting her on how tanned and rested she looked. She shook each of their hands, received their compliments, and sent them back to their desks, save her secretary, the trusty Martha, who had been with her for her entire career as a columnist.

"Ready for your messages?" Martha asked, holding up a batch of yellow slips.

"Not yet," Amanda replied, slipping behind her little French desk. She loved the desk. Sister Parrish, the doyen of New York interior designers, had found it especially for her when she had done the apartment a few years before her death. "Before I do anything else, get me Bill Eggers at Woodman and Weld. He should already be at his desk."

Martha returned to her desk, and a moment later the green light on Amanda's phone flashed; her party was on the line, waiting. Amanda did not converse with other people's secretaries.

"Bill," she breathed into the phone. "How are you, darling?"

"I'm wonderful, Amanda," the lawyer replied. "How was your holiday?"

"Just perfect. I'm fully rested and raring to go.

What was Hickock's reaction to our latest contract proposal?"

"I called him on Friday, but he's putting me off," Eggers replied. "He says somebody in the legal department is on vacation, but to tell you the truth, I think he's just not giving it his full attention. After all, he's got another two months and three weeks before your contract expires. He's used to negotiating with the print unions right up to and past deadlines."

Amanda frowned, then forced her facial muscles to relax. Having recently had some lines surgically removed, she didn't want new ones cropping up. "He's not going to have that luxury," she said.

"You want me to call him again?"

Amanda though for a moment. "No," she replied. "Meet me in the lobby of the Galaxy Building at precisely ten minutes past one this afternoon."

"Do you already have an appointment?"

"No, but he'll see me."

"If you say so, Amanda, but listen, I have to give you my best advice on this before you do anything rash; that's my responsibility."

Amanda sighed. "Go ahead, Bill."

"Okay, you're in a good negotiating position; your readership is slightly up in the home paper, and well up in syndication. You're not overpaid, at the moment, and what we're asking for is not out of line with the numbers involved. However, it's almost never good to appear eager when you're dealing with Dick Hickock; he'll have you for breakfast, if he thinks he has any sort of edge. My advice is to wait, not even call him, just wait for his call. He knows exactly when your contract is up, and he won't ignore the deadline and risk losing you to another paper. Sit tight, and you'll get most of what you want. There, I've said it; what do you want to do?"

"Precisely ten past one, at the Galaxy Building."

"See you there."

Amanda hung up and began doing something she had forced herself to put off: She went through the New York and L.A. papers quickly, looking for any reference to the incident of the night before. As she had suspected, there was nothing. Every paper had closed well before the photographs were taken at the hotel, and nobody would have been fool enough to print the story without substantiation. She breathed a heavy sigh of relief; she had until early evening, when the show biz news programs came on, after the evening news.

Amanda got up, walked to the door, and leaned against the jamb, looking out into the open bay where her secretary and two assistants sat. Of the three, only Martha had known where she had spent the past weekend, and nobody, but nobody, could torture the information out of that woman. While the others hadn't known, they might have somehow picked up something around the office. Still, each of them was well paid and, apparently, happy in his or her work. One, Helen, was a young woman of thirty who had been with her for three years; the other, Barry, was a gay man who had been with her for eight. There was not a naive bone in Amanda's body, but her best judgment told her that the news had been leaked from some-where else, most likely from her lover's end, al-though he had denied any such thing. Most likely his wife had put a detective on them, but that re-mained to be seen.

"All right, Martha," Amanda said, "let's go through the messages."

At nine minutes past one the elderly Cadillac glided up to the main entrance of the Galaxy Building, and Amanda stepped out; Bill Eggers was waiting in the lobby. It was lunch time, and the two were alone together in the elevator.

"Amanda, won't he be at lunch at this hour?" Eggers asked.

"Dick Hickock always has lunch at his desk on Mondays," she replied. "Always."

"Are you sure he'll see you?"

"He won't have a choice," Amanda said.

"Jesus," the lawyer said under his breath.

They stepped out on the thirtieth floor, into a paneled and hushed hallway. The receptionist's desk was empty; a sign on the desk said, THIS FLOOR IS CLOSED UNTIL 3:00 P.M. FOR ASSISTANCE, PLEASE GO TO THE MAIN RECEPTION DESK ON THE TENTH FLOOR. "Follow me," Amanda said. She strode down the hall, her footsteps silenced by the thick carpeting, through a double door marked "Chairman," across a reception room, and into the office of Richard M. Hickock, chairman of the board of Galaxy Media. Dick Hickock sat at his desk in his shirtsleeves, his necktie undone, the *Wall Street Journal* open before him, eating a huge sandwich.

"Hello, Dick, darling!" Amanda enthused, walking behind the desk and planting a kiss on his cheek, leaving a smear of cerise.

Hickock had just taken a large bite out of his sandwich, and he struggled to get it chewed and swallowed so that he could speak. By the time he had, Amanda and her lawyer were seated in a pair of chairs to his right.

"You know Bill Eggers, don't you?" Amanda asked.

Hickock nodded and washed down food with a glass of beer.

"Amanda, what the hell..." he began.

"I do apologize for interrupting your lunch, Dick," Amanda said contritely, "but I hope you will understand that this just won't wait."

"Amanda," Hickock said, shaking his head in disbelief, "there's a thirty-eight in my desk drawer, and I would have used it on *anybody* who walked in here like that." He smiled benevolently. "Anybody but you. Now what can I do for you?" He nodded at the sandwich. "My Milton Berle is waiting."

"What's in a Milton Berle, Dick?" Amanda asked, apparently fascinated.

"Corned beef and chopped liver with Russian dressing on pumpernickel, and this." He held up a huge pickle. "The reference to Berle," he said, grinning.

Amanda blushed. "Oh, Dick! You are awful!"

"It's true," Hickock said to Eggers. "I am awful."

"It's about our contract proposal," Amanda said without further ado.

"Amanda, your contract has another three months to run," Hickock replied. "What's your rush?"

"Oh, it's not me, darling, it's SI Newhouse."

Hickock's face instantly became expressionless. "SI who?" he asked disingenuously, his eyes narrowing.

"Dick, it's been awful; I've spent the whole weekend fending him off. *Somehow,* he got my phone number, and he would *not* be put off."

"Don't listen to a word he says," Hickock said.

"Oh, I've tried not to—he's such an awful flatterer—but I must admit, when he started throwing numbers around...."

"That absolute shit," Hickock said, almost to himself.

"Oh, I don't want to go with SI, Dick; that's why I came to see you. He's practically forced me to have a drink with him later today—God knows, I don't want to alienate him—and I'm planning to tell him, as sweetly as I possibly can, to go away."

"Right, my dear," Hickock said, smiling. "That's exactly what you should do."

"But I can't, Dick darling, not with things just... *hanging* the way they are with my contract."

"Just say no, Amanda."

"Well, I can't very well do that, if I don't know for sure that I have a deal with you, can I? I mean, my God, I don't want to leave Galaxy, but when he's dangling all that money in front of me and all those *perks*...."

"Perks?" Hickock asked, looking alarmed.

"Oh, you know how lavish SI can be when he really wants somebody."

"Amanda, it's wrong of you to press me like this."

"Dick, my darling, *I'm* not pressing; I'm the soul of patience. SI, unfortunately, is not."

Hickock rummaged in his desk and came out with the contract proposal that Eggers had sent him. He put on his reading glasses and began leafing through it. "You really think you're worth this sort of money, Amanda?"

Eggers jumped in. "Her numbers support everything in that proposal," the lawyer said.

"You want five percent more of the syndication?"

"Syndication income is *way* up," Eggers said.

Hickock seemed to be collecting himself, Amanda thought.

"Tell you what, Amanda, my legal guy is back from vacation next Monday; we'll get back to you the end of next week, all right?"

Amanda stood up and smoothed her skirt. "Dick, my darling, I can't *tell* you how sad this makes me," she said, dabbing at the corner of an eye, where an actual tear had appeared. "I had *so* wanted it to work out. I want you to know that I have no hard feelings whatsoever." She turned and started toward the door, with Eggers at her heels, then stopped. "Oh, can you and Glynnis come to dinner on Friday? Just a small dinner, we'll only be eight, but it's a good crowd."

Hickock was on his feet. "Now, Amanda, come back and sit down."

Amanda and Eggers returned to their chairs. "I'm sitting, Dick," she said.

Hickock was reading the proposal again. "A

13

Mercedes *Six Hundred?* What's the matter with the Five Hundred? Or, come to that, with the Four-twenty? The Six Hundred is a hundred-and-thirty-seven-thousand-dollar car, for Christ's sake!"

"Oh, that's right, you drive one, don't you, Dick? Isn't it such a wonderful car? I mean, the Six Hundred has the burled walnut and the separate air conditioner for the back seat. You know how warm-natured I am."

"Amanda, be reasonable."

"Dick, I despise cheapness in a man, I really do."

"Oh, all right, you have a deal," Hickock said. "We'll sign something when my legal guy gets back."

Eggers instantly produced a small stack of documents. "I've prepared a deal memo," he said. "We'll work out the final language when your man gets home."

Hickock read the document quickly and signed all four copies. Amanda signed them, and Eggers left two with the publisher.

Amanda stood up. "I'm so *thrilled* that we're going to be together for another four years, darling," she said. She met him halfway around the desk, and they embraced. "And don't forget dinner, Friday, at seven." She turned to Eggers. "Can I give you a lift, Bill?" She took his arm and steered him toward the door. At the threshold she turned and looked at Hickock, who was gazing at his sandwich. "Oh, Dick, they have just the car I want at that Mercedes showroom on Park Avenue." She returned to the desk and laid a card on it. "The man said they could deliver it at five; all it takes is a phone call from you."

"We'll be trading your Cadillac, right?" Hickock asked.

"Oh, Dick, you *are* funny; I've already sold it." She swept out of the office.

In the car, Bill Eggers wiped his brow. "Amanda, I don't know why you need me at all," he said.

Amanda patted his hand. "Somebody has to do the boilerplate, dear."

Chapter 3

Richard Hickock left his office at four o'clock, stopping briefly at his secretary's desk. "Anybody calls, tell them I'm in the building somewhere for a meeting, you don't know where, and I won't be back at my desk by the end of the day."

"Yes, sir," the woman replied.

Hickock took his private elevator to the basement garage, where his white Mercedes S600 was waiting. "Ralph, I think I'll take a walk in the park," he said to his chauffeur.

"Of course, Mr. Hickock," the chauffeur replied. "You've been walking in the park a lot lately. Good for the heart."

"Right," Hickock said, taking one of his magazines, not his favorite, from the leather pocket on the back of the front seat. He leafed idly through it, making mental notes, one of them to fire the magazine's art director. He wasn't seeing enough

tits in the book these days, and the man had ignored his request for more.

Presently, the car stopped at an entrance to
Central Park on Fifth Avenue in the sixties.
Hickock opened his own door. "Hover around
here, and pick me up in an hour and ten minutes." He knew from experience exactly how long
this would take. The car pulled away; Hickock
crossed Fifth Avenue and walked briskly to an
elegantly restored townhouse apartment building,
using his key to open the downstairs door. As it
was about to close, a young man stepped into the
hallway behind him, holding what appeared to be
a sack of groceries.

"Thanks," the young man said. "I didn't have a
hand free to look for my key."

"Don't mention it," Hickock said, stepping into
the elevator. The young man followed him into
the car.

"Nice day out there," the young man said.

"Great time of the year." The elevator stopped
on the fourth floor, and Hickock got out. "See
you," he said.

"You bet," the young man replied.

The young man got off the elevator on the floor
above and walked down a flight, peeking over the
banister rail to see Hickock letting himself into
an apartment. He noted that there was only one
apartment on the floor, so he was unlikely to be
disturbed. He walked to the apartment door, set
his grocery bag on the floor, removed a loaf of
bread, and pulled out an electronic stethoscope.
He placed the receivers in his ears, switched it

on, and held the listening part against the apartment door.

Inside, Hickock was greeted by a very beautiful young woman wearing a silk dressing gown.

"Oh, Dick," she breathed, taking his face in her hands. "I've been so excited ever since you called."

Hickock kissed her lightly, then untied the gown's sash, exposing her naked body underneath. He caressed her large breasts and felt the nipples rise. "Then you must be ready for me," he said.

"Oh, yes," she sighed, taking him by the hand. "Come with me." She led him into the bedroom, kicked the door shut, and locked it.

"I don't know why you always lock the door," Hickock said, tearing at his clothes.

"I don't know either," she said, letting the dressing gown fall from her shoulders. "It just makes me feel more secure." She held out her arms to receive him, and they toppled onto the bed.

Outside in the hall, the young man with the stethoscope heard the bedroom door lock engage. He moved along the hall toward the bedroom wall and placed the stethoscope there. When he was certain that the couple were erotically engaged, he went back to the door, removed what appeared to be a small manicure kit from a pocket, took out two small tools, and began to work on the front door lock. In half a minute he was inside the apartment with his grocery bag. He removed a leather tool box from the bag and went to work.

In the bedroom, Hickock lay on his back, breathing deeply as he recovered from his orgasm. She went into the bathroom, came back with a hot face cloth, and began to wipe his penis. Hickock made a little noise.

"Oh," she said, "I believe there's something still there."

This was the part Hickock liked best; while he had been essentially impotent with his wife for years, this girl could always get him going for a second round. "Use your mouth," he whimpered.

"Why, of course," the girl replied.

The young man listened at the bedroom door with his stethoscope, smiling. He'd better get out, he thought; Hickock would be finished in another few seconds. He picked up his grocery bag, let himself out of the apartment, and walked down the stairs to the basement, checking carefully on each floor that he was still alone. In the basement he found the building's central telephone box and went to work. Half an hour later he let himself out of the building and walked off down the street.

Hickock looked both ways on Fifth Avenue for his car. Not seeing it, he crossed the street, walked a few feet into the park, and waited. A couple of minutes later he saw the white Mercedes turn a corner onto Fifth Avenue. He stepped out of the park, went to the curb, flagged down the car, and got in. "Let's go home, Ralph," he said.

"Enjoy your walk in the park, sir?"

"Oh, yes," he replied. "It always refreshes me."

Chapter 4

Amanda swept into her office suite, wearing a smile that telegraphed good news to her staff. She waved Martha into her office and pushed aside the stack of items Helen and Barry had assembled for tomorrow's column.

"It must have gone well," Martha said, taking a seat and getting her pad ready.

"It went extremely well, my dear," Amanda replied. "So well that there's a ten percent raise for you when the new contract begins."

"Oh, thank you, Amanda," Martha gushed.

"And tell the others that there'll be another five percent in their pay packets on the day."

"They'll be delighted."

"Oh, tell Paul to sell the Cadillac, and he can keep ten percent of what he gets for it; I don't want to see it again." She handed Martha the car salesman's card. "Call this gentleman and tell him I'll want the new Mercedes delivered no later than four-thirty, and tell him to get the car phone number changed over. Call a music store and get a dozen CDs delivered for the new car's stereo—you know the kind of thing I like—at least two Bobby Shorts and some Michael Feinstein and some chamber music. Give them to Paul so the salesman can show him how the CD player works. Make sure the salesman gets my vanity plates changed over, too."

"Right." Martha was making notes. "I'll deal with the insurance; what value do you want to put on it?"

"A hundred and thirty-seven thousand dollars."

Martha's eyes widened. "Hickock sprang for the Six Hundred?"

"Of course he did. You'd better let the garage man know about the change; the doorman, too. Let's not have any glitches."

"It shall be done," Martha said, rising. "You ready for lunch?"

"I'll have a salad, then send Helen and Barry in, and we'll get started."

Martha disappeared, still writing on her pad.

Amanda still had the sick feeling in her stomach that had begun the night before, but her elation over the new contract and the Mercedes helped to drive it away. She felt very much better now.

When the salad dish had been taken away, Helen and Barry shuffled into the office and took seats.

"Anything really good?" Amanda asked, starting to leaf through the stack of items, each on a page to itself. They would need twenty-five to thirty for tomorrow's column.

"Three high-profile pregnancies that together might make a good lead," Barry said. "They're on top."

"Good; I like to start with good news," Amanda replied. She held up a page and frowned. "Ivana Trump is buying a yacht? Why would anyone care?" She crushed the page in her long fingers and tossed it into a wastebasket. Her people knew she had little time for the Trumps.

"I got a call," Helen said. "The *Infiltrator* is starting in again on Michael Andress; this time they've got a waiter from some drive-in restaurant in Long Beach who says they've been sleeping together for three years."

"The boy's straight as an arrow," Barry said. "I have it on good authority, and anyway, I can always tell. How many children does he have to father before they leave him alone?"

"And his wife is one of the pregnancies on the list," Helen said.

"Good chance to stick it to the *Infiltrator*," Amanda mused, marking the item. "Say something about the unjust pursuit of the boy; you know how it should go." She went rapidly through the stack of items, keeping some, tossing others out. "That's it, I think," she said, tossing the good ones onto the desk. "I'll have my lead for you in half an hour." She glanced at her watch.

Helen and Barry left, and Amanda turned to her computer to compose the paragraphs that would lead the column. She had planned to enthuse about St. Bart's and what a wonderful time she had had on her weekend, but the incident of the wee hours was still on her mind, and until she found out what it was all about, she would hedge her bets. She had been writing for ten minutes when she looked up and saw Martha standing at the door. She had turned pale, and she had a sheet of paper in her hand.

"Martha, what's wrong, dear?" she asked.

Martha approached the desk slowly and put the paper on the desk. "This just came in on the fax machine," she said.

A death, Amanda thought, but she was wrong. She picked up the sheet of paper and saw a photograph of herself, taken early that morning. The sheet was set up like the front page of a tabloid newspaper, and the lead story was:

DIRT

Greetings, earthlings! Look who we caught with her knickers down and her forked tongue erotically engaged in a love nest in a chic East Side hotel. None other than gossip's high bitch, Amanda Dart, who, after revealing others' peccadilloes for years, has revealed remarkable appetites of her own. She checked into the elegant hostelry last Friday night after having concocted an elaborate ruse to make the world at large (you and I) believe that she was lolling at the St. Bart's beachfront compound of the Duke of Kensington. (Write this down should you ever want to disappear for a couple of weeks.) Dear Amanda set up an answering machine to receive calls from those who were clever enough to get her holiday number, then she phoned the machine daily for her messages. When she returned her calls, she no doubt had a wave machine running in the background to lend verisimilitude. What a hoot!

Her companion in bed was a prominent out-of-towner whose wife will, no doubt, have a few questions to ask him on his return home. Certainly, after servicing the indefatigable Amanda for a whole weekend, he'll not have much energy left for the wronged lady in question.

Just how great are dear Amanda's appetites? Enough to last until late Sunday night, when we snapped the pics above. Will she ever show her neatly carved face in the Big Apple again? We should know tonight when she's promised to appear at a book party for her pal Norman Barton of the *Times* at Mortimer's, the East Side *boite,* where *tout le monde* of Gotham journalism will gather to honor dear Norm and get his scribble in their very own copy.

Will dear Amanda show? I certainly will! I wouldn't miss this one for a million-buck advance on my no-holds-barred bio of the delectable Dart!

Amanda put down the fax and looked at Martha. As she did, every phone in the office started ringing. Barry appeared, breathless, at the door. "Amanda, there's apparently some sort of fax being sent to half the town. Do you know anything about it?"

"Half the town?" Amanda asked, appalled.

"Apparently. We're hearing from every columnist in the city, and some from L.A. asking for a comment."

"Tell them to read tomorrow's column," she said. "Martha, will you excuse me for a few minutes? I have to rewrite tomorrow's lead."

Martha vanished.

Amanda turned back to her computer, stunned,

and deleted what she had written. She sat, staring at the screen, wondering what to write. She had only twenty minutes until deadline.

Chapter 5

Amanda got into the back seat of the spanking new Mercedes S600 and settled herself. She found the switch for the rear seat air-conditioning, and cool air flooded the rear passenger compartment. She touched the glassy surface of the burled walnut trim on her door and squirmed on the leather seat; she asked Paul for music, and the sounds of Bobby Short's singing materialized around her. She might have been sitting at ringside at the Cafe Carlyle, she thought. "Mortimer's, please, Paul," she said. Then she settled back into the soft, two-toned leather and tried to compose herself.

She could not remember the last time she had felt such anxiety; in fact, she could not remember the last time she had been so vulnerable. Amanda had conducted her life for a very long time in such a way that no one could have any ammunition to fire at her. She was the soul of discretion, especially where her own personal life was concerned, if not that of others. Outwardly, she was always charming, concerned, sweet, or grateful, whichever the circumstances called for. Inwardly, she was well aware that the scandal sheet's reference to her as a "high bitch" was entirely justified. Half the satisfaction of being a bitch was to be sure that no one could ever prove it of her.

Tonight, though, there were allegations in the

air. She had, over the past ten years, been slyly critical of any prominent woman with a well-known sex life. Now she herself would be subjected to a great deal of unwanted scrutiny and, probably, a very messy divorce.

She had decided to press on with her column's lead about her time in St. Bart's; all she could do now was brazen it through. After all, though the sheet had been entirely factual, proving the allegations would be quite another thing. With computer-generated photographic editing available to almost anyone who desired it, she could claim doctored pictures, in the hope that whoever was doing this would not want to reveal himself in order to provide further evidence. If it came up in court—well, she'd cross that abyss when she came to it.

"Lovely car, Miss Dart," Paul said. He rarely spoke unless spoken to, but Amanda received the compliment gratefully. It added another whit to the confidence that would be needed to face the crowd at Mortimer's.

"Thank you, Paul," she replied. "I hope you will enjoy driving it."

The car slid to a halt in front of the restaurant, and after a moment, Paul had opened the door for her. She stepped out, smoothed her skirt, took a deep breath, and plunged into the East Side's most fashionable hangout. She had timed her entrance for a moment when half the guests would have already come; that way she could easily spot those already there, then watch the others arrive.

As the door closed behind her there was an audible pause in the conversation as people glanced her way, then a resumption as they pretended not to see her. In a trice she had located the Walter Cronkites, the Mike Wallaces, the Abe Rosenthals, and the Richard Clurmans, all friends of Norman Barton's, who was rumored to be in line for the executive editorship of the *Times* when the present occupant of that office retired. She headed toward the honoree, giving a happy wave and a smile to acquaintances along the way.

Norman was standing in the back room, surrounded by friends and admirers, autographing copies of his book. After only a brief pause, Amanda strode forward, and the others gave way like yachts before the Queen Mary. "Norman! How exciting this must be for you!" Someone from the publishing house handed her a book. "I can't wait to read every page!"

"Amanda!" Barton cried, touching his cheek to each of hers. "I'm so pleased you got back in time!"

"Oh, I got back early this morning," she replied.

"I didn't know the airlines arrived from the islands at that hour," someone said.

Amanda turned her gaze on a short, plump woman who collected gossip items for a news syndicate. "One doesn't always fly the airlines, dear," she replied sweetly. "Sometimes one's friends provide."

"Oh, a private jet," the woman cried. "You landed at Teterboro?" Obviously looking for something she could check.

"No," Amanda replied dismissively, then reached forward, took Barton's elbow, and deftly plucked him out of the group as a cow pony cuts a steer from the herd, and, by her proximity to the honoree, placed herself at the center of the party.

They chatted enthusiastically for a moment, and then, as Amanda had planned, people began to approach, greeting them both, complimenting Amanda on her tan, asking about her holiday.

"Did you try that new little restaurant?" a rival columnist asked cattily.

"Oh, my dear, no," Amanda sighed. "All I did was work. I got up every morning, played the tennis ball machine for half an hour, worked for three hours, had lunch at the pool, then worked another three hours. The staff cooked every bite I ate."

"And what work kept you so occupied?" the woman asked.

"Why, I finished my book, darling," Amanda sang back. "It goes to my publisher's tomorrow!"

The woman blinked. "Congratulations," she said, then disappeared.

Amanda worked the crowd for an hour, then, at the moment when the tide seemed to turn toward dinner, she made her goodbyes and headed toward the door, nearly colliding with Bill Eggers.

"Oh, Bill," Amanda said, "you are just the man I want to see. Come with me, you're taking me to dinner." She hustled him to her car.

"Good thing I didn't have plans," Eggers said.

"I'd have kidnapped you anyway," Amanda said, sliding her arm through his. "Paul, we're going to Elaine's."

"Yes, ma'am," Paul replied.

"I see you got the car," Eggers said, looking around admiringly.

"Of course I did, darling," Amanda giggled.

"I don't think Dick Hickock knew what hit him."

"Of course not, darling." She made small talk all the way to Elaine's, while simultaneously formulating her next move.

Chapter 6

Amanda swept into Elaine's, automatically casting an eye about for who was there and where they were seated. Elaine herself was way in the back of the restaurant, seated at a customer's table. She lifted an eyebrow and Jack, the headwaiter, seated Amanda and her lawyer at a favored table up front. Amanda was just as happy not to have been greeted by Elaine, who she found hard to read, never quite sure whether she was being insulted. She came to the restaurant only for her work; before they were seated she had three items for tomorrow's column.

Bill Eggers ordered a double Jack Daniel's on the rocks, and Amanda ordered a large bottle of San Pellegrino mineral water. She always kept her wits about her, relaxing enough to drink alcohol only when she was among trusted friends in her home or theirs. They chatted idly as they selected from the menu and ate two courses. Only when they had both declined dessert and received their coffee did Amanda choose to begin.

"Bill, you must know about this scandal sheet that was circulated to a lot of fax machines this afternoon."

"I believe I caught a whiff of it."

"Well put; it was all so much dung."

"Certainly was, Amanda. I mean, I would have known if you weren't in St. Bart's."

"Of course, darling." She paused for effect. "I want to hire a private detective; I'd like you to recommend one."

The lawyer's nose wrinkled. "Is it that important to know who sent the fax?"

Amanda gazed across the room. "It might become that important; if so, I intend to be ready."

"Amanda, let me give you my lecture, the short version, on private detectives."

"All right, Bill; I'm listening."

"I suppose I've dealt with a couple of dozen of them in one way or another over the past twenty-five years, and I haven't found one yet who could be trusted to keep a confidence." He held up a hand before she could reply. "I'm not saying there are not ethical private eyes out there; it's just that I've never run across one. They tend to be failed cops whose ethics were too ripe for the police force—and that's very ripe indeed. They dress badly, smell awful, and drink in the morning; they charge you by the day, then spend half the day at the track; they charge you for information, then make you pay them not to reveal it to others."

"This is the short version?"

"All right, I've said it, and having said it, I have a much better idea."

"I can't wait to hear it."

"Does the name Stone Barrington ring a bell?"

Amanda wrinkled her brow before she caught herself. "That police detective who was involved in the investigation of the Sasha Nijinsky disappearance four or five years ago?"

"Your memory always astonishes me."

"It's not *that* good; tell me about him. The long version, past and present."

"Born somewhere in New England to a mill-owning family who went bust during the thirties; father dropped out of Harvard to become a carpenter and a political leftist in Greenwich Village, thus becoming the black sheep; mother was Matilda Stone...."

"The painter?"

"Right. Stone went to law school, but during his senior year he hung out with some cops and became besotted with their profession. When he graduated, he didn't take the bar; instead, he went to the police academy. He had made it as far as detective second grade over fourteen years—no better than average—when Sasha Nijinsky disappeared. He was practically on the scene when she vanished and thus caught the investigation. His theories didn't square with the department's—he had never really been one of the boys—so at the first opportunity they retired him for medical reasons. He had taken a bullet in the knee on an earlier investigation."

"Was he crippled?"

"Not really; they were just looking for an excuse."

"What has he done since?"

"For a while he spent his time restoring a Turtle Bay townhouse left to him by a great-aunt, until he ran out of money. Then he crammed for the bar examination and passed it well up on the list, top ten percent. I'd known him in law school; I took him to lunch and offered him a deal with us."

"He joined Woodman & Weld?"

"Not exactly. He became of counsel to us, set up his own office at home, and began handling our client-related criminal cases and the occasional investigation."

"Client-related criminal cases? I don't understand; you don't represent criminals, do you?"

"Typically, a valued client's son involved in a date rape—that sort of thing."

"I see. And what sort of investigations?"

"Again, client-related—divorce, adultery, runaway daughter, theft of company funds, industrial espionage—whatever comes up."

"Is he good?"

"He combines a good policeman's curiosity and tenacity with a good lawyer's discretion and restraint. And he's socially acceptable."

"Then why don't I know him?"

"He lives a quiet life, dates a lady judge; he's better known in courtroom circles than in society."

"Wasn't there a lot of publicity about him over the Nijinsky case?"

"A great deal, but he went to ground very quickly, and the press forgot about him, not having any reason to remember."

"He *sounds* good."

"Why don't you go and see him? I'll be glad to make an appointment."

"Bill, people usually come to see *me*."

"It would perhaps be more discreet for you to go to him."

"Make the appointment; I'll go for tea tomorrow at four."

"*Tea?*"

"Bill, if he can't mount a decent tea, why would I want to know him?" Amanda looked up to see a television actor come into the restaurant with a woman who was not his wife. She made a mental note for the column.

Chapter 7

The young man stood behind the stone wall that separated Central Park from Fifth Avenue and watched the front door of the apartment building from across the street through a pair of pocket binoculars. It was just before 2:00 a.m., and a couple were being deposited at the curb by a hired limousine.

The night doorman got the car door, then rushed ahead to open the building door for them. The young man watched him see the couple onto the elevator, then return to the lobby. The doorman picked up a clipboard, made some sort of mark, probably next to the couple's name, then tossed the clipboard onto a desk, tipped his uniform hat back on his head, stretched and yawned, then sat down at the desk and rested his head on his arms. He had obviously checked in the last people for the night—all present or accounted for—and now there would be no one to disturb his sleep until the early birds went for their jogs.

The young man waited for another twenty minutes, checking the doorman frequently through the binoculars; finally, the man was clearly deeply asleep. The young man set a paper bag on top of the wall, placed his hands on the wall, and vaulted lightly over it. He picked up the paper bag and crossed Fifth Avenue. Traffic was very light at this hour. He checked his watch: just past 2:30 a.m.

He approached the door of the building without stealth, as if he were about to enter, then stopped and again checked the doorman, who was still sleeping soundly. He looked at the lobby floor: marble. Then he stepped into the shadows beside the door of the building, shucked off his sneakers, pulled out a pair of soft leather-soled bedroom slippers, put them on, then put the sneakers into the bag. He couldn't afford squeaking noises from rubber soles on the marble floor. He checked the doorman again, then walked silently across the lobby to the elevator, which he already knew was very quiet, and pressed the button for the fourteenth floor. The young man already knew a lot about the building and the apartment he was about to enter.

He stepped out of the elevator car and into a private vestibule. Only one apartment to a floor in this building. The door took nearly two minutes—a very good lock—and when he heard the bolt slide back he stopped, put away his lockpicks, took a stopwatch from his pocket, and pressed the start button. He had forty-five seconds, and he didn't want to use more than thirty, if he could help it.

He opened the door, closed it behind him, and sprinted down a hall, across a large living room, and into the study. He knew that the occupants

33

were away and that the maid's room was all the way at the rear of the apartment, behind the kitchen. In the study, he opened a closet door, switched on the light, found the burglar alarm central control box, and fixed the stopwatch to it with a magnet glued to its back. Twelve seconds gone.

He opened the control box and began the process of disconnecting first the telephone line to the box, then the wire to the siren. This was necessary because he didn't know the disarming code sequence. He looked at the watch; thirty-two seconds had passed. Not bad. The alarm would go off in thirteen seconds, and since he had done all he could, he would just have to wait and see what happened. At forty-five seconds there was an audible click and the sound of tone dialing from the central computer unit. No siren, and, since the telephone line had been disconnected, no phone call to the central security station of the alarm company. There was the possibility, though, that the disconnecting of the phone line had sent some sort of code to central security, so he would not dally.

The safe was conveniently located in the same closet as the alarm control box; he had examined it briefly on his previous visit. It was sturdy and electronically operated, requiring a four-digit code and a key to open the door. The key was absent, but the lock would not be a problem. He retrieved a small screwdriver from his tool kit and removed the battery access panel from the front of the safe, then took a palmtop computer from a jacket pocket. A wire attached to tiny alligator clips ran from the computer, and he attached the clips to the safe's battery terminals. He had written a simple program for the computer that would start at the lowest possible four-digit number, then go to the highest possible four-digit number and back and forth until the safe clicked open. The process would be shortened by the fact that most of these electronic safe keypads would not allow the repetition of a number in the code, so there would be fewer codes to try. He had test-run the program, and he knew that it required nine minutes and eighteen seconds to try all the possible codes. He tapped the instructions into the small keyboard, and the program began to run. He set the computer on top of the alarm control panel and settled in to wait. Four minutes and nine seconds into the program, he heard a click from the safe, and the program stopped.

Quickly, in case there was a time limit, he picked the safe's conventional lock, and the door swung open. Inside were two delightful surprises. The first was three thick stacks of one-hundred-dollar bills, with a rubber band around each, and another stack of fifties. The bills looked well used, and a cursory inspection revealed that the serial numbers were not consecutive. He estimated that they totaled approximately thirty-five thousand dollars, but this was no time to start counting; he stuffed them into one of his jacket's large pockets. The other surprise in the safe was a small, nickel-plated automatic pistol, with, of all things, a silencer! He stuffed that into a pocket, then opened a jewelry box, which was full of a lot of junk that didn't interest him, except for a Cartier watch with a gold bracelet. That he kept; he loved watches.

He had just closed the safe door and was putting away his equipment when from a distance he heard a noise like the front door opening, followed by voices. No time to reconnect the alarm system; he closed the cabinet door, switched off the light, and left the closet, closing the door behind him. While he was doing all this he wondered if he had somehow caused this to happen. His heart was racing; he loved it. The voices came closer, and he dove into the kneehole of the desk, pulling his knees up to squeeze in.

"We got a disconnect signal," a voice said. The lights came on in the study. "If somebody cuts the phone line or disconnects it, we get a signal. Usually means a burglar has visited."

"Do you really need a gun?" another voice asked, sounding nervous.

"There might be somebody in the apartment right now," the other voice replied. "If there is, I'm going to be ready."

The voices were muffled slightly, and the young man thought they were probably in the closet by now.

"See right here?" the first voice asked. "The phone line was disconnected."

Time to go, the young man thought. He peered around the corner of the desk and saw the backs of the two men.

"He's probably had a shot at the safe," the first voice said. "Electronic job."

The young man crawled quickly, silently toward the door of the study; in doing so, he had to move past the closet. As he made the door, the first voice spoke again.

"You stay here," the voice said, and there was the sound of the action of an automatic pistol being worked. "I'm going to have a look around. You might use the phone on the desk over there to call nine-one-one and tell them there's been a break-in."

"Right," the other man replied.

The young man sprinted nearly soundlessly through the living room, his soft slippers making only tiny noises on the carpeting. He made it down the hall to the front door, opened it, and stepped into the hallway. The elevator and the front door seemed like a bad idea; if there was already a cop car on the block when the 911 call went in, he might meet them going out the door. The elevator door stood open. He stepped inside, pushed in the emergency button to activate the car, pressed the button for the ground floor, and stepped out of the car just as the doors closed. The elevator started down, and he made for the stairs. Holding his paper bag of tools, he bounded down flight after flight, past the lobby floor to the basement. There had to be a back door for service purposes.

He emerged into a dimly lit hallway that seemed to have a row of doors leading to storage rooms. He raced past them, made a turn at the end of the hallway, and came up against a door. He put his ear to it, and could hear the sound of a garbage truck outside. Carefully, he opened the door, and as he did, a loud bell began to ring. Coolly, he put his head out and looked around. He was in a sort of concrete pit, with steps leading up to the side street. He closed the door behind him, but the bell continued to ring, both inside and outside the building. Worse, a red light over his head was flashing relentlessly. Now he began to panic. He charged up the steps and ran head-on into a garbage collector holding two empty cans.

The two went down together, the garbage man hollering, the cans bouncing around the sidewalk.

"Hey, get that guy!" somebody yelled.

The young man got to his feet, grabbed his paper bag, and sprinted down the block toward Fifth Avenue, pursued by the garbage men. He ran straight across Fifth, nearly being run down by a police car, its lights flashing. Funny, he hadn't heard the siren until now. He heard the car doors opening, and somebody shout, "Stop! Police! Stop!"

Only one choice here, he thought. He ran straight at the park wall, throwing his paper bag ahead of him, vaulted over the wall, hit the ground on the other side, grabbed the paper bag, and was gone into the brush. They'd never get him now. Cops were too fat to run far. He emerged onto a walkway and ran down it toward Central Park South. The sound of police sirens faded into the distance.

He had gotten away with it again.

Chapter 8

Amanda got out of the Mercedes and looked ap-approvingly up and down the tree-lined block. The nineteenth-century development known as Turtle Bay comprised three sides of a city block between Second and Third Avenues in the Forties; all the houses opened to the rear on a common garden. She knew half a dozen people with houses on the block and recognized it for the highly desirable place to live that it was.

She climbed the steps of the brownstone and rang the bell. The door was answered almost immediately by a Mediterranean-looking woman. Amanda followed her through an entrance hall and a formal drawing room into a book-lined study at the rear of the house, with a bay window overlooking the gardens.

"Will you please be comfortable for a moment," the woman said. She spoke with a rather heavy accent. "Mr. Barrington will be with you quick."

"Thank you," Amanda said, taking one of a pair of leather wing chairs before the window.

"I'll get some tea," the woman replied, then left.

Amanda stood up and had a look around the room. It contained a great deal of original oak paneling, in addition to the bookcases, and there was an antique Persian rug on the floor, with old-fashioned parquet showing around its edges. A leather-topped walnut desk occupied a corner, and there were a number of silver-framed photographs on a shelf beside the desk, of people Amanda assumed to be Barrington's father and mother. On the wall behind the desk were three good-sized oils, all New York scenes, that Amanda would have bought on the spot. They were, she realized, all by Matilda Stone, who, she knew, had died fairly young and had left only around fifty canvases, all in private hands. She wondered what these three might be worth.

Stone Barrington finished his phone call and hung up. "Alma," he called to his secretary, "I'm going upstairs to meet my four o'clock; hold all my calls."

"Right, Stone," Alma called back from her adjacent office.

Stone climbed the spiral staircase that led to the rear hall of the first floor of the house and entered his study. A tall, handsome, beautifully dressed and coiffed woman, who appeared to be in her early forties, stood before his desk, looking at his mother's paintings. "Good afternoon," he said.

She did not turn around immediately, but went on looking at the paintings. "I don't suppose I've seen more than a dozen of her pictures in my whole life," she said, "but I've loved every one of them."

"Thank you; she'd be pleased to have the compliment."

She turned and walked toward him, holding out her hand. "I'm Amanda Dart."

He took her hand. "I'm Stone Barrington; won't you sit down?"

They each took a wing chair and, as if on cue, the servant appeared with a silver tray containing a matching teapot, two cups and saucers, and a plate with several slices of pound cake and some cookies.

"This is my housekeeper, Helene," Stone said. "She makes the best pound cake on the Eastern Seaboard."

"In the Western Hemisphere," Helene said blithely.

"Helene is Greek; humility does not come easily to her."

"And what would I have to be humble about?" Helene asked. "You bet not my pound cake."

Amanda smiled appreciatively. She wanted the strange woman to be gone. "Tell me about this house," she said, so they'd have something to talk about while Helene poured. Anyway, she was interested.

"Of course. It was built in the eighteen-nineties by the father of my great-aunt on my father's side. I suppose that makes him my great-grandfather? The architect was a man named Ehrick Rossiter, who worked from the eighteen-seventies through the nineteen-thirties."

"He had an eye for proportion," Amanda said, looking around the room.

"Yes, and he filled the house with interesting detail. I'll give you the tour someday, when you have the time."

"Thank you, I'd love that, but not today. Did you choose the furnishings?"

"About half of them, I suppose. The rest came down from family or were in the house when my great-aunt left it to me."

"You're very fortunate in your family's tastes."

"I am."

"Has Bill Eggers told you why I'm here?"

"No, he said he'd let you explain everything."

Amanda opened her alligator bag and handed him the scandal sheet. "Recently, I had a weekend in St. Bart's; the day of my return this was

41

sent to at least several dozen fax machines around the city—perhaps farther abroad, who knows?" She waited while Stone read it.

"Where were these photographs taken?" he asked.

"At a hotel in Manhattan."

"What is it that you'd like me to do for you, Ms. Dart?"

"I want you to find out who produced this...document," she said.

"Why?"

"Because I want to know, of course."

"Why do you want to know?"

She looked at him blankly. "Because when someone is publicly telling gratuitous lies about me I want to know who it is."

"I see." Stone looked at the photographs carefully. "Ms. Dart," he said, "are you saying this isn't you in the photograph?"

"Of course that's what I'm saying," she replied.

"Ms. Dart, I am principally a lawyer, and when I am representing someone it is essential that I know everything there is to know about the situation in question."

"I don't want to hire you as a lawyer, but as an investigator."

"There is little difference from my point of view. You see, if a client withholds information from me, I tend to spend too much of my time trying to find out why he is doing so. It would be much less expensive for you to save me that trouble. I expect Bill Eggers told you that I used to be a police detective."

"Yes, he did."

"Well, old habits die hard; I can usually tell when a person is lying to me."

"Oh, all right, it was...I was...." She seemed unable to go on.

Stone looked at the photographs again. "And I believe I recognize the front door of the Trent in the background. You are not the first of my clients who has made use of it. After all, it's the best, isn't it?"

"Yes," she said, "it's the best."

"As a lawyer, Ms. Dart, I am ethically bound to respect my clients' confidences; and if I have your confidence I will be better able to help you."

Her shoulders sagged slightly, then she recomposed herself. "All right, the statements in the sheet are accurate; I wasn't in St. Bart's, I was at the Trent, with a friend."

"Thank you for your candor. Now, why do you want to know who circulated this sheet?"

"Mr. Barrington, until very recently I was in negotiations for a new contract with my newspaper and their news syndicate. The fax arrived at a very awkward time, so much that I had to accelerate the negotiations, and at very great risk to my career."

"How did the negotiations go?"

"I got exactly what I wanted."

"Did your newspaper see this sheet before you reached agreement?"

"I very much doubt it; I moved too quickly for that."

"So you are safe on that count, for the moment."

"For the next four years. However, revelations

of the sort in that sheet tend to undercut my credibility, and credibility is the basis of my success in my work."

"I understand. So you would like me to try and stop this person or persons from doing this again?"

"No. You find out who it is, and I'll do the stopping, believe me."

"That sounds rather ominous, Ms. Dart. I hope you aren't thinking of doing anything foolish."

"I am not a foolish person, Mr. Barrington, I assure you." She suddenly smiled. "And I would be pleased if you would call me Amanda."

"Of course; please call me Stone."

"Will you assist me in this matter, Stone?"

"If I may be sure of your continued full cooperation."

"You may indeed."

"Then I will begin by asking you a great many questions," Stone said.

"Let's get started," Amanda replied.

Chapter 9

The gardens were lovely now, Amanda noticed, half in sunshine and half in shadow. A lone gardener knelt and pulled at weeds.

"Amanda?" Stone said quietly.

"I'm sorry," Amanda replied, returning her full attention to him. "I was just admiring the light in the garden."

"It is lovely, isn't it?" Stone said. "I've sat whole days watching it."

"Please ask me your questions," Amanda said, crossing her legs and adjusting her skirt. She was aware of Stone's glance at her legs, which she knew were one of her best features.

Stone knew he had been caught looking at her legs, but she didn't seem to mind. "How many people knew you were going to spend the weekend at the Trent?" he asked.

"Only my secretary, Martha," Amanda replied. "Martha always knows where I am, in case of emergency."

"Last name?"

"McMahon."

"And how long has Martha been with you?"

"For fifteen years; she's my most trusted employee."

"Do you think Martha could be bought?"

"Absolutely not. Anyway, she's *extremely* well paid. She earns on a par with a secretary to a top corporation head."

"Who else besides Martha knew?"

"No one."

"How did you travel to the hotel?"

"Oh, well, Paul, my driver, took me."

"So Paul knew where you were going?"

"Not exactly. I mean, he knew the address, but I don't think he could have known the significance."

"Did he know you were supposed to be in St. Bart's?"

"Well, yes; he had been told that, in case anyone asked."

"So he knew you didn't go to the airport, that you were doing something unusual."

"Yes, I suppose, but he never asked any questions. Paul never does."

"Last name?"

"Brennan."

"How long with you?"

"Nine years."

"Trustworthy?"

"Absolutely."

"So that's two people who knew something. How about at the hotel? Whom did you see there?"

"No one; the desk clerk had turned his back when I ran for the elevator."

"No maid, no anyone?"

"A maid did bring some sheets and towels a couple of times, and, of course, there were room service waiters, but I was always in the bathroom when they arrived."

"They knew that Mr. Bell was with someone, though."

"I suppose they did; the meals were for two, after all, but they would have no reason to know it was me."

"Did you carry a handbag there?"

"Yes, a small clutch."

"Where did you place it in the suite?"

"I...dropped it on the floor when I entered the first time."

"Did it remain there?"

"No, when I left, it had been put on a table, by the maid, I suppose."

"Might she have had time to open it?"

"Possibly; my driver's license was inside, and some credit cards."

"I see."

"I'm beginning to see, too, I think," she said. "It's hard to go anywhere without *someone* knowing, isn't it?"

"It is. With that in mind, can you think of anyone else who might have known?"

"I can't think of anyone else."

"Bill Eggers?"

"No; I told him nothing."

"Let's look at the St. Bart's end, then."

"How do you mean?"

"In the same way that certain people in New York knew you were remaining in the city, certain people in St. Bart's would have known of your absence there."

"Oh, I see. Well, certainly my, ah, putative host, the Duke, knew of my absence, though he didn't know why. The staff at the house would have known I was not there, had anyone asked. They would have known about my message on the answering machine, conceivably."

"Was the Duke in residence at that time?"

"No, he was in London. I believe he's in St. Bart's this week."

"I think you might call him and ask if anyone inquired about your presence or absence there during the time you were at the Trent."

"Good idea," she said, making a mental note.

"Have you visited the Duke's house before?"

"Twice."

"How many staff?"

"A butler, a housekeeper, three maids, and a cook and kitchen staff. Oh, a driver. They've all been with the Duke for years, and he made a point of their discretion."

"Good."

He was very thorough, Amanda thought, and she liked that. She liked his looks, too—tall, slender, blond hair going gray. She liked the good suit and shirt—not custom-made, perhaps, but fine quality. She liked the house. She could make this man very well known, if she chose to. He was the sort of man she might like to be seen with. She would think about that.

"You would have made a good police detective," Stone said.

Her eyebrows went up. "Why do you think so?"

"You've very observant, very analytical," he replied. "At least as much so as I."

"Thank you," she said, smiling. "Only an observant person would see that."

"Amanda, I think you may have it in you to solve this mystery without my help. Certainly you know the people involved better than I. You know who might wish to hurt you."

Amanda laughed ruefully. "They are legion," she said. "In my business I make enemies every week, even though I try very hard not to."

"I can see how it might be difficult not to make enemies."

"Not difficult, impossible. I run the most innocuous item about someone's marriage or divorce and, at the very least, I'm perceived as having taken sides in the matter, sometimes by both parties."

Stone laughed, and she joined him. She had seemed a bit stiff at first, but now she had loosened up, and she was charming. He was forty-two, and he tended to be attracted to women a decade younger, but she must be around his age, he thought, and he found her appealing. Careful, this was business, at least for the moment. He had been on the point of offering her a drink.

Amanda glanced at her watch.

"Am I keeping you from something?" Stone asked. "I think we're about finished for now, if you have to leave."

"I have another hour," she said, "if you do; and the sun is well over the yardarm. I wonder if I might have a drink?"

"Of course," Stone said. Mind reader! "What would you like?"

"Oh, something light."

Stone picked up the phone and pressed a button or two. "Helene, there's a bottle on the bottom shelf of the small refrigerator. Would you bring that and a couple of glasses?"

Helene appeared with a bottle of champagne in a silver wine cooler and a pair of flutes.

"Just set it on the desk; I'll open it," Stone said.

Helene departed; Stone opened the champagne and poured.

"Veuve Clicquot," Amanda said. "My very favorite."

"I'll keep that in mind," he replied.

Amanda lifted the thin glass and took a sip. And Baccarat crystal, too, she thought. "Enough of business," she said. "Tell me about you."

"Not much to tell. Grew up in the Village; P.S. Six, NYU, law school, joined NYPD, made detective, took early retirement, practiced law. That's me in a nutshell."

"Stone," she said, "men like you don't fit into nutshells."

He laughed.

"I'm having some people for dinner on Friday evening. Will you come?"

"I'd be delighted."

She dug a card from her purse and handed it to him. "Come at six-thirty; that'll give us time to talk a bit before the others arrive."

"All right."

She looked around the rooms. "Your books tell me more about you than you do."

Stone shrugged. "I've nothing to hide."

"We'll see," she replied.

Chapter 10

Stone arrived at Elaine's at eight-thirty, having only just sobered up from the champagne with Amanda Dart. Jack, the headwaiter, seated him at the table just beyond the newly painted no-smoking line and brought him a Wild Turkey on the rocks without being asked. Dino was late, which didn't surprise him. They had dinner once a week, usually at Elaine's, but Dino had a lot of demands on his time these days. Lieutenant Bacchetti, formerly Stone's partner on the force, now ran the detective squad at the Nineteenth Precinct on East Sixty-seventh Street.

Elaine pulled up a chair and sat down. "You meeting Dino?"

"Yep."

"He might be late; his kid had a birthday party earlier."

"Then I'm surprised he's coming at all."

"I'm not," she chortled. "He'd do anything to get out of something like that."

"You're probably right. Elaine, do you know Amanda Dart?"

"Doesn't everybody?"

"What do you think of her?"

Elaine shrugged. "I don't, much. She comes in here a couple times a month and eyeballs the crowd, but she doesn't write much about the place. If she ever printed anything nasty about a regular, I'd kick her ass into the street."

"Do you know her at all, as a person?"

"Not at all; strikes me as one cold dish, though. What's your interest in her?"

"Oh, I met her recently, and she surprised me. Just wondered what your take was on her."

"She behaves herself in here; she's fine with me," Elaine said, then she grinned. "You heard about this *DIRT* thing that's making the rounds?"

"I heard about it."

"Now, *that's* funny, to see one of these broads getting a dose of her own venom." She looked toward the door. "Here comes Dino." She stood up, allowed Dino to give her a peck on the cheek, and wandered off toward somebody else's table.

"Lord Barrington, I believe," Dino said in an execrable English accent. He hung his coat on a hook along the wall and sat down, taking care not to wrinkle the jacket of his fine Italian suit against the chair.

"You made chief yet?" Stone asked.

"I woulda, if the mayor had any brains."

"I just wondered; don't you have to be a chief to rate a driver these days?" Dino traveled in an unmarked car, driven by a rookie detective.

51

"I like to give these kids the experience, you know?"

"Why don't you invite him in for a cup of coffee, at least?"

"Let him freeze his ass off; when *I* was a rookie nobody ever invited me in for a cup of coffee."

"That's because you never paid."

Dino looked outraged. "*I* should pay?"

"I hear little Angelo had a birthday today."

"Yeah, he's four, if you can believe it. His grandfather wanted to give him a piece of ass for a present."

Stone laughed. "I guess that's the sort of thing you have to expect when you knock up a capo's daughter."

"The kid'll make his bones by the time he's six, if the old man has his way."

"How's Mary Ann?"

Dino made a face. "She wants to move into Manhattan."

"Sound like a good idea."

"Are you *nuts?* She'll want eight rooms on the East Side; who can afford that on a lieutenant's salary? Let me tell you something, Stone; don't ever marry into a royal family. The princess will want to live like a queen."

"Wouldn't her daddy kick in for a place on the East Side? I mean, doesn't he love his little girl?"

"You bet your ass he would, but I can't take that from him. Next time we get some commission looking into corruption on the force, they'd have me by the balls."

"Not if the place is in her name, paid for with her money."

"Shit, you think he's just going to write her a

check and say, 'Here, honey, buy yourself a co-op'? Nah, he'd have to screw somebody out of the place, or he wouldn't feel right about it, you know? I mean, he'd find some schmuck with a nice apartment who owes him a hundred grand on the book, and he'd take it away from him. That's how the goombahs operate."

"I guess you're right. Still, if you're living in Manhattan, Mary Ann wouldn't have to see so much of her family, would she?"

Dino brightened at the thought. "You got a point there, pal. Anything I could do to get out of those family dinners would be fine by me. I walk into the house and everybody stops talking, you know? It's like they been talking about burning down a building or clipping somebody, and now I'm there, and they have to talk about the weather. It's uncomfortable, you know?"

Stone shoved a menu at him. "Want to start with some calamari?"

"Yeah, sure."

Stone waved a waiter over.

They were on coffee when Elaine came their way, clutching a sheet of paper and laughing heartily. "Stone, you made the papers," she said, handing him the paper. Dino leaned over to read along with him.

DIRT

Flash, earthlings! Our favorite bitch queen, Amanda Dart, has hired herself a shamus to track us down! Don't you love it? No kidding, she's retained ex-cop, now an East Side shyster, Stone Barrington, to find out how we know so much. You remember dear Stone: He was the cop who broke the Sasha Nijinsky disappearance case a few years back. For his trouble, the department shipped him out. Now he's supposed to catch us at our work! Lotsa luck, Stone!

"What's going on, Stone?" Dino asked.

"I don't believe it," Stone said. "This happened only this afternoon, what, five hours ago?"

Elaine was loving it. "I love it!" she crowed.

"Tell me," Dino said.

Stone told him.

"You got nothing better to do with your time than to track down somebody for an old dame who got caught with her knickers down?"

"She's an important client of Woodman and Weld, or maybe just an important person; I'm doing it as a favor to them. And she's not so old."

Dino shook his head. "Give me a good homicide anytime." He drained his coffee cup and set it on the table, glancing at his watch. "I gotta be somewhere," he said.

"Oh?" Stone asked, looking at his own watch. "You're going home to Brooklyn so early?"

"Not directly home, no."

"Dino." Stone shook his head. "You're going to get yourself in trouble."

"What're you talking about, trouble?"

"I know you; this unscheduled stop has something to do with a lady."

"So?"

"So, if your father-in-law should hear about it, you won't have anything to offer the ladies anymore."

"Stone, don't say stuff like that," Dino said, shivering.

"You know I'm right."

"The old man has too much to worry about that he should take an interest in my social life."

"Don't be so sure, pal."

"I'm always careful," Dino said, slipping into his coat.

"I hope you're right," Stone said.

Chapter 11

On the West Coast, as Dino left Elaine's, Allan Peebles arrived at his Beverly Hills home after a long editorial board meeting at the "newspaper" he edited, *The American Infiltrator*. His editorial board consisted of a dozen writers and editors who had failed at real newspapers and magazines and had ended up, as Peebles had, at the last stop for a journalist, a seamy tabloid. They were consoled by the fact that they were considerably better paid than their counterparts at real newspapers.

Peebles was an androgynous Scot who had fled his native Glasgow, pursued by rumors about his sexual orientation, for London, where he had acquired an English accent, an English wife, and, apparently while holding his nose, two English daughters. When the marriage failed, his father-in-law, who owned a London tabloid, had sent him to America to found a similar organ there, on the condition that he not return to England until his daughters were of age.

To his father-in-law's surprise, Peebles had succeeded in putting together a highly profitable, if highly disreputable, publication, which specialized in exposing those parts of the lifestyles of the rich and famous that they had hoped would remain secret. Peebles did this with some glee, while, in the permissive atmosphere of La-La Land, indulging his own rather specialized appetites. Tonight, Peebles was hungry for pizza.

Upon entering his empty house, he shucked off his jacket, picked up a phone, and pressed an unlabeled speed-dial button.

"Jiffy Pizza," a whiskied female voice said.

"It's number two zero two; how are you, sweets?"

"Fine, baby; what's your pleasure tonight?"

"I'm in the mood for the special."

"'Round-the-world?"

"You bet."

"With sausage?"

"*Lots* of sausage."

"That's going to run you twenty," she said. Twenty meant two hundred.

"And cheap at the price, I'm sure it will be."

"Half an hour, sweets. Your order is in the oven."

"The sooner the better. Bye." He hung up and walked into the kitchen. Opening the freezer door, he extracted a bottle of lemon vodka and poured himself a double. He always had to be a little drunk for pizza.

Three miles away, Sheila consulted her book and dialed a number.

"Hey, talk to me," a husky male voice said.

"It's the pizzeria," Sheila said. "I've got an order for a 'round-the-world, with *lots* of sausage; I thought of you."

"Of course you did, baby."

"You available immediately?"

"How much?"

"Ten; you won't be there long, believe me."

"I can do it."

She gave him the address. "Oh, and pick up a pizza on the way; we want this to look good, don't we?"

"Sure we do."

"And be sure to get paid before he starts eating."

"You know it."

Allan Peebles finished his drink, poured another, then went to his bedroom and stripped off his clothes, donning a terrycloth robe. He was looking at himself in the mirror, playing with his hair and sipping his drink, when the doorbell rang.

When he opened the door, a muscular young man in shorts and t-shirt was leaning against the jamb, holding a pizza box. He smiled broadly, revealing good dental work. "Delivery," he said.

"Why don't we dine out by the pool?" Peebles said, waving the young man to follow.

The young man entered the house, kicking the door behind him. It did not quite close.

Peebles led the way through the house and out to the pool, switching on the underwater lights as he went. The garden was suffused with the soft glow of the pool lighting. Peebles let his robe drop to the ground. "I never dine clothed," he said. "Do you?"

"I never complete a delivery until the check's been paid," the young man responded. "Nothing personal."

Peebles picked up the robe, extracted two one-hundred-dollar bills from the pocket, and handed them to the young man. "There's a nice tip in it for you, if the service is good."

The young man dropped the pizza and got out of his clothes in a trice. "The tip's about to be in it for *you*, darling," he said.

Out on the street, another young man got out of a car and opened the trunk. Inside was a large aluminum case, which he opened to reveal a selection of photographic equipment. He selected a machine-operated 35mm single lens reflex camera and a small video camera, fixing them both to a bar containing two floodlights. Getting into a battery belt, the young man plugged in the lights, closed the car trunk, and started toward the front door of the house, where he could see a crack of light.

He opened the door an inch and peered inside. Nothing. Emboldened, he stepped into the house and listened. A strange sound reached his ears; it seemed to be coming from the rear of the house. On tiptoe, he crossed the living room and approached the sliding doors to the garden. Outside, in the soft light from the pool, he could make out what he had come for. "Oh, Jesus," he said. "This is absolutely fab."

As he stepped through the doors he was able to

see clearly, without the reflected glare from the sliding panes. Perched on the diving board were two figures, one on his hands and knees, the other in more of a riding position. The one on top was slapping the naked ass of the one on the bottom with his open hand.

"Giddyap!!!" the rider cried.

The one on the bottom made loud, horsey noises.

The intruder made sure the microphone on the video camera was operating, then pointed his equipment and switched on the floodlights.

"Ride 'em cowboy!!!" he crowed as he began to photograph and tape. "Give him the crop!!!"

Confusion ensued. The equestrian took one look at the floodlights, disengaged, swept up his shorts, and fled across the garden, plowing straight through a privet hedge.

The figure playing the equine role looked wide-eyed over his shoulder and rolled off the diving board into the water. A moment later he surfaced, peering shyly over the rim of the pool and shouting, "Get out! Get out! Get out!!!"

"Glad to oblige, Old Paint! Got all I need!" He turned and vanished into the house, then onto the street.

Chapter 12

Stone arrived at Amanda's building at 10:00 a.m. for his appointment. He had phoned her earlier that morning and asked to see her in her office.

The doorman looked at him appraisingly be-

59

fore allowing him into the lobby, and the man inside at the desk called upstairs and announced him before allowing him into the elevator. They both looked like retired cops. He was impressed with the building's security.

He was met at the elevator by a plump woman with pale red hair who appeared to be in her late thirties or early forties.

"Mr. Barrington? I'm Martha, Amanda's secretary. Will you follow me, please?" She led the way down a hall and through a heavy door.

Stone had noticed another, double door; that must be her apartment, he thought. He followed the woman into an open office area containing three desks; one was empty—obviously Martha's, the other two were occupied, respectively, by a young woman and a young man, both of whom were on the phone. He followed Martha into a comfortably decorated office where Amanda, seated behind her desk, was on the phone. She waved him to a seat and dismissed Martha with a shooing motion.

"Yes, darling, I understand," Amanda was saying. "Not a word to anyone until you're ready, and I *do* appreciate your confiding in me alone. It is me alone, isn't it? Yes, I'll see you soon." She hung up the phone and gave him a wide smile. "So, you found your way to my aerie."

"I did, and it's a very cozy working arrangement, even nicer than I'd imagined."

"You know the joys of working at home, don't you?"

"I do."

"Well, then, what would you like to see here?"

"Your diary page for yesterday," Stone replied. She laughed, then handed it over.

Opposite four o'clock was written, "Stone Barrington, investigator," and his address. He handed back the diary. "To whom did you speak between the time you left my house and, say, eight-thirty last night?"

"Everybody?"

"Let's start with those you saw face to face."

"Well, there's Paul, my driver, of course, then I returned here and saw the doorman and the lobby man, then came upstairs in time to see Martha and my two other people before they left for the day."

"Did you say to any of them that you'd seen me?"

"No, but Martha knew I had, of course. Martha knows all."

"Anybody else before eight-thirty?"

"No, I was home alone until nine, when I left for a dinner party."

"Do your employees commonly come into your office when you're out?"

"Yes, I suppose; they leave me notes or copy to read."

"Do you ordinarily leave your diary open on your desk?"

"Ahhhh," she said. "Yes, I do." She produced the scandal sheet with the mention of his assignment. "Have you seen this?"

"I saw it at eight-thirty last night. When did you write my name in your diary?"

"When I made the appointment with you, earlier yesterday."

"Do any outside people come into your offices?"

"Messengers, visitors."

"Did you have any visitors yesterday?"

"No."

"Messengers?"

"There's a constant stream of them, but there's no way Martha would have let one of them into my office."

"Does Martha keep a duplicate diary of your day?"

"Yes, in her middle desk drawer."

"Does she ever leave it on her desk?"

"Possibly. I could ask her. You think, then, that someone saw your name in my diary?"

"So far, it seems the only possible way that anyone could have known you brought me into this."

"You think it's one of my people, then?"

"Not necessarily, but it's a possibility to keep in mind. Who cleans your offices?"

"My live-in maid, Gloria; she does my apartment, too."

"Could she have leaked the information?"

"She wouldn't have come into the office until this morning."

"What about yesterday afternoon?"

"No, I don't think so, but I'll ask Martha."

"I think you should ask Martha to keep a log of every person who comes into your offices, no matter how briefly—messengers, repairmen, anybody."

"All right."

Stone reached into his briefcase and took out a black plastic box. "Do your phones have the Caller ID feature that the phone company sells?"

"Yes; I don't know how we ever did without it."

"On the fax line, too?"

"I'll have to ask Martha."

"If you don't already have it for that line, ask Martha to arrange it, then plug this unit into the line between the wall socket and the fax machine. Let's see if we can see where this…newsletter is being faxed from."

"An excellent idea," Amanda said.

"Among your three employees, who is married?"

"None of them; Barry is gay, Helen is divorced, and Martha is single."

"Does any of them have a regular companion?"

"Helen sees somebody, I believe; Barry, who knows? Martha doesn't seem to have a social life, except vicariously, through me."

"I'd like to know who Helen sees and, to the extent possible, who Barry's closer friends are."

Amanda frowned. "I don't see how I can learn that without tipping them off, if one of them is involved."

"Give me their addresses and phone numbers, then; I'll have it checked out."

"Discreetly, I hope."

"Of course."

Amanda flipped through her address book and wrote down Helen's and Barry's addresses. "I really don't believe that either of them could have anything to do with this; they've too much to lose."

"Then it will be best if we can eliminate them as suspects. We have to be sure."

"You know best," she said, handing over the addresses.

He looked at them. "What about Martha?" he asked.

"Oh." She scribbled down the information and handed it over. "But believe me, investigating her would be a waste of your time."

"Then I won't bother until I've exhausted any other possibilities."

Martha appeared in the doorway, clutching a sheet of paper. "Excuse me for interrupting, Amanda, but I thought you'd want to see this." She handed her boss the paper.

Amanda read it quickly and handed it to Stone.

DIRT

Greetings, earthlings! Check out our dear Allan Peebles in the snaps below! Nice to know, isn't it, that the fellow who has outed so many folks over the past couple of years is now out himself! This little photo op occurred in Allan's back-yard only last evening. The "rider" was booked by a very discreet Beverly Hills service that provides company for the lonely in the guise of pizza deliveries after dark. Word is, you can order just about any combination of goodies your little hearts desire!

Allan, who's been playing the part of a divorced gentleman and father, was married to the boss's daughter, you know. We hear that in order to get pregnant the lady had to very carefully calculate her moment, then wear a sailor suit to arouse dear Allan's interest long enough for a transfer of seed!

Let's see if this makes the front page of this week's *Infiltrator*!

"Well," Stone said, "it looks as if this little sheet has coast-to-coast coverage, doesn't it?"

"It does," Amanda said, taking back the fax and staring at the photographs, which made her want to vomit, because they were so similar in nature to the one of her that had appeared in the sheet. "Mind you, it couldn't happen to a nicer guy."

"I don't doubt it."

"What does this do for your investigation?" she asked.

"Broadens it considerably, I should think," he replied.

Chapter 13

Arnie Millman waddled into Stone's office and plopped into a chair. Arnie had been retired from the force for fifteen years, and he looked like half a million elderly Jewish retirees in New York City, making him ideal for surveillance.

"You putting on weight, Arnie?" Stone asked.

"Always. It's my wife's cheesecake; I can't help myself."

"You up for a little work?"

"Why not? The money I can use."

Stone handed him a sheet of paper. "Two people: Helen Charlson and Barry White. They both work for a client of mine, a gossip columnist type, and some confidential information is leaking out of the client's office. The girl has a boyfriend, I'm told, and the guy is gay; don't know who he sees. I want you to find out who their principal social contacts are and run brief checks on those people—employment particularly. I'm especially interested in anybody working in the media, especially entertainment."

"When you need it?" Arnie asked, making notes.

"Soonest; a week, outside."

Arnie nodded. "You want me to wire them?"

"Arnie, I've still got a license to practice law, and I want to keep it."

"Stone, you know I'd never let it get back to you. I'm just a meddlesome old man who knows a lot of cops who wouldn't turn him in for something like that."

"I'll leave it to you, then, but we never talked about it."

"Of course not."

"I'd like to know whether either of them has a lot of debt, is very short of money, or has been spending beyond his or her means, especially in cash. Let's extend that to their lovers, as well."

"If you want all this that fast, I'm going to need to bring in a couple guys."

"As long as they never hear of me."

"Budget?"

"Ample, but not open-ended."

"Gotcha." Arnie got up and sauntered out of the office.

Stone's secretary buzzed him. "Line one, here come de judge."

Stone picked up the phone. "Your Honor, how are you?"

"So-so," she replied. "Can I buy you lunch today?"

"Sure. Downtown?"

"Let's do it in your neighborhood; I'd just as soon not be seen together around the courthouse."

"The Box Tree at twelve-thirty?"

"Good."

"I'll book."

The Box Tree was a dark, cozy restaurant not far from Stone's house. He got there first and ordered half a bottle of wine. It was all the two of them would drink at lunch.

She came in five minutes later and, once again, he thought how attractive she was—small, blonde, pretty, and very fit. He sought her lips, but she offered her cheek. *Uh-oh,* he thought. "How are you, Sara?"

"I'm all right."

He hadn't seen her for a week, a long time for them. They usually spent two or three nights a week together. "You look wonderful today." He poured her a glass of wine and waved at a waiter, who brought menus.

"I'll just have the wine," she said. "I can't really stay for lunch."

"You came all the way uptown for a glass of wine?"

She looked him in the eye. "It hasn't been going well, Stone, you and I."

"Funny, I thought it was going extremely well," he replied.

"You would think that," she said. "Fact is, I don't like sneaking around so the other lawyers I deal with won't know; I don't like recusing myself from your cases and not being able to say why; and good sex isn't enough."

"I thought we had more going than sex," he said.

"I thought so, too, for a while, but I was wrong. We meet each other's needs, to a point, and that point ends right after sex."

"You've met somebody, haven't you?"

She shrugged.

"Haven't you?"

"All right, I have; actually, it's somebody I've known for a long time but am getting to know better."

"It's the real thing?"

"I don't know about that yet. It might be, if I can devote some time to it."

Stone nodded. "And I'm using up a lot of time."

"You're using up a lot of *me,* Stone, and I'm not getting enough back."

"I'm sorry."

"No need to be sorry; you've always been straight with me. I know you don't have any interest in marriage, and I thought that was okay, but it's just not. I need something in my life with a future. I'm thirty-four, and I want kids before I'm forty."

"I can understand that," Stone said into his wine glass.

"Not really," she said. "It's just not something you can empathize with. You're a sweet man, Stone, in lots of ways, but deep down inside you're

68

very...contained. I almost said cold, but that would be a bum rap. You're just not...easy to reach. I'm probably not the first woman to tell you something like that."

Stone shrugged. He didn't want to confirm it, but she was right. "So, who's the guy?"

"Tom Bill."

"Judge Thomas Bill?"

"Right. Don't worry, I won't ever tell him about us. He's the jealous type, and he could make your life miserable in court."

"That he could. What about you? Are you going to make my life miserable?"

"Not in court," she said, allowing herself a small smile. "You'll be miserable later, when you figure out what you've lost."

"I'm already miserable," he said.

"Not really, but you will be. That'll be my little revenge for your not taking me seriously."

"I always took you seriously."

"Not seriously enough." She shrugged. "Your loss."

"My loss," he agreed.

She sighed. "Well, that's about it, I guess."

"Sure you don't want some lunch?"

"I'm due back in court at two; I'd better get going." She stood up.

He stood up with her, at a loss for words.

"See you in court," she said, and left.

Stone sat quietly, staring at the tablecloth.

A waiter approached. "The lady won't be lunching?" he asked.

"The lady won't be lunching,"

"And what would you like, Mr. Barrington?"

"Sometimes I wonder that myself," Stone replied.

Chapter 14

On Friday evening Amanda stood naked before her dressing room mirror and regarded her body. She had exercised her whole life, and never more regularly than during the past ten years. The effort showed in her trim figure; what few defects had appeared with age she had had adjusted—a little off the tops of the thighs, a slight lifting and augmentation of the breasts, and she was not all that different from the girl she had been at eighteen, during her first year at Barnard.

She had been born Ida Louise Erenheim in Delano, Georgia, to a father and mother who had both worked their whole lives at Delano Mills, one of a group owned by the prominent Delano family of Atlanta, who had founded her home town and for whom it had been named. The girl's earliest memories were of her mother picking lint from her hair after a ten-hour day among the looms.

Ida Louise had discovered early the importance of her beauty, at first to the girls who were her social betters in the town and later to the boys from the better families. She had also been a very bright child, good in school and mature beyond her years. At a time when her girlfriends were giggling about sex at pajama parties, Ida Louise had been enthusiastically practicing it in various back seats, usually of Cadillacs and Lincolns. Word had quickly spread among the richer boys that Ida Louise responded well to shows of wealth.

By the time her girlfriends were thinking of offering up their virginity, Ida Louise had acquired a sexual repertoire that had astonished a number of athletic stars and one teacher. The teacher had filled out her scholarship application for Barnard and written his proposal letter while she had knelt under his desk and fellated him to higher flights of endorsement. Shortly after she had foolishly confided this incident to an athlete lover, she had found herself trapped in a locker room with the first string, and, faced with gang rape, had decided to enjoy the experience. She had, indeed, enjoyed it right up to the moment when they had beaten her senseless and left her naked and battered on the cold cement floor, to be discovered by a janitor, who had called the coach. The business had been hushed up, and Ida Louise had missed giving her valedictory address at graduation, departing early for New York and Barnard, caring not who saw her bruises in the day coach of the Atlantic Coast Line Railroad. For the rest of her life, the smell of sweaty athletic clothing would cause her to have unreasoning panic attacks. She had never again entered any sort of locker room, preferring to exercise outdoors or at home. The event had, though, instilled in her the iron determination that for the rest of her life it would be *she* who controlled every aspect of her sex life. She had made the mistake of allowing someone else to do that, and she would never make that mistake again.

Her first act on arriving in New York had been to find a lawyer and legally change her name to Amanda Delano, which name her cooperating high school teacher had already placed in her school records and scholarship application.

Amanda had a much nicer ring than Ida Louise, and thereafter she had not disabused her college friends from thinking that she was one of the mill-owning Atlanta Delanos.

At Barnard, Amanda had remained celibate for a year while pouring her sexual frustration into her studies and the school newspaper, for which she wrote a column on campus social life. When she could no longer tolerate a life without sex, she began to seek out older, often married men—assistant professors, usually, who demanded no full-time relationship and who could recommend her for the best classes and teachers. After graduation from Barnard she got a job on the old *Journal-American* and, very soon afterward, began an affair with a forty-year-old assistant managing editor, one Robert Dart, who she knew was headed for a top job at the paper. Within a year he had promoted her twice, given her her own column, and divorced his wife of fifteen years to marry Amanda.

The marriage was hell for both of them, but it had ended well for Amanda when Bob Dart had dropped dead on a squash court and left her his name, a cooperative apartment in a good neighborhood, and two hundred thousand dollars in life insurance. She had hardly been set for life, but now she had a career, a certain respect as the widow of a well-known journalist, and, above all, the column. When the *Journal-American* had folded, Dick Hickock's predecessor had recruited her and syndicated the column. Amanda Delano Dart had made herself powerful.

Amanda pulled on a pair of stockings and secured them to her garter belt. Her legs were too long for most pantyhose, and she felt somehow more alluring in a garter belt anyway. She slipped silk panties over the stockings and stepped into a short, low-cut black dress from her favorite, Chanel, that showed off both her good legs and her firm breasts. She needed no bra, and with the twitch of a shoulder she could give a properly attentive man a glimpse of nipple. A pair of black alligator Ferragamos and a modest diamond necklace and earrings completed her outfit.

She walked into the living room and gave it a quick once-over. She had long since trained her housekeeper, Bela, to perfection, but knowing that Amanda noticed kept her that way. She strolled into the dining room and checked the place settings, then toured the kitchen to see how the caterers were coming along. The television was on in the kitchen, and she was stopped in her tracks by the lead story on *Gossip Tonight,* which followed the evening news. An "anchorman" was saying:

"Word is out around New York and L.A. that two of gossip's leading figures have figured unflatteringly in a newsletter-by-fax called *DIRT,* which has been going out to a list of movers and shakers over the past week. The lady was allegedly caught in a most compromising position in a New York hotel, and the gentleman, who has taken part in a number of public outings of gay men and women, was said to have been photographed during a sex act with a pizza deliveryman. Can libel suits be far behind? It will be interesting to see."

Amanda kept moving, but her heart was pounding. She glanced at her Cartier watch. Stone

Barrington was due for an early drink in fifteen minutes.

Stone was knotting his tie when *Gossip Tonight* followed the news and Amanda's indiscretion was mentioned. Not by name, though, thank God. That would have certainly played hell with Amanda's dinner party. He didn't know who all her guests would be, but chances were at least some of them would have seen *DIRT*.

He slipped into his jacket and surveyed himself in the mirror. Dark, chalk-striped suit by Ralph Lauren, black baby calf shoes from E. Vogel, an old family shoemaker in Chinatown, a cream-colored silk shirt from Turnbull & Asser in London, and a reasonably sober necktie and pocket square from the same people. His cufflinks were old gold, his wristwatch a Cartier Tank. Perfect East Side dinner party garb, he thought. He gave his hair a final brush, tucked his gold reading glasses into his jacket's breast pocket, and let himself out of the house, whistling down a passing cab. That loud whistle, learned in boyhood, had served him well in New York City.

Amanda heard the elevator chime as it stopped in her foyer. She smoothed down her dress and banished nervousness. She was ready for her first guest.

Chapter 15

Amanda opened the door, and Stone was very taken with what he saw. Before him was just about the most perfectly turned out woman he had ever seen.

"Stone, darling, come in," Amanda said, offering him a cheek to peck. She turned and led him into the living room, a vision of chintz and good pictures.

"What a beautiful room," Stone said, knowing he was saying the right thing.

"Thank you, kind sir."

"And an even more beautiful hostess."

"For that, you get a real kiss," she said. Amanda took his face in his hands and planted upon his lips a soft kiss, with only a hint of tongue. Her carefully blotted lipstick remained unsmeared. "And now a drink," she said.

"Bourbon on the rocks, please?"

"Jack Daniel's? Wild Turkey? Old Crow?"

"Wild Turkey, please."

"A man after my own heart," she said. "You must have southern blood."

"No, just southern tastes in some things."

"As a Georgian, I thank you," she said, deftly pouring two drinks at a butler's tray across the room. "I'm so glad you didn't wear an overcoat. Gloria is busy in the kitchen, and I hate dealing with coats."

"I wear coats only when I am likely to be cold," he said, lifting his drink.

"New friends," Amanda said, raising her glass.

"I'll drink to that."

They did.

Amanda took his hand and led him to a soft sofa. "I hope you have nothing to report," she said.

"Nothing yet."

"Good; I'm in no mood to talk business. That is a very handsome suit; who made it?"

"A Mr. Lauren runs them up for me."

"Can't go wrong there, can you?"

"Nope. Who's coming to dinner, besides me?"

"Bill and Susan Eggers, whom you know, of course."

"Bill since law school; Susan only from a few law firm parties."

"Dick and Glynnis Hickock."

"He owns your paper?"

"Right, and don't kowtow to him, whatever you do, or he'll consider you his inferior forever."

"I'll try not to be impressed. Anyone else?"

"Vance Calder and some girl or other."

"Now I'm impressed."

"Be sure and let him know it, or he'll be hurt."

"I don't think I've ever had dinner with a real live movie star."

"Superstar, darling; if you forget, he'll remind you."

"And his girl?"

"One never knows with Vance. She might be a princess or a whore—more likely both." She sipped her drink. "I've not asked you, Stone; is there a woman in your life?"

"There was until yesterday."

Amanda smiled. "How convenient. I hope you're not too crushed."

"I'm managing."

"Something I should mention before the others arrive: don't be the last to leave, all right?"

"Whatever you say."

"It's not that I wouldn't want you to stay, it's just that I don't want to start any rumors."

"As you wish."

"As a reward for giving up a late evening with me, how would you like to drive out to the country tomorrow?"

"Sounds lovely."

"It will be. The autumn leaves are at their peak, and the weather forecast for tomorrow is perfection."

"I'll look forward to it."

"Will you meet me downstairs at nine sharp? We'll take my car; it's new, and I can't get enough of it. Do you drive?"

"I do, but I've always thought of a car as a liability in this city."

"It is, unless you have a convenient garage and a driver."

The doorbell rang, and Amanda looked at her watch. "That will be Dick Hickock," she said. "He always comes to dinner exactly on time, damn him."

A moment later, the maid ushered in the Hickocks and introductions were made. A man appeared to mix drinks while the maid went to answer the door again.

Hickock was a stocky, balding man in an expensive suit; his wife, Glynnis, looked expensive, too.

Hickock fixed him with a stare. "What do you do, Barrington?" he asked.

"I'm a lawyer, and please call me Stone."

"You can call me Mr. Hickock."

"Thanks, Dick."

Hickock managed a small smile. "What firm?"

"I'm of counsel to Woodman and Weld, but I practice privately, too."

"What sort of practice? Financial?"

"Only if the transaction is perceived as being of a criminal nature."

"Ah, a mob lawyer, eh?"

"No, my clients seem to arrive one at a time."

"But they're criminals?"

"I represent only the innocent, even if they're proven guilty."

Hickock laughed aloud. "And what did you think of this O.J. business?"

"If I should ever be charged with a double murder, I would be very pleased for Johnnie Cochran, Bob Shapiro, and Lee Bailey to represent me."

Bill and Susan Eggers entered the room and greeted everyone. Stone liked Bill, but had always found Susan to be cold, even haughty. She had been Bill's entree to the Four Hundred, such as they were. She shook Stone's hand and seemed ready to ward off any attempt at a kiss.

Vance Calder arrived last, no doubt to make an entrance, and Stone found him to be just as handsome and charming as he was on the screen. He had been called the new Cary Grant, and Stone thought that appropriate. He also thought that Calder's date was probably the most beautiful woman in New York. She was as tall as Calder, which wasn't as tall as Stone had expected; she had shoulder-length hair the color of ranch mink and was wearing a mannish pinstriped, double-breasted suit. "This is Arrington Carter," the actor said after he had shaken Stone's hand. "Arrington, this is Stone Barrington."

"Mr. Barrington," the young woman said with

a pleasingly southern accent, "you and I must never, *ever* marry."

Stone and Calder both erupted with laughter, while she regarded them coolly. "Gentlemen, you make my point for me," she said.

Stone had an urgent desire to sweep her out of the room someplace where he would not have to share her company with anyone else. Then he reminded himself who her date was, and what his own chances were of taking her away from a man whom *People* magazine, only the week before, had dubbed "the most beautiful man in America."

They sat at a beautifully set round table and dined on caviar, followed by a crown roast of lamb, with béarnaise sauce on the side, and very good, fairly old wine. Stone was placed between Amanda and Arrington, and his hostess gave him the distinct impression that she would have arranged things differently if she had met the other woman beforehand.

Hickock was holding forth about the newspaper business. He took a swig of the Opus One '89 and addressed Stone. "Do you read my newspaper?"

"Only for Amanda's column," Stone replied.

"Isn't he sweet?" Amanda said, squeezing Stone's thigh under the table.

"What about my editorial page?" Hickock asked.

"I only read your editorial page if I want to be annoyed," Stone said.

Everybody laughed but Hickock. "I take it you're a Democrat," he said.

"A liberal Democrat," Stone replied.

"These days nobody *decides* to become a liberal Democrat," Hickock said. "It must run in your family."

"On the contrary, my father was a Communist; so was my mother."

Hickock looked genuinely shocked. "You can't be serious."

"Entirely," Stone said. "I can't really complain about it, because their politics brought them together. Where would I be if one of them had been a Republican?"

Vance Calder spoke up. "What work did your father do?"

"He was a carpenter."

Bill Eggers broke in. "...and something of a genius as a maker of furniture and cabinet work. If he had been working in this country during the eighteenth century, Sotheby's would be selling his work for very high prices today."

"Why did he become a Communist?" Hickock asked.

"He had a Republican father," Stone explained.

Amanda spoke up. "Stone's mother was Matilda Stone."

Hickock and Calder looked blank.

"The painter," Amanda explained.

Arrington Carter was smiling broadly. "I own one of her pictures," she said to Stone. "Of Washington Square in winter."

Stone was surprised. "What good taste you have."

"I certainly do."

"Arrington has a very good collection," Vance Calder said.

"I explained that to Vance," Arrington said to the table. "He only knows about clothes, scripts, and leading ladies."

Coffee was served in the library, and Stone declined brandy. "I really have to be leaving," he said, rising. "I have an early appointment tomorrow morning." He collected a grateful smile from Amanda, shook hands with the other guests, and went home.

As he lay in bed, waiting for sleep, he thought of Arrington Carter, but tried to dismiss her from his mind. He couldn't compete with the likes of Vance Calder.

Arrington Barrington. He laughed aloud.

Chapter 16

Stone took the wheel and pulled away from Amanda's apartment building. "Wonderful car," he said, heading across Seventy-ninth Street toward the West Side Highway.

"Isn't it?" Amanda agreed. "This is the first time I've sat in the front seat."

As he accelerated onto the highway, Stone realized for the first time what twelve cylinders meant. "Unbelievable," he said.

Amanda smiled. "Don't get a ticket; I don't want to waste a minute of today."

After paying the toll as they left Manhattan, Stone set the cruise control at a reasonable number and relaxed, letting the amazing car do the work. The leaves along the Sawmill River Parkway were beginning to change color, but as they drove north, the colors intensified. By the time they were north of Danbury, the maples were so brilliant as to be distracting. Following Amanda's instructions, Stone ran the car along the winding Connecticut roads through Brookfield and Bridgewater. South of Washington, they turned down a narrow road into the woods, and after two miles they came to a beautiful little colonial house set back from the road behind a screen of birches and flaming maples. A handful of geese sunned themselves beside a small pond.

"Spectacular," Stone said, as they got out of the car.

"I bought it twelve years ago for peanuts, and I've been redecorating ever since," Amanda said. "After Sister Parrish died, I did it mostly myself. Will you get the basket from the trunk, please?"

Stone followed her through the front door and to the kitchen, where he deposited the basket. Amanda got a bottle of Krug Brut from the fridge and poured them both a glass. "Ready for lunch?" she asked.

"I'm ready for anything," Stone replied.

"I'm delighted to hear it. Why don't you light the fire in the living room, and I'll be in in a moment. Take the champagne with you."

Stone followed instructions, kneeling on a deep sheepskin rug to fan the fire. He tossed his jacket onto the sofa and sat cross-legged on the sheepskin, staring into the crackling flames.

"I love a fire," Amanda said, setting down a silver tray and joining him on the rug. Having shed her coat, she was wearing a red cashmere jumpsuit that zipped up the front. The tray contained a lobster salad and a loaf of French bread, and they dug into it. When they had finished, Amanda pushed the tray aside and stretched out on the rug, her head in Stone's lap. Sunlight streamed into the room, bringing out the soft colors in the carefully chosen furnishings. "Mmmm, I feel almost perfect," she said.

"What would make you feel completely perfect?" Stone asked.

She laughed a low laugh and turned on her side. Gently, she put her mouth on his crotch and softly bit at his penis through his trousers. "That would," she said. "Why are we wearing all these clothes?"

"I can't imagine," Stone replied.

She sat up and began working on his buttons. When she had stripped him of all his clothing, she stood, tugged at the long zipper, and stepped out of her jumpsuit. He was already fully erect, and she knelt on the sheepskin and took him into her mouth.

"If you do that much longer there won't be anything left," Stone panted.

She stopped and climbed on top of him. "I'll be the judge of when there's nothing left," she said, taking him inside her. For better than half an hour they lay on the sheepskin, changing positions occasionally, experimenting, until she let out a sharp cry and began her orgasm. Stone rose to meet her, and they came nearly together, noisily, groping and gasping. Finally she fell, panting, beside him on the rug. "What a wonderful first time," she breathed, stroking his damp penis.

"Wonderful is the word," Stone agreed.

"Let me tell you how it's going to be with you and me," Amanda said.

"All right, tell me."

"We're not going to become an item around the city," she said. "We're not going to fall in love. We're going to be friendly, maybe even friends, and we're going to meet when we feel like it, not out of any sense of mutual obligation, but when we both feel like fucking each other, and when we do, we're going to do it well. Can you live with that?"

"Oh, it'll be a struggle, I suppose, but I think I can manage."

"Not too cold and hard a relationship for you?"

"A fellow needs all sorts of relationships. Why don't we try it and see how it goes?"

"I'd love that, but you have to understand, I don't get involved. My life is too complicated for anything beyond sex."

"I'll keep that in mind."

"Keep this in mind, too: there isn't anything you can do to me, excepting violence, that I won't enjoy, and there's nothing you could want that I wouldn't love doing to you. All my life I've had a voracious sexual appetite, and I love doing to just as well as being done to. Am I beginning to sound like the perfect woman?"

"Just about."

She laughed. "I'm not jealous, either; you can fuck whomever you like, and it won't bother me. But please understand: discretion must be absolute. Nobody knows we're together or where we are, and that's the way I want to keep it."

"Not even Martha?"

"Not even Martha. With this scandal sheet thing happening I must be very, very careful. We can fuck at my apartment or at your house or here, but only when we're absolutely alone, agreed?"

"Agreed."

She was kneading his penis, then she swallowed it for a moment and stopped. "Do you particularly like this?" she asked.

"Particularly," he managed to reply.

She found an orifice with a finger. "And this?"

"Oh, yes."

She returned to his penis, but did not remove her finger.

Stone found her buttocks with his hand and returned the favor. For the next several minutes they used only lips and fingers until both came again. When they had exhausted their orgasms, Amanda left for a couple of minutes and came back with a basket of hot towels. Slowly, they sponged the sweat and fluids from each other's body; then they stretched out again onto the sheepskin and relaxed.

"I wish we could stay the night," Amanda said, "but I have to be back in the city this evening for an important engagement."

"It's all right," Stone replied. "If we stayed the night I might be dead by morning."

She giggled. "But you'll be ready again when we've dozed for a while, won't you?" She took a light hold on his penis and squeezed.

"I am entirely in your hands," Stone breathed.

She laughed. "Easy now; rest for a little while."

"Amanda, I've never met anyone quite like you," he said.

"My darling, you have no idea, as yet, just how true that is. But you will."

Somehow, he knew she was right.

Chapter 17

Stone was home by dark; he came into the house at dusk, feeling oddly empty inside. Drained might be a better word, he thought, reminding himself of how he had spent the afternoon. He switched on the living room lights and walked to the study, sinking into a leather wing chair.

Stone had always thought of himself as having a large appetite for sex, but he had never before met anyone as voracious as Amanda Dart. He remembered, in a high school science class, seeing a captive black widow spider as it came upon a fly in its web and watching as the spider had sucked the life out of the fly. Now he thought he knew how the fly felt.

He was about to go upstairs when a red light on the telephone beside him began to flash. It was the fax machine in his office, and he wondered who could be faxing him on a Saturday evening. He walked downstairs, switched on the office lights, and went to the machine. It was just spitting out a sheet of paper, and he picked it up.

Oh, God, he thought, *what now?*

DIRT

Greetings, earthlings! Fabulous dinner party at dear Amanda Dart's last evening, just fabulous! A roster from the A-list, distinguished one and all. There was Richard A. Hickock, dear Amanda's publisher, whose nineteen-year-old mistress, one Tiffany Potts (no kidding) was, somehow, not invited. Tiffany resides in nineties splendor in a lovely brownstone apartment not a condom's throw from Dickie's own digs on Fifth Avenue, and she is not trotted out on such occasions. Though top-heavy, Tiffany's tits are her own, not the gift of a quack, and we are reliably informed that they are what keeps Dickie coming back for more. The publisher's mammary complex is well known—what's the matter, Dickie, didn't Mommy do right by you as a baby?

The gorgeous Vance Calder was there, too, sporting one of the lovelies he hopes will keep folks from asking too many questions about his erotic preferences. This one is said to have a brain, too!

Finally, there was the handsome lawyer-cum-gumshoe, Stone Barrington, who Amanda has retained to uncover little old us. Watch out, Stone, even though Amanda has just turned fifty, she's as horny as ever she was. The former Ida Louise Erenheim, who hails from the downscale side of some small-town Georgia tracks, has bounced from bed to bed for thirty-odd years, improving her station with each hop. She's discreet, we'll give her that, but keep your fly zipped, Stone, or dear Amanda will be on you like a bunny rabbit!

Stone's ears reddened as he read the sheet. The phone rang, and he picked it up. "Hello?"

"Stone, it's Amanda. Another of those horrible

faxes just came in, and I've got the number from the Caller ID box attached to my fax machine."

"Give it to me." She dictated the number, and Stone wrote it down. "I'll check it out and get back to you," he said.

"I'll be out all evening, but you can get me first thing in the morning."

"Right." He hung up and switched on his computer. From a box on his desktop he selected a CD-ROM disk and inserted it into the computer. A few keystrokes later a window appeared on the screen. "Name or phone?" it asked.

He selected PHONE and typed in the number Amanda had just given him. "Searching," the screen said. A few seconds later a name and address appeared on the screen. "Eddie's Mailboxes." The address was on Lexington Avenue in the upper seventies. Stone wrote it down, left the house through his office door, and hailed a cab. Less than ten minutes from when the fax had come in he was walking into Eddie's Mailboxes. A young man stood behind the counter.

"Evening," Stone said.

"Yeah," the young man said. "Help you with something?"

Stone put the scandal sheet on the counter. "This was faxed to me a few minutes ago; can you tell me who brought it in here?"

"Well, the way I look at it," the young man said, "that's kind of confidential information."

Stone put a twenty on the counter. "Describe the person."

The twenty disappeared. "Hispanic, late teens, on the short side."

"Male or female?"

"Male."

"How long ago?"

"About forty-five minutes. He gave me the sheet and a list of numbers. The machine is still faxing them."

"Can I see the list of numbers?"

"Well...."

Stone produced another twenty.

The young man produced a sheet of papers with around fifty numbers on it. Some were in New York, some in L.A.

"This Hispanic teenager; he ever been in here before?"

"I never seen him."

"You ever fax something like this before?"

"First time. Entertaining, ain't it?"

"Thanks," Stone said, and turned to go.

"I'll tell you this for free," the young man said.

Stone stopped and turned. "Yes?"

"I think somebody gave the kid a few bucks to bring it in here, you know?"

Stone nodded and left, tucking the list of phone numbers into his pocket. He got a cab home, went back to his study, and poured himself a bourbon. The message light was flashing on his answering machine. Probably Amanda, he thought, pressing a button. The machine rewound quickly; only one message.

"This is Arrington Carter," a woman's voice said. "Give me a call when you get a chance." She left a number.

"My goodness," Stone said aloud while he dialed the number. "It certainly pays to stay home on a Saturday night." The phone rang, and there was a click.

"Hi, I'm out, leave a message," her recorded voice said.

Stone slumped with disappointment. He must have just missed her. "It's Stone Barrington, returning your call," he said. "I'll look forward to hearing from you."

He hung up, and the phone rang almost immediately. He grabbed it on the first ring; it must be her. "Hello?"

"Barrington?" a man's voice said. He sounded angry.

"Yes."

"This is Richard Hickock."

"Hello, Dick."

"Is it true that you're working for Amanda on this thing?"

"What thing?"

"This *DIRT* business. The goddamned thing came in on my home fax machine. My *wife* could have seen it."

"I'm afraid I can't discuss that, Dick. You'll have to talk to Amanda."

"I'll do that, don't worry; I just want to say this: You find out who's doing this, and I'll double whatever Amanda's paying you."

"As I said, I can't discuss it."

"I'll get back to you," Hickock said, slamming down the phone.

Stone sighed. He'd rather it had been Arrington Carter. He went downstairs, started his computer, and began identifying the phone numbers on the *DIRT* distribution list. They were pretty much

90

what he had expected—newspapers, TV shows, columnists. Halfway through he tired of the list, shut off the computer, and crawled into bed with a book.

Chapter 18

Stone was awakened by the ringing telephone. He opened an eye and looked at the beside clock: nine-thirty. He didn't usually sleep so late. "Hello?" he grumbled into the phone.

"It's Amanda; what did you find out last night?"

"The fax was sent to a distribution list from a mailbox and copy shop on Lex in the Seventies. Apparently our man gave some kid a few bucks to deliver it; he's being careful."

"Damn!" she said. "I was hoping for a break."

"So was I. I think we'll find the next one will be sent from a similar place by similar means. I did get a copy of the distribution list, though."

"Who was on it?"

"Just who you'd think—anybody who might spread the word. Nothing to be learned from the list, I'm afraid."

"So we're back to square one?"

That was an embarrassing question, and Stone didn't answer it. "I got a call from Dick Hickock last night. He's interested in finding out who the publisher of *DIRT* is, too."

"I'm not surprised, after the contents of last night's fax. He's already been onto me this morning. I don't mind in the least if you work for him, too."

"Well, so far I don't have anything more to tell him than I have to tell you."

"Keep at it," she said, and hung up without another word.

Wide awake now, Stone brushed his teeth, took his vitamins, and got into a robe. He went to the little kitchenette outside his bedroom, got some English muffins and coffee going, then retrieved the *Sunday Times* from his front doorstep. He was back in bed, eating breakfast and reading the paper, when the phone rang again. "Hello?"

"It's Arrington Carter," a low voice said.

"Morning."

"You had breakfast yet?"

"Nope," he replied, setting down his half-eaten muffin.

"Can I buy you brunch?"

"Why don't you come over here; I'll fix you an omelette."

"I'd rather meet you at the Brasserie in half an hour."

"Make it an hour; I haven't really gotten started this morning."

"An hour it is," she said, "and brunch is on me."

"Yes, ma'am." They both hung up.

She was waiting at the top of the stairs that descended into the restaurant; they shook hands and got a table immediately. She ordered a pitcher of mimosas, sat back in the booth, and looked at him through large, dark glasses. "So," she said. "Tell me about you."

"What do you want to know?"

"More than you're probably willing to tell me."

"I'm an open book," Stone said, "but I'd rather talk to eyes than shades."

She took them off, revealing large green eyes, a little red around the rims, no makeup.

"Late night?"

"Swine," she said equably. "I reveal myself, and you point out my weaknesses."

"I don't see any weaknesses."

"Good. Now, you were going to tell me about yourself."

Stone gave her the sixty-second version of his biography. "Now," he said, "who you?"

"Me Jane," she said.

"Who Tarzan?"

"No Tarzan, just me."

"Good news."

"I'm glad you think so. Who your Jane?"

"She took a hike last week."

"You all broken up?"

"No, just mystified."

She laughed. "I'll bet she told you exactly why she was dumping you."

He shrugged. "You're right, she did, and she was specific."

"Not enough of a commitment?"

"Something like that; how'd you guess?"

"Attractive men your age who've never been married nearly always come up short in the commitment department."

"You were telling me about you," Stone said.

"In sixty seconds or less, like you?"

"If you like."

"Virginia girl from old Virginia family, Virginia schools, et cetera, et cetera."

"You've got fifty-five seconds left."

"Came to New York to be an actress, didn't like the process, wrote about it, wrote other stuff, still writing."

"Fiction or non?"

"Non, although there's half a novel somewhere in my computer."

Something rang a bell. "Did you once write a piece for *The New Yorker* about being an actress in New York?"

"Guilty."

"I liked that piece; I guess I'd never given any thought to what a tough life it can be."

"Thank you for the kind review."

"Were you any good as an actress?"

"As a matter of fact, I was."

"Why didn't you stick with it?"

"You read my piece."

"I find it hard to believe that someone so beautiful would have a hard time making it if she had talent, too."

"Let me tell you something: Being beautiful is hard work, maybe even harder than acting."

"I'd always thought beauty was a great advantage in any field."

"There are advantages, God knows, but they are offset by the liabilities."

"Such as?"

"The difficulty of hanging on to one's soul. There are lots of people out there who are in the market for it, and some of their offers are hard to turn down."

"I see your point."

"You probably don't, or at least not much of it,

but you'll just have to take my word for it, because the subject is too boring to be discussed while sober. Let's order some breakfast."

They both ordered eggs Benedict, and passed the time until their food came discussing the variety of people sitting around them in the restaurant.

"What made you call me?" Stone asked, finally.

"You fishing for compliments?"

"Apart from my devastating attractiveness, I mean."

She laughed. "I haven't spent very much time with men as gorgeous as Vance Calder," she said, "but it occurred to me that meeting me in the company of somebody like that might slow a man down when it came to calling me. You didn't, for instance, ask me for my number, or even ask me anything that might tell you how to get in touch with me."

"You're right; I judged the competition to be impossibly tough."

"Well, relax; Vance isn't competition."

"What is he?"

"A friend, sort of; sometimes. He's mostly on the coast; sometimes he calls me when he's in town and he needs a date."

"It never occurred to me that Vance Calder would ever need a date."

"Well, he does, and he doesn't like bimbos. Vance is a very bright man, as anyone who has ever negotiated a contract with him can tell you, and he likes bright company. That's not so easy to come by, even for him."

"Is he gay?"

"Not so's a girl would notice," she said. "I've

95

never known a more attentive man. There are rumors, but there are always rumors about people in his position, even when they've been married and divorced a couple of times, as he has."

"I hope I'm not being inattentive. May I have your number again? I'd like to call it often."

She fished a card from her bag and handed it to him. "See that you do."

He put the card into his jacket pocket.

"What is it with this *DIRT* thing?" she asked.

"Where'd you hear about it?"

"Vance had a copy in his pocket on Saturday night, the one about Amanda's little hotel rendezvous."

"Oh, that one."

"She hired you to run it down, then, like the sheet says?"

"I couldn't confirm that, even if she had."

"Well, I'm glad you're not a blabbermouth."

"By the way, did you know that you made the latest edition of *DIRT*?"

Her eyes widened. "What are you talking about?"

He produced last night's fax and handed it to her. She read it with bated breath.

"Jesus, that was fast, wasn't it?"

"It was."

"At least it didn't mention my name."

"I wonder why," he said.

"Why do you think?" she asked.

"I don't know. It would seem that the publisher's information was good enough to do so, if he wanted to, but he didn't. He did pay you the compliment of calling you bright, though."

"How would he know?"

"Maybe the publisher is somebody who knows you. Did you tell anybody you were going to the dinner party?"

"No; Vance only called me on Friday, and he didn't say who'd be there, except for Amanda."

"What did you think of Amanda?"

"I think she's predatory," Arrington said.

Stone's ears were burning, and he hoped she didn't notice. "I don't really know her well enough to confirm that," he lied.

"Trust me; a girl knows about these things."

"I think I do trust you. Why do you think that is?"

She smiled. "Because you have good judgment."

As they left the restaurant, she immediately flagged down a cab.

"I was hoping we could spend the day together," Stone said.

"Sorry, I've got plans. I'd like to see you soon, though; will you call me?"

"I certainly will."

She pecked him on the cheek, got into the cab, and rode away.

Stone walked slowly home, facing a Sunday alone with the papers and *60 Minutes*. Well, he thought, it wouldn't be the first.

Chapter 19

First thing Monday morning, Arnie Millman eased himself carefully into a chair in Stone's office. "Hemorrhoids," he said without being asked.

"It's all those years sitting on your ass at the Nineteenth Precinct," Stone said. "What've you got for me?"

"The girl, Helen, first," Arnie said. "She's seeing a guy; he's an advertising art director at Young and Rubicam."

"How do they spend their time together?"

"Screwing, mostly; the relationship is only a couple of weeks old, but neither one is seeing anybody else. They go out, they grab a pizza, they go home, usually his, and they screw. Noisily."

"Any connections to the publishing or entertainment industries?"

"Not that I could see. His accounts are an airline and a hand lotion; neither one is good for much show biz contact, far as I can see."

"Still, advertising people mix with actors and other people who cross over into entertainment."

"Not this one, apparently."

"Okay, what about Barry?"

"Barry is a different story; Barry mixes with anybody he thinks is cute. I saw him buy a gross of condoms at his neighborhood drugstore—they had ordered them for him. He hangs out at a bar in the East Village called the Leather Room, and he takes home somebody different just about every night. These boys are all over the place—actors, dancers, directors—he seems to prefer those in the business."

"Did you pick up on any pillow talk?"

"I put a cup mike on his bedroom window, and I heard it all, and I mean *all*, believe me. Something I don't understand about these people, these

98

pansies: How come they can do it every night, two or three times a night? I could never do that, even when I was his age."

"The younger generation seems to be in better shape."

"Tell me about it."

"And you can't call them 'pansies' anymore, Arnie; too many people find that offensive."

"Tell me about it," Arnie replied.

Stone changed the subject. "Is Barry chatty about his work?"

"The CIA should be so tight-lipped. The boy tells his new friends who he works for—that always gets a reaction—but he doesn't blab about what he does for her, or about her. Strikes me as intensely loyal to his boss."

"I'm disappointed," Stone said. "He seemed the likely one to me, and the multiple relationships would underscore that. But if you feel strongly…."

"I kid you not, Stone, the guy's a regular monument to discretion." Arnie shifted painfully in his seat. "What about the other one?"

"What?"

"You said there was a third employee."

"Yeah, but she doesn't look promising." Stone sighed, wrote down Martha's name and address, and handed it to Arnie. "About five-five, a hundred and fifty, pale red hair, not pretty."

Arnie read it and looked up. "You want me to check her out?"

Stone thought about it for a minute. "My client feels strongly that she's not the leak, and I have to agree with her."

"Can't hurt to check," Arnie replied.

"I guess not. Maybe I'll take a look at her later, if I don't come up with anything else."

Arnie shoved the address back across the desk. "This is something to do with this *DIRT* business, isn't it? And so I guess I know who your client is."

"Arnie, you really get around, don't you?" Stone asked, surprised. "How'd you come by this?"

Arnie shrugged. "Friend of mine is on the features desk at the Post. They been handing the sheet around the newsroom."

"You got any theories?"

"Sounds like somebody tight with one of the people getting burned, maybe with more than one of them. I think you should check out Martha there." He pointed at the piece of paper on Stone's desk. "You can never tell what motivates a person."

Stone nodded. "You've got a point; maybe I will."

His secretary buzzed. "Richard Hickock on line one. You in?"

"I'm in," Stone replied. "See you soon, Arnie; give my girl your bill on the way out, and she'll write you a check." He picked up the phone as he watched the retired detective trudge out. "Dick?"

"Okay, I talked with Amanda," Hickock said, not bothering with a greeting.

"She told me."

"What have you learned so far?"

"Not much; I'm checking out a few leads."

"Any of them lead to me?"

"Not so far. Tell me, who else knows about Tiffany Potts?"

"Not a goddamned soul, that's who."

"Not your secretary?"

"No. We don't communicate through her."

"How do you communicate?"

"Cellular phones, and she has a beeper."

"Cellular can be leaky, Dick. All somebody needs is a scanner."

"We never use names. If somebody was listening, they wouldn't know who was talking. We also keep it very brief."

"I think I should talk with Miss Potts."

"Stone, she's very *very* discreet."

"Nevertheless, Dick, if you want me to get to the bottom of this...."

"Oh, all right; I'll have her call you."

"Good. Are there any other...intimates I should talk with?"

"None. Get back to me." Hickock hung up.

Ten minutes later, she was on the phone. "This is Tiffany," she said. "A mutual friend says we should talk." Her voice was quiet, shy.

"May I come and see you?" Stone asked.

"Sure; when?"

"Half an hour?"

"I guess I can get myself together by then." She gave him the address. "It says Dunhill on the bell. Ring twice, then once; the intercom's not working."

The townhouse had a limestone facade and only four bells; each apartment occupied a floor, and Hickock's mistress was on the third. Tiffany Potts had done very well for herself. Stone rang the bell twice, paused, then once more. The lock clicked, and he was inside a mahogany-paneled foyer. The elevator door stood open; he took it to the top floor.

She was smaller than he had thought she would be, less blonde, and prettier; the scandal sheet had been right about her bustline. She was wearing well-fitted jeans and a chambray shirt. She stepped back and held the door open. "Please come in," she said, offering her hand. "I'm Tiffany Potts."

The apartment was quite handsome—crown moldings, nice curtains, good furniture, good pictures, lots of books. She showed him to one of a pair of sofas facing each other before the fireplace. "You have a very nice place," Stone said. "Who's your decorator?"

"I am," she said shyly.

"You have very good taste."

She rewarded him with a small smile. "Thank you."

"What did Mr. Hickock tell you about me, Miss Potts?"

"Please call me Tiff; everybody does. He said you're looking into this *DIRT* thing for him. Are you a private detective? You don't look like what I'd imagined."

"I used to be a police detective, Tiff; now I'm a lawyer."

"What should I call you?"

"Stone will be just fine."

"I like that name. Names are important to actors."

"Is Dunhill your professional name?"

"Not really; Dick didn't want my name on the bell. I chose Dunhill; it's sort of a joke. Believe me, I wouldn't call myself Tiffany Dunhill; it sounds like a stripper."

Stone smiled. "You're an actress?"

"An actor," she corrected. "A student, really."

"Where are you studying?"

"At the Actor's Studio."

"That's very impressive; you'd have to be very promising to be accepted."

"Dick got me the interview, but I got in because of my audition," she said. "I expect all you know about me is what you read in that *DIRT* thing, but I'm not a bimbo, Stone. I have talent as an actor."

"Have you appeared in anything yet?"

"Two off-Broadway plays, one of them a lead; I got good reviews."

"Do you mind answering my questions?"

"No; Dick said to tell you the truth."

"How long have you known Dick?"

"About fourteen months. He came to a backer's audition for one of the plays I did."

"Did you start seeing him right away?"

"No; I knew he was married, so I refused to go out with him. But he came to our opening a few weeks later, and to the party afterward, and I really liked him. I decided to overlook his wife. I know that doesn't sound very moral, but I'm a big girl; I take full responsibility." She waved a hand. "He gives me this, and I give him...companionship. Sex is only part of it. He leads a very pressured existence, and he's able to relax completely with me. I don't expect him to leave his wife; at some stage it will end, but right now it suits us both."

"How often do you see him?"

"Somewhere between once and three times a week, depending on when he can get away."

"Where do you go?"

"Usually here. I cook for him. Once or twice

picked me up at the Studio, and we've gone for dinner in the Village."

On any of these occasions did you run into anybody who knew him?"

"No. When he's not wearing a business suit, he's really quite anonymous."

"Anybody who knew you?"

She shook her head.

"Has there ever been a mention of you two in any of the gossip columns?"

"Not once; not until this *DIRT* thing. Dick is very upset about it; his wife doesn't seem to know yet, but he thinks she'll find out now, that some 'friend' will mention it to her. The fact is, he loves his wife. He just needs something more than she's giving him."

"Tiff, have you ever had the feeling that somebody was following you?"

Her brow wrinkled. "No, I haven't; do you think somebody might be?"

"It's a possibility; after all, whoever is publishing this sheet seems to know where you live."

She looked worried now. "I hadn't thought about that. Do you think I'm in any danger?"

"No, I shouldn't think so. In fact, you may have already heard the last of this. Whoever's doing it just wanted to needle Hickock; I don't think you were the target."

She looked relieved.

"Have you ever discussed your relationship with Dick with anyone else—a friend, maybe—somebody at the Studio?"

"No, never; it's always been our secret. God, I wouldn't want anybody I know to think that I'm the mistress of a married man, which is—let's face it—what I am. I come from a small town, where people don't do this sort of thing. I would never want this to get back to my parents. They wouldn't understand at all."

"I don't think it will get back to them," Stone said. He handed her his card. "I don't want you to get paranoid about this, but if you ever feel that someone is following you, or if anyone tries to photograph you on the street, please go straight to a pay phone and call me. I'll try to find out who it is."

"Thank you, I'll do that," she said.

Stone stood up. "Well, that's all I need to know for the moment," he said. "I'm sorry to intrude on your privacy."

"That's all right," she said, smiling. "To tell you the truth, if I weren't seeing Dick, I'd welcome the intrusion; sometimes I get a little lonely." She opened the door and held out her hand. "I hope you'll come and see me if I ever get in another play."

Stone took her hand. "I'm sure you will, and I'd like that very much."

She closed the door behind him, and he took the elevator down. He liked the girl; he thought Hickock was a lucky man. If his wife didn't find out about Tiffany Potts.

Chapter 20

Arnie Millman came out of the movie house on Third Avenue and checked his watch; nearly five.

105

Arnie had spent the day at the movies because he didn't have any work to do. It kept him out of the house, and that was okay with his wife. Tonight was her bridge night, and his apartment would be full of cackling hens. He always ate out on her bridge night, but he wasn't hungry yet.

It occurred to him that he wasn't all that far from the address Stone had shown him, Amanda Dart's place, where the secretary, Martha, worked. Maybe he'd give Stone a couple of free hours; after all, he had nothing else to do until dinnertime. He walked briskly uptown and west, until he came to the apartment building where Amanda Dart lived.

He hung around outside until Martha came out, just after five-thirty. She was as Stone had described her—plump and a little on the plain side— and he began to follow her home. Except she didn't seem to be going home. Martha lived on Third Avenue in the Sixties, but she crossed Third and walked uptown to Second Avenue in the Eighties. Her step was light; Arnie thought she must be in a very good mood.

She went into a fancy grocery store, and Arnie followed her. He picked up a basket and began idly dropping things into it, watching her as she moved through the aisles. She spent most of her time at the deli counter, buying a big chunk of smoked salmon, a small tin of very expensive caviar, and some cheeses, testing them for ripeness. She picked up a bunch of fresh flowers and, finally, a bottle of very good domestic champagne. Somehow, Arnie didn't think she was planning supper alone at home. He put down his basket and ducked out of the store as she stopped at the checkout counter.

A few minutes later, she came out and headed uptown, carrying a shopping bag in one hand and her purse and the flowers in the other. Arnie followed, half a block behind her. He was right in the middle of the 19th Precinct, his old beat, and he knew virtually every shop and restaurant along the way. He was enjoying the walk.

Then something peculiar happened: the hairs on the back of his neck stood on end. It used to happen when he was in a dangerous situation, when he was hyperalert, going down a dark alley after somebody with a knife, that sort of thing. Now it was happening for no apparent reason.

Martha stopped at a corner for a traffic light, and Arnie turned toward the window of an antique shop, apparently studying its contents. With little visible motion of his head, he checked down the street in the direction from which he had come. He had the odd feeling that he was being followed.

The streets were busy, lots of people on the way home from work, many of them with briefcases or groceries. He could detect no one who made him suspicious. Normally, if he had thought he were being followed, he would have checked the other side of the street as well, but he dismissed the notion from his mind. He remembered an occasion, many years ago, when he had been followed, on Second Avenue, right around here. Some part of his brain must have reacted to that memory.

The light changed, and Martha continued uptown, turning east down a street in the low Nineties. Arnie crossed the street and followed her down the other side, continuing when she stopped at a building. He saw her open a wrought-iron gate and disappear down a flight of steps to what must have been an outside door to the basement. He crossed the street, walked to the building, and looked down the stairwell, just in time to see her entering the apartment, stopping on the threshold, apparently to give someone a kiss. He couldn't see who it was. The door closed, and Arnie was left standing on the sidewalk, frustrated.

He walked up the front steps of the building and checked the mailboxes; the one for the basement apartment was marked "Dryer." Arnie stood on the stoop and looked up and down the street. It looked as though Martha was there for dinner, at the very least, and while it wasn't his own dinnertime yet, he had no great wish to spend the next two or three hours standing in the cold outside this building waiting for Martha to come out, especially since he wasn't being paid to do so. Even if he did wait, what would he accomplish? What he wanted to know was, who was Dryer, and what were they talking about in that apartment?

Arnie walked down the steps, tipping his hat to a middle-aged woman who was on her way up, and at the bottom turned right. There was a narrow alley beside the building, and he walked down it, hoping there might be a window opening into the basement apartment that he could see through. He found nothing but a solid brick wall.

Still, basement apartments often had gardens, didn't they? He took out a penlight and shone it down the alley; it stopped at a brick wall another forty feet along. He walked on down the alley until the brick changed to a concrete block wall, which went up only a couple of feet higher than his head. The wall seemed to separate him from a garden, and there would be windows on the other side of it.

Arnie found an empty garbage can with a lid and carried it over to the wall. He steadied himself against the concrete blocks and tried to step up on top of the can, but it was too big a step for him. A few years ago, he'd have had no problem doing that, but now....Using his penlight, he found a wooden box full of excelsior down the alley. He carried it back and placed it next to the garbage can; it made a nice step up.

Arnie stepped onto the box and, grabbing the top of the wall with his fingers, stepped up onto the garbage can. He was head and shoulders above the top of the wall now, and he could see a row of glowing windows on the back of the building, with shadows moving across them. Must be the kitchen; Martha and her friend, Dryer, would be preparing the things she had brought from the grocery.

Arnie figured that, in spite of his years, he could hoist himself to the top of the wall and down the other side, so he could look through the windows. He was about to try this when the hairs on the back of his neck began moving around again. Then there was a tug on the tail of his raincoat, and, alarmed, he turned around to see who was there.

"What the fuck..." he managed to say aloud, before he began to fall off the garbage can.

Chapter 21

Stone worked late on a memo advising a Woodman & Weld client how to handle a drunk driving charge for an employee's wife. It was nearly eight when he had finished the memo and faxed it to Bill Eggers, and he had just turned out his office light when the phone rang. He switched the light on again and picked up the phone. "Hello?"

"Stone, it's Dino."

"Hi, Dino."

"Can you meet me at Elaine's in half an hour?"

"Sure."

"Good." The detective lieutenant hung up.

Dino could be curt when under pressure, Stone remembered; he wondered what was going on. He felt grungy, so he had a quick shower and changed into some casual clothes before leaving the house and hailing a cab uptown.

Dino was already at a table along the right wall when Stone entered, and he looked grim. Stone's immediate thought was wife or father-in-law trouble, but he was wrong. He sat down, ordered a bourbon, and looked at his former partner. "So, what's going on? You look a little down."

Dino nodded. "Down is a good word for it. Somebody wasted Arnie Millman around six this evening."

Stone stared at Dino. "Jesus, I saw him only this morning."

"Not since then?"

"No, not since nine-thirty, ten, I guess. This is terrible; has somebody called his wife?"

"I drew that duty," Dino said glumly. "I sent a

policewoman out there to be with her until some family could be rounded up."

"What happened, Dino?"

"Was he working on something for you?"

"No."

"Stone, your check for sixteen hundred bucks was in his pocket."

"He was working on something; we finished up this morning, and I paid him."

"Any loose ends?"

Stone thought about Martha, but dismissed the idea. "No; he checked two people out for me, gave me his report this morning, and that was it."

"Anything about these two people that could have hurt Arnie?"

Stone shook his head. "It was a straightforward surveillance, a background check. Both people were no problem to my client, so that was it."

"Any chance either of them could have known Arnie was following them?"

"You know Arnie better than that, Dino; he was good."

"Yeah." Dino opened his notebook and showed Stone an address in the low Nineties. "That address mean anything to you?"

Stone shook his head again.

"Yeah. You sure this address doesn't match up with either of your people?"

"Absolutely; one lives in the West Fifties, the other in the East Village. Who lives there?"

"My guys talked with all the tenants, but nobody admitted knowing Arnie or anything about him. One woman saw him coming down the front steps as she was going up; that was about five-forty-five. Arnie bought it in an alley beside the building shortly after that."

"How?"

"Small-caliber handgun, looks like. He took two in the head. It wouldn't have made much noise."

"Robbery, maybe?"

"Maybe. They took his gun; I remember Arnie using the old standard Smith & Wesson thirty-eight, two-inch barrel. His wallet was beside him and the money was gone, but who knows? That could have been window dressing."

"Look, Arnie wasn't the sort of guy to attract a pro hit. He worked Robbery for most of his career, never had anything to do with the wiseguys."

"I know, I know."

"It just doesn't make any sense."

"What was he working on for you?"

"Are we off the record here, Dino?"

"Sure, it's just between you and me."

"You remember that *DIRT* thing. He was checking out two of Amanda Dart's employees; both of them came up clean. It isn't the sort of business to end up with a shooting like this one. It's all ego, vanity."

"Two good motives for murder."

"Not in this case. Neither employee had any thought of being followed by Arnie; he'd have known it if they did. There's only one other employee, and I didn't assign Arnie to her; I was going to check her out myself, if it came to that. I don't think it will."

"Where does that employee live?"

"Third Avenue in the Sixties."

"Nowhere near, then."

"No. She's a secretary; not the type to shoot a retired cop."

"I'll take your word."

"When do you get the ME's report?"

"He's working on Arnie's body now; he'll call me here when he's finished."

"No witnesses, of course."

"None. Like I said, it wouldn't have made much noise, wouldn't have attracted any attention unless somebody had been walking right by the alley at the very moment."

"And nobody was?"

"Nope. Let's have some dinner while we wait for the ME to call." He signaled a waiter for a menu.

They ate in glum silence. It was a ritual with them; in the circumstances they were either supposed to talk about Arnie, or not at all. Stone tried to remember some anecdote or other about Arnie, but he couldn't. "Funny," he said after a while, "all I can remember about him in the squad room is he never took his overcoat off in winter. He'd sit there in his coat with the steam heat going and type arrest reports."

"He had some good busts," Dino said. "I never partnered with him, but I remember he had a reputation for being tenacious, for not giving up on a case, for going the extra mile in an investigation."

"I knew that, I guess. That's why, when he called me for work—this was three, four years ago—I gave it to him when I could. He was reliable, he had a good nose. That's why I don't think either of the people he was working on for me could have been involved. Arnie would have smelled something. Do you think this could connect to some old case of his?"

"What, fifteen years after he retired? I can't buy that."

The pay phone on the wall rang, and they both stopped eating and watched a waiter answer it. He waved Dino over.

The conversation lasted less than a minute, and Dino's expression never changed. He came back and sat down.

"What's the news?"

"Like I thought, two shots, small caliber—a twenty-five automatic."

"Don't see many of those anymore."

"Yeah, these days every punk on the street has a Glock or something better. There was an abrasion on Arnie's left knee, too, like he fell down, but no marks to show that somebody hit him first."

"Where'd he take the bullets?"

"Left temple and back of the head."

"An execution, then. Well, I suppose it could have been some junkie with some trash piece he'd copped in a burglary. He sees Arnie, an old guy, easy mark, and he's desperate enough to pop him, even for just a few bucks."

"He didn't take your check," Dino said.

"Where was it, in the wallet?"

Dino shook his head. "Left inside jacket pocket. The guy went for the cash, didn't worry about the rest. Arnie was wearing a Rolex we chipped in for when he put in his papers."

"I remember that," Stone said. "I bought a piece of that watch. The guy didn't take that?"

Dino shook his head. "This doesn't look good for clearing."

"Pull in your snitches, put the word out on the street. The twenty-five handgun is something, at least. Not a lot of them on the street, I'll bet."

"Oh, we'll treat it as a cop killing, which means all the stops out," Dino said. "I'm just not optimistic."

"Maybe you'll get lucky."

"Funny," Dino said, playing with his food. "I don't feel lucky today."

Chapter 22

Stone said goodbye to Dino on the sidewalk, declined a lift home, and walked up Second Avenue. He turned right in the low Nineties and found the building. There was nothing in particular to distinguish it from any of the other houses on the street. Most of them looked better now than they had when he was working out of the 19th; gentrification had had its way with the block.

The alley was dark, and he used a pocket flashlight that had been part of his wardrobe since his first day as a detective nearly twenty years before. There didn't seem to be much reason for the alley—it was a dead-ender, and neither of the adjacent buildings had a door opening onto it. At the back, after the buildings ended, there was a wall on either side of the alley, affording some privacy to the gardens at the rear of the houses. Stone's light fell on a garbage can and a wooden box.

It was a funny place for a garbage can, not near a back door, where it might be used, or the street, where it might be emptied. He turned and looked back toward the street. Half a dozen other cans rested there. Why was this one at the opposite end of the alley? Certainly, no New York City garbage collector was going to walk the few extra yards to pick it up.

Stone stepped onto the box, then onto the garbage can, and looked over the wall. Small garden, untended, dark windows at the back of the building. Could Arnie have been interested in those windows? He remembered that the old detective had used a cup microphone on one of the other two surveillances. He looked up and saw a fire escape disappearing upward into the darkness. If he stood on top of the wall and jumped, he could make the fire escape. Was Arnie contemplating that? The idea seemed preposterous for a man of his years; his even going over the wall seemed unlikely.

Stone hopped down, then remembered that the Medical Examiner had said that Arnie's body had had an abrasion on a knee. Could he have gotten that jumping or falling from the garbage can? He played the light around once more, hoping for something that the cops had overlooked, but there was nothing.

He walked back to the front of the building and put his light on the mailboxes; none of the names sounded at all familiar. He wrote them down for future reference, then walked back down the steps to the street. He looked over the iron railing at the basement apartment; a dim light glowed behind the windows. That apartment would own the garden out back. He walked down the stairs and rang the bell, waited, then rang it again.

The door opened the length of the security chain and a young man, half in silhouette, looked back at him. Six feet, a hundred and eighty, hair on the short side, wearing only a pair of faded jeans; Stone registered all this automatically. He checked his notebook for the name. "Mr. Dryer?" he asked, flashing his badge. His ID had "RETIRED" stamped on it, but the badge didn't.

"Yeah?"

"Mind if I come in? It's about what happened here tonight."

"I've already answered all the questions I'm going to," the young man said. "What is this, anyway? It's after eleven."

"Sorry to inconvenience you; there are just a few more questions. I don't have to come in; you can answer them right here."

"Look, I've cooperated, answered everything you people asked me, now I'm going to get some sleep. Don't bother me again." He slammed the door shut.

Stone heard the lock work. He played his light around the front door, saw nothing, and walked back up to the street. He didn't think much about Dryer's refusal to talk to him. Lots of people didn't like talking to cops, especially twice in one evening. Unwilling to leave yet, he walked around to the alley and looked in the garbage cans. They were all empty but one; that had a paper grocery bag filled with the usual kitchen detritus, an empty champagne bottle on top. He moved the bottle, and his light fell on the lid from a caviar tin underneath it. Whoopee, he thought; somebody had had a big night; he wondered if it were Mr. Dryer. Stone walked down to First Avenue and got a cab home.

As he approached his house, Stone saw somebody sitting on his doorstep. He readied himself to send the usual vagrant on his way, but as he got nearer, he saw that the vagrant had shoulder-length dark hair and was very beautiful. "Hello, Arrington," he said.

"I camped on your doorstep," she said, sounding just a little drunk.

"I'm flattered. Come camp inside awhile."

She got to her feet and followed him into the house, back to his study.

He hung their coats in a closet and showed her to a sofa. "How about some coffee?"

"How about a drink?" she said.

"You've already had a drink or two," he said. "I like my company reasonably sober."

"Oh, all right, coffee then," she said wearily, and began to cry softly.

He sat down next to her. "Want to talk about it?"

"You make the coffee, and I'll stop crying, I promise."

He went downstairs to the kitchen, made a pot of coffee, and came back upstairs with a tray. He set it on the coffee table and poured some for her.

"Black will do," she said, picking up the cup.

Stone poured himself a cup. "So, how have you spent your evening?"

"Getting rid of Tarzan," she said.

"I thought there wasn't a Tarzan."

"There isn't anymore; I was a bit previous the other day, that's all."

"Having regrets about cutting the vine?"

She shrugged. "There was a time when I thought it might go somewhere. I've known for a while that it wouldn't; I guess I'm just feeling sorry for myself."

"Did all this take place in the neighborhood? Is that why you stopped by here?"

"It took place way uptown," she said, sipping her coffee. "You weren't on the way to anywhere. I just wanted to see you."

"I'm glad you did."

"I behaved stupidly tonight. I went over to his place to tell him it was all off, and quite to my humiliation, there was somebody else there with him."

"Oh. So you didn't have that final satisfaction of telling him where to get off."

"Exactly. You see, I wasn't crying because I'm sad, but because I'm angry. I set myself up for that, and it annoys the hell out of me."

"I get the picture. I've had pretty much the same experience in my time. It gets funny later."

She giggled. "It's already funny," she said. "Listen, I don't want to sleep alone tonight. Can I stay here with you?"

"Sure you can."

"I don't want to make love or anything; I just want somebody next to me. I'll be fine in the morning."

"Delighted to have you—I mean, to be your host."

"Have you got something I can sleep in?"

"Sure."

He gave her one of his nightshirts. She went to the bathroom, washed her face, and came back wearing the nightshirt, the sleeves rolled up.

Stone was already in bed. He lifted the covers for her, and she crawled in next to him, snuggling on his shoulder. He reached over to turn off the light, and when he turned back, she was sleeping like a child. He extracted his arm from under her, so it wouldn't go numb, put a pillow under her head, and tried to go to sleep himself. He shouldn't have had that coffee so late, he reflected.

It took at least two hours of staring at the ceiling and thinking about the girl next to him, but he finally dozed off.

Chapter 23

When Stone awoke, Arrington was in the shower. He put an extra pillow under his head and waited, hoping; a moment later, he was rewarded with the sight of her stepping out of the stall, water running down her tall body, not bothering with a towel. She stood before the mirror, squeezing water out of her hair, then reached for the towel, disappointing Stone. But his luck was holding; she wrapped it around her head and began brushing her teeth, her long back arched over the sink, her breasts dangling, her trim buttocks protruding. Stone began to get an erection.

His first impulse was to get up and take her from behind, but he stopped himself. He wanted this to go well; if it did, no doubt he would have the opportunity of jumping her on some other occasion.

She came out of the bathroom rubbing her hair with the towel, apparently not conscious of her nudity. "You're awake," she said. "I've been awake since six."

Stone looked at the bedside clock; it was after nine. "I got to sleep later than you did," he said.

"How much later?"

"A couple of hours. The coffee, I expect."

"Poor Stone." Her hair as dry as she could get it, she began toweling her body.

"Just for the record," he said, "you're a beautiful girl."

"Woman. Thank you."

"I know you're too accustomed to being told that, but I thought you ought to know how I felt about it."

"Coming from you, I consider it a great compliment." She held the towel between her legs, rubbing thoughtfully for a moment, staring into the middle distance.

Stone breathed more deeply, to keep from breathing faster; he shifted some covers to hide his rising interest. "Would you like a hair dryer?" He wanted to keep her naked for as long as possible.

"No thanks; it'll dry soon."

"Will it look the way it looked the first time I saw you?"

"Pretty much; it behaves well. I get it cut every couple of months; that's about it."

"Amazing," he said.

She laughed. "You're exhibiting an awful lot of control for a man who's in the same room as a naked woman he finds beautiful. Or is it disinterest?"

"It's an awful lot of control," he said, honestly.

She laughed again. "I'm impressed."

"So am I."

There was just a moment's hesitation; then, before he could decide what to do, she picked up her jeans and slipped them on, not bothering with underwear. "I'm sorry if I was maudlin last night," she said.

"Don't worry about it," Stone replied.

She followed the jeans with her black turtleneck sweater, then she picked up her underwear and stuffed it into a large handbag.

"How about some breakfast?" he managed to say, sorry to see her breasts disappear and anxious to hold onto her a little longer.

"Thanks, but I'm expecting a call from an editor this morning, and I don't want to miss it. How about dinner instead?"

"Gee, I'll have to check my calendar."

She laughed aloud. "Seven, at my place; Ten-Eleven Fifth Avenue, dress sloppy."

"Seven it is."

"Dare I kiss you goodbye?"

"Not unless you want to spend the day here."

"I'm gone," she said, running for the door.

The phone rang.

"Hello?"

"It's Dino; the funeral's at two o'clock, in Brooklyn; you want to ride with me?"

"Two o'clock? That's quick."

"Jews have to be buried within twenty-four hours, or something terrible happens, I forget what."

"Oh, right. Yeah, pick me up."

"One-thirty," Dino said, and hung up.

By noon a steady drizzle had enveloped the city, and by the time they left the synagogue a hard rain was falling. Stone sat in the back of the big Ford police car with Dino, while two young detectives took the front. The drive to Brooklyn was painfully slow.

"Traffic always goes to hell in this city when it rains," Dino said.

"Yeah."

"You sure this business can't be connected somehow with what you're working on?" Dino asked.

"I've thought about it again and again," Stone replied, "and I don't see how it could be. Arnie had finished the job with me."

"Arnie's wife said he went to the movies yesterday afternoon, and he was planning to eat out; it was her bridge night."

"Does that sound like he was working for me?"

"I guess not. I'm sorry to harp on this, Stone, it's just that I don't have anywhere else to go with it."

"Maybe it really was some stupid junkie."

"Maybe it was, but it just doesn't sit right."

"I know; it doesn't sit right with me, either."

"You know if Arnie was working for somebody else? Some other PI?"

Stone shook his head. "He didn't say anything about it if he was."

They drove on in the rain. As they crossed the bridge, the sky suddenly began to clear. They buried Arnie Millman in bright sunshine, under a cloudless sky.

Stone stood at the graveside with fifty other cops and looked up to see Amanda Dart standing on the other side, at the rear of the crowd. When the service was over, Stone said to Dino, "I won't need a ride home." He hurried after Amanda, who was walking quickly toward her waiting car.

"Hi," he said, catching up to her. "Can I catch a lift back to Manhattan?"

"Hello, Stone. Sorry, I'm not going back to Manhattan for a while; I have some business on this side of the river."

"I'm surprised to see you here," he said. "Did you know Arnie Millman?"

She nodded. "He was an occasional source for me."

"*Arnie?*"

"Yes, and I liked him. Why are you so surprised?"

"Somehow, he didn't seem the type to be hobnobbing with newspaper columnists."

"Stone, Arnie didn't hobnob with me; he called me on the phone when we had to talk. I really only met the man face-to-face on one occasion. Anyway, you would be amazed to know who some of my sources are." She glanced at her watch. "I've got to run, darling. Want to get together later this week?"

He knew what that meant, and he thought of Arrington.

"Ah…I'll call you, if that's okay."

"That's okay." She got into the back of her car, and the driver closed the door.

Stone sprinted toward Dino's departing cruiser, barely catching it in time.

"Ride didn't work out?" Dino asked.

"Nah, she wasn't going back to Manhattan."

"You know a woman who gets chauffeured around in a Mercedes?"

"That was Amanda Dart."

"What the hell was she doing here?"

Stone nodded toward the two young detectives in front. "I'll tell you later."

They drove back to Manhattan in silence. When they reached Stone's house, Dino got out of the car with him.

"So, what was Amanda Dart doing at Arnie Millman's funeral? She his ex-wife or something?"

"Funny. She said Arnie used to be a source for her."

"For a gossip columnist? I don't believe it."

"She apparently has some fairly unbelievable sources."

"That don't add up," Dino said flatly.

"She's probably got a source or two in every station house in Manhattan," Stone said. "How do you think these people get the story so fast when somebody of note gets arrested? It makes sense; it's just funny that Arnie was one of them."

"Well, I guess he liked a few extra bucks as well as the next guy."

"I guess so. I gotta run. See you."

Dino waved goodbye and got back into his car.

Stone put Arnie and Amanda out of his mind and started thinking about his dinner date.

Chapter 24

Stone arrived at Arrington's building on time and was announced by the lobby man. On the way up he reflected on the fact that he had once known another woman who had lived in this building, and the memory of that experience made him uneasy.

She came to the door wearing an apron over white pants and a white turtleneck sweater, seeming a negative image of the girl in black he had last seen that morning. There was a glass of wine in her hand. "Hi, come on in."

He followed her into a small apartment, especially small for such a posh building. There seemed to be only a living room and, through an open door, a bedroom. A counter divided the larger room into living and kitchen areas. She waved him to a stool at the counter and poured him a glass of red wine from an open bottle that was already nearly half empty. "Or would you prefer booze?" she asked belatedly.

"This is fine," Stone said, settling on the stool. "Smells good; what are you cooking?"

"A lamb dish," she said. "One of a repertoire that includes only half a dozen recipes, all easy."

"Easy is okay when it smells like that."

"How was your day?"

"I went to a funeral in Brooklyn, that's how my day was."

"Oh. Somebody important to you?"

"Somebody I knew when I was a cop. Another cop, retired."

"Are you sad?"

"I didn't know him all that well, but he sometimes worked for me. He was a likeable guy."

"I'm not sad anymore," she said. "Again, I'm sorry about last night."

"Last night had its rewards. And this morning."

She smiled a little. "I'm glad you think so. Dinner will be ready in about ten minutes; good thing you were on time."

"I'm compulsively on time."

"Not I."

"I'll keep that in mind."

She checked something in the oven, then pulled a stool up to face him. "I don't get you," she said.

"What do you mean?"

"I mean, you don't add up."

"No?"

"No. You're this extremely polished man; you live in this very impressive house; you dress beautifully; you have something to do with a prestigious law firm, but you don't actually work there; and yet you're retired, at an early age, from a blue-collar job that doesn't produce a whole lot of polished men."

"I was something of a misfit on the force," he said.

"That I believe."

"And I was never allowed to forget it."

"How so?"

"Well, as my former partner once said to me, 'Stone, the police force is a kind of mystic lodge, and you never joined.'"

"You didn't buy into the cop culture?"

"Not really. I found the work fascinating and often rewarding, but, I confess, I was unable to become one of the guys. I knew it, and they knew it. The only cop I was ever really close to was my ex-partner, Dino."

"Dino Bacchetti?"

Stone blinked. "How did you know that name?"

"I wrote something for *New York* magazine once, about a case at the Nineteenth Precinct. I interviewed him for it."

"I'm surprised you got out of his office with your virtue."

She laughed. "I nearly didn't; Dino is very smooth."

"That he is."

"So you were white bread among the Italians, the Irish, and the Hispanics in the department?"

"That's about the size of it."

"What, exactly, do you do for Woodman and Weld?"

"Their dirty work, mostly; the odd criminal case, the odd investigation."

"Now I'm getting the picture."

"So I add up now?"

"The house doesn't add up."

"I inherited it from a great-aunt, my grandfather's sister."

"Money, too?"

"Just the house. I did a lot of the restoration myself, but it damn near broke me."

"I'm glad you're not filthy rich," she said.

"I'm not glad," he replied. "I've got nothing at all against filthy rich. My father, God rest his soul, would be deeply ashamed of my attitude."

"Your father the Communist?"

"Father and mother; they met at a Party meeting. They were idealistic; they had both broken with their families in New England and had been through a depression."

"Your polish must have come from them."

"Unlike some of their colleagues in the Party, they had abandoned a lifestyle, but not the manners acquired therefrom."

"Good for them."

"You would have liked my mother."

"I love her work. How about your father?"

"He'd have been deeply suspicious of you."

"Why?"

"He knew class when he saw it, and he wanted to live in a classless society."

"I'll take that as a compliment."

"You should."

She went to the oven, removed an iron pot, and set it on a small table in the living room that had been carefully set. "Open another bottle of wine, will you? It's right there on the kitchen counter."

Stone found a corkscrew, opened the bottle, and took it to the table.

She poured them another glass of wine and raised hers. "*Bon appétit.*"

"*Bon appétit.*"

They sat among the ruins of dinner, sipping coffee.

"That was wonderful," he said.

"Thanks; if you only cook half a dozen things, they have to be wonderful."

"Tell me about this guy you just broke up with."

She looked into her wineglass. "I'm embarrassed. Why do you want to know?"

"I just want to know where you are and how you got there. It seems to have become important to me."

"I'm still embarrassed. He's younger than I am."

"How much younger?"

"A couple of years."

"Not so bad; lots of men date women a lot younger."

"It's not the same for a woman."

"Why not?"

"Men see younger women for sex, whereas...." She stopped.

"Whereas....?"

"Well, all right, I did it for the sex, too, mostly."

"Is sex in such short supply for you?"

"It's not that; I mean, anybody can get laid. For some reason, I was feeling old, so I was vulnerable."

"How old are you?"

"Thirty-one. Do you always ask women that?"

"Always."

"Why? It's supposed to be rude."

"It's not important to know how old a woman is, but it's important to know if she'll tell you. It's a matter of character."

"Do you know how old Amanda Dart is?"

Stone shrugged. He could feel the tops of his ears turning red.

"She's fifty; I have it on the best authority."

Stone was surprised, but not shocked. "Why are we talking about Amanda Dart?"

"Because you're involved with her."

"Am I?"

"I could tell at dinner that night; not from your behavior, from hers."

"You were wrong; we weren't involved, except professionally."

"Liar."

"Not until the next day. We spent that...together."

She shrugged. "I can't say that I blame you. After all, you had just broken up with somebody, and she is quite attractive." She looked at him levelly. "Everybody's entitled to a sex life."

"You have me at a disadvantage; you know more about me than I about you."

"All right," she sighed, "his name is Jonathan. He's one of those young men who seem to earn their living by...being charming and attractive."

"You mean, he was paid?"

"Not exactly. Men like Jonathan don't ask for money; they just seem always to be broke. I picked up a lot of tabs."

"I've known women like that," Stone said. "Still, it's more embarrassing for a woman paying for a man."

The phone rang; Arrington didn't move. On the third ring, the answering machine kicked in.

"It's Jonathan," a disembodied voice said. "I want to see you. I want...."

She got up and grabbed the phone. "Hello?"

Stone could no longer hear the young man's voice.

131

"No, thanks," she said. "I've no intention of doing that. I dropped by last night to tell you." She listened for a moment. "It's over, Jonathan. I have no desire to see you again."

He was obviously giving her an argument.

"Jonathan," she broke in. "It's over; accept the fact and get on with your life." She hung up and turned to Stone. "I'm sorry you had to hear that," she said.

"I'm glad I heard it," Stone said. He stood up and started clearing the table. Together, in silence, they put the dishes in the dishwasher and cleaned up the kitchen.

"He's going to call back," she said, but she was wrong. Instead, the house phone rang. She picked it up. "Yes? No, Jimmy, don't send him up; put him on." She waited a moment. "Listen to me very carefully," she said. "I have company; I have no intention of seeing you, now or ever again. Please go away." She hung up, seemingly on the verge of tears.

Stone took her shoulders and turned her toward him. "Are you all right?"

She buried her face in his chest. "I'm afraid of him," she said. "When you leave, he'll still be there."

"Then I won't leave."

"I don't want to stay here tonight," she said. "Will you take me back to your house?"

"Of course. Is there a way out of the building, other than the front door?"

"Yes, we can take the elevator to the basement; there's a door that opens onto the side street."

"Get your coat and your toothbrush."

She went into the bedroom, put some things

132

into a duffel, got her coat, and came back, brushing away tears.

"There's nothing to worry about," Stone said. "Come on, let's go."

She double-locked her door, and they took the elevator to the basement. She found a light switch, but it didn't work. "Come on," she said, "follow me. I have cat's eyes." A moment later they were at the side door of the building. "Will you look out and see if anyone is there? I don't want him following us."

"Sure." Stone opened the door and stepped into the street while she hung back. A taxi came down the block and he whistled it to a halt. There was no one else visible in the street. "Come on, Arrington," he called. They got into the cab, and Stone gave the driver the address. He watched out the back window, and he thought he saw someone, a man, come around the corner from Fifth Avenue, but in a moment they were gone.

For the second successive night, she slept in his bed, falling asleep immediately. Again, they did not make love.

Chapter 25

Stone was awakened by the smell of coffee brewing. He sat up in bed in time to watch Arrington, wearing his robe, come into the bedroom with a tray containing orange juice, coffee, and an English muffin.

"Good morning," she said. "I hope you're ready for breakfast." She set the tray on his lap.

"Actually, I'm more ready for you," he said, stroking her cheek.

She kissed him on the forehead. "That's a sweet thought, but I have an early appointment with my agent. I've got to run." She stood up and sloughed off the robe, standing naked at the foot of the bed.

Stone set the tray aside and started to get up.

"Oh, no," she said, grabbing for her underwear, "you get right back into bed."

Stone fell back onto the pillows, watching her. "It seems to be my lot in life to watch you walk naked around my bedroom while I do nothing about it."

She smiled, hooking her bra. "Bad timing," she said.

"You've spent the past two nights in my bed…."

"Sweetie…" she pulled her sweater over her head and brushed her hair back with her fingers. "You've just caught me at a bad time in my life, and I need some time to sort things out."

"How can I help?"

"By not pressing me."

Stone picked up the tray and returned it to his lap. "Consider yourself unpressed," he said.

"Stone," she said, sitting next to him on the bed. "I like you, I really do; I want this to go somewhere…."

Stone took a bite of his muffin. "Arrington, it can't go anywhere until it goes *somewhere*."

Her shoulders slumped. She crossed her arms, took hold of the sweater, and yanked it over her head. "All right," she said, "let's do it."

Stone took another bite of the muffin. "No

thanks," he said, his voice muffled by the food. "I'm eating."

"Tell me what you want," she said.

Stone washed the muffin down with some orange juice. "I don't know what I want, beyond the immediate urge to make love to you, but I know what I don't want; I *don't* want to be kept at arm's length."

"I don't mean to do that."

Stone sighed. "I think what we need to do is start over."

"Okay."

"When would you like to do that?"

"Oh, Jesus, it's a really bad time for...."

"Arrington, you owe me nothing; you don't have to change your life to make room for me."

"But I *want* to make room for you."

"Then what you have to do is figure out what's clogging up your life, and *do* something about it."

"That's just like a man," she said. "Figure out your life, rearrange it, *order your existence.*"

"This may have escaped your attention, but I *am* a man, and I don't see what's wrong with ordering your existence. *Everybody* has to order his existence, just to get through the day."

"Well, if that's how you feel about it," she said huffily, struggling back into the sweater.

"It certainly is," he said. "You go and take a look at your life, and if you find some room in it, call me."

"Typical," she said, throwing things into her duffel.

"*Typical?*" he nearly shouted.

135

"Don't raise your voice to me!"

Stone's bedside phone buzzed, and the intercom light flashed. He ignored it and took a deep breath. "I'm sorry," he said.

"Good for you."

"Is this our first fight?"

"It could be our last one," she shot back, getting into her coat.

The intercom buzzed again. Stone picked it up. "Yes?" he said.

"Stone, I'm sorry to disturb you," his secretary said, "but Bill Eggers left a message on the office machine last night. He wants you to be at his office this morning at ten for a meeting; he said it was important."

"Thanks," Stone said and hung up.

"Now you're being rude to your secretary," Arrington said.

Stone looked at his bedside clock and got out of bed. "I've got a ten o'clock appointment," he said, "and it's nine-thirty now."

Arrington looked at him. "So now you're going to parade around naked and try to turn me on."

"It's a desperate move, but it's the only card I have left to play."

"It's working," she said, walking over to him, dropping the duffel.

She made a grab at his crotch, but he dodged her and ran toward the bathroom. "Oh, no," he called back, "you're going to have to wait until I can make room in my busy schedule for you."

"Bastard!" she yelled after him. "I'll call you tonight." She picked up the duffel and left.

Stone arrived at Woodman & Weld five minutes late and went directly to Bill Eggers's office.

"Come in, Stone, and have a seat," Eggers said, pointing at a chair next to the sofa. "You know Glynnis Hickock from Amanda Dart's dinner party last week."

Dick Hickock's wife sat primly at one end of the sofa. "Good morning," she said.

Stone sat down. "Of course. How are you?"

"Just great," the woman said through clenched teeth.

"Would anyone like some coffee?" Eggers asked.

"I would," Glynnis responded.

"Bill, could I speak with you outside for just a minute?" Stone asked. He had an idea of where this might be leading, and he wanted to head it off before it got started.

"Stone, don't worry, anything you've got to say you can say in front of Glynnis." He set a cup on the coffee table and poured from a Thermos. "The short version of this is, Glynnis needs some surveillance on her husband, in preparation for divorce proceedings."

"Bill, I really have to speak to you alone, and right now."

Eggers looked at him, surprised. "Glynnis, I'm sorry, will you excuse us for just a moment?"

Glynnis crossed her legs and picked up her coffee cup but said nothing.

Stone walked into the adjacent conference room, waited for Eggers, then closed the door. "I can't be involved in this," he said.

"*Now* you tell me," Eggers cried. "Do you know how big a divorce this is going to be?"

"I can guess, but I can't be involved. I have a conflict."

"What kind of conflict?" Eggers was working up an anger now.

"I'm representing her husband on this *DIRT* thing."

"What? You're supposed to be representing Amanda on that, not Dick Hickock."

"Hickock called me when he saw the sheet; I told him I couldn't represent him, so he called Amanda, and she called me and told me to go ahead."

"As an investigator, then, not as a lawyer?"

"Same thing, as far as I'm concerned. If you'd talked to me ahead of time, I could have explained it to you."

"What am I going to tell Glynnis?"

"The truth; do you want me to do it?"

"I'd appreciate it."

Stone went back into Eggers's office and sat down. "Glynnis, I'm sorry, but I have an ethical conflict in representing you in this matter."

Her hackles went up. "You're working for Dick, aren't you? Good God, you've been following *me?*"

"No, I have not been following you, nor have I been asked to. I'm representing Dick in another matter, and that creates a conflict for me; I hope you can understand that."

She swiveled her head and looked out the window, saying nothing.

"Glynnis," Eggers broke in, "this doesn't mean that the firm can't represent you, just that Stone can't. He's not employed by the firm; he is only of counsel. I promise you we'll deal with this matter in a manner that will represent your interests to the highest possible degree. Stone, I think that will be all," he said.

Stone made a brief goodbye and left the office.

He was barely back at his desk when his secretary buzzed him. "Tiffany Potts is on the phone."

Stone punched the flashing button. "Hello?"

"Hi, remember me?" she asked cheerfully.

"Of course."

"You said to call you if I thought somebody might be following me."

"Yes."

"Well, somebody is."

"Where are you calling from?"

"My apartment."

"Let's not meet there."

"How about the Oak Bar at the Plaza in an hour?" she asked.

Chapter 26

She got there first. When he entered the high-ceilinged, dark-paneled room she was sitting at a window table wearing a gorgeous fur coat, a Perrier before her, looking out the window. It was early yet, and except for the bartender and a waiter, the two of them were alone in the big room. Stone sat down.

She rewarded him with a broad smile. "How are you?"

"Very well; and you?"

"I'm just fine. Sorry to get you out on such short notice."

"Not to worry; I'm at your beck and call."

She liked that. "How nice."

The waiter approached. "I'll have one of the same," Stone said, nodding at the Perrier. They made small talk until the drink came. "Now," Stone said, "tell me about it."

"I was at Bloomingdale's yesterday afternoon when I saw him. I was browsing in several departments, and whenever I looked up, he was there."

"What did he look like?" Stone asked.

"Tall."

"How tall?"

"Not as tall as you."

"I'm six-two."

"Six feet, then."

"How built?"

"Slender."

"Hair?"

"Light brown, tending to be sun-bleached at the ends. Collar-length."

"Clothes?"

"Fashionable. A long raincoat, below the knee."

"Describe his face."

"Long, straight nose, eyes a little close together, strong jaw, wide mouth, full lips."

"That's very good," Stone said, impressed.

"I can do better," she said, bending down and taking a copy of *Vanity Fair* from a large purse. She put the magazine on the table, flipped through the early pages and turned it toward Stone. "That's real close," she said, tapping a full-page photograph. "It's not him, but it's real close."

It was an ad for a men's cologne, and the model fit her description perfectly.

"You're sure it's not him?"

"I'm sure. I don't make mistakes about men as good-looking as that. The guy who followed me could be doing that kind of work for a living."

"Modeling?"

"Or acting, or both. He's the type who turns up in classes at mediocre acting schools."

"Did he follow you when you left Bloomingdale's?"

"Yes. I walked home, and he was with me all the way. At first, I thought he was just interested, you know? But he never approached me, always stayed well back. A couple of times he was on the opposite side of the street, but he was always there. When I got home I looked out the window, and he was half a block down the street, watching."

"When did you last see him?"

She glanced at her watch. "Ten minutes ago."

Stone sat up straight. "He followed you here?"

"Yep. He was out there this morning. Change of clothes, but the same raincoat."

They were only a couple of feet above the sidewalk. "Do you see him now?"

"Nope, but he was down that way a couple of minutes ago." She pointed toward Fifth Avenue.

"I'll be back in a minute," Stone said. "Don't leave."

He left the room and walked outside. Traffic was heavy on the sidewalk. Stone walked purposefully, west on Central Park South as far as the corner of Sixth Avenue, then all the way back to the front of the Plaza, checking every face coming and going. Nothing. He entered the hotel by the front door and made a sweep of the hallways and the Palm Court, but the man was not in sight. He returned to the Oak Room.

Tiffany was still at the table, but the Perriers had been replaced by two martinis. "I switched," she said. "I ordered one for you, too."

Stone fingered the glass, but did not pick it up. "It's a little early for me," he said.

"Then leave it; I'll drink it."

"Have you told Dick about this man?"

"Not yet."

"Tell him, but don't use the phone in your apartment; it may be bugged."

"Dick was always careful about that." She pulled a tiny cellular phone from her coat pocket. "That's why he gave me this."

"Be careful, even using that, and don't see him until I get a handle on this."

"He won't like that," she said with a small smile, taking a large swig from her martini.

"I'll talk to him. In fact, can I borrow your phone?"

She handed it over.

"What's his number?"

She gave it to him. "That's his cellular. Let it ring once, then hang up; that's our signal. He'll call back as soon as he can."

Stone followed her instructions, then set the little phone on the table. "How long will he take?"

"Depends; if he's in a meeting, it could be a while."

Stone eyed the martini but didn't pick it up.

"Oh, go on; it's good for you. There was an article in the *Times* this morning, said it's good for you."

"I've got to keep a clear head," Stone said.

She leaned forward, and her cleavage made an entertaining sight. "A clear head is not always an advantage," she said.

Stone managed a chuckle.

"Tell me about you," she said.

"Not much to tell."

"Are you seeing anybody?"

"Yes, as a matter of fact, I am."

She looked disappointed. "Pity."

"It's flattering that you think so."

"I spend so much time alone," she said. "Quite frankly, Stone, I'd like some company."

The phone rang, and Stone silently thanked God. "You answer," he said, "then I'll talk to him."

She picked up the phone and punched a button. "Hey," she breathed. She listened for a moment, then smiled. "I'd really love to, but someone sitting here says we shouldn't. I'll put him on." She handed the phone across the table.

"It's Stone."

"What the hell are you doing with her?" Hickock demanded.

"Someone has been following her, and I'm checking it out."

"Following her? Oh, God."

"Exactly. And I have to tell you that someone is likely to be following you in very short order."

"What do you know that I don't know?"

"Your wife is considering divorce."

"How do you know that when I don't know that?" he demanded.

"I can't go into that, but it's a fact. For God's sake, don't let her know that you know; just play it out, and for the time being, don't go anywhere near the young lady or her apartment."

There was a groan from the other end of the phone.

"I know that's tough, but it'll be tougher still if you're seen together. I'm going to send someone over to her apartment to find out if there's any electronic surveillance in the building."

"If there is, can you get rid of it?"

"If there is, I'm going to leave it in place. As long as we know it's there, it can't hurt, and it could be useful."

"I've got to see her," Hickock said, and he sounded pathetic.

"Please take my advice, and don't. And it would be best if you didn't talk on the cellular phone, either, unless you're willing to be overheard. It's not that tough to listen in."

"How long is this going to last?"

"Until either your wife tells you she wants a divorce, or until you make up with her."

"God. Listen, I appreciate this."

"I know it's going to be tough, but you could make a bad situation a lot worse."

"I understand. Let me speak to her."

Stone handed the phone to Tiffany.

"Hey, baby," she said. "I'm so sorry. Yes, I know, I feel exactly the same way, but maybe our friend has a point."

Stone drew a finger across his throat.

"He says we have to hang up. I hope I'll see you before very long. Me, too." She broke the connection and put the phone back into the pocket of the fur. "Well, I guess it's just you and me," she said.

"Oh, no, it isn't," Stone replied. "I don't know if we've already been seen together, but if we are it will just complicate the situation. Now we've got two problems—the scandal sheet and Dick's wife, and both are very dangerous for Dick." He pushed the martini across the table. "I have to leave now. If you see the guy again, call me *immediately,* and I'll see if I can have a word with him." He scribbled a number on a card and handed it to her. "This is my cellular number; I don't usually carry it around, but I'll start." She looked awful, and he felt sorry for her. "You going to be okay?" he asked.

"No," she said, "but I guess there's nothing to be done about it." She took a key from her bag and pushed it across the table. "You'll need this if you're going to check out my apartment. Or for any other reason you'd like to use it."

"I hope this won't last too long."

"*You* hope," she said, and her eyes filled with tears.

"I'll give you some advice," he said, "and don't tell Dick I said this to you. Get yourself a boyfriend, even if only temporarily. If Dick's wife puts somebody on you, it'll look a lot better. And," he said, "you'll have a lot more fun."

She managed a small smile. "You know how a girl thinks," she said.

I wish to God I did, he thought. He left some money on the table and left the girl sitting alone in the room, which was now beginning to fill with the noontime trade. He didn't think she'd be alone for very long.

Chapter 27

Stone called Dino after lunch. "Who's your tech these days?" he asked.

"Don't say that over the goddamned telephone," Dino said, sounding tense. "We'll talk in person; you free for dinner?"

"Yes."

"Eight-thirty at Elaine's; I'll book."

Dino was a little touchy, Stone thought. The detectives always had a guy around who could do illegal technical work—tapping, bugging—when they couldn't get the job done any other way.

He worked on cases through the afternoon, having a sandwich at his desk, and just after six, when he was almost done for the day, the phone rang.

"It's me," Arrington said.

"Hello there."

"I understand you've been hanging out with Dick Hickock's girlfriend."

"Oh? What makes you say that?"

"Have you checked your fax machine lately?"

"Hang on." Stone went to the closet where the machine was kept and found a single sheet there.

DIRT

Greetings, earthlings! The plot thickens: Gorgeous Tiffany Potts, who has lately been the favorite plaything of Richard Hickock, was seen today tête-à-tête with shyster/shamus Stone Barrington, over martinis at the Oak Bar. Looks as though Dickie may have been inattentive to poor Tiff lately, which is just as well, because his dear wife, Glynnis, is on the warpath. Informed of her husband's dalliance by us, she is Taking Steps.

Stay tuned for more!

Stone picked up the phone. "It was strictly business," he said.

"That's what they all say, but I believe you. Listen, I've spent most of the day clearing the decks of my life, and I think I'm ready to curl up with a good detective."

"I can recommend somebody."

"Tonight suit you?"

"I'm seeing Dino for dinner at Elaine's, and Dino always leaves early. Why don't you join us, and we'll go on from there."

"Sounds good. I'll bring my toothbrush."

"You do that. We're meeting at eight-thirty, but I need half an hour with Dino. Nine?"

"Nine it is." She hung up.

Stone allowed himself a very deep breath.

Dino sat down, and he looked pissed off. "What's this 'tech' shit?"

"I need a tech to...."

"Stone, you don't talk about that on the phone these days, not when there's a commission looking into police corruption."

"Sorry, Dino, I...."

"They're all over us like flies, you know, even though the Nineteenth is clean as a whistle."

"As far as you know."

"I know, pal, believe me."

"About the tech."

"What about him?"

"I need a man to go over an apartment, see what he finds."

"He's not planting anything?"

"Not a thing; I just want to see what somebody else might have planted."

"Does he have to break in?"

"I've got a key, and the occupant is expecting him."

"Give me the key and the address. I'll contact him."

Stone produced the key and wrote down Tiffany's name and address. "Tell him to call first and say I sent....Wait a minute. No, tell him just to show up, having already written on a piece of paper that I sent him. No names, in case the place is wired."

"Okay."

"What's it going to cost?"

"Since he's not planting anything, I'll make him do it for five hundred."

"Steep. I haven't got it on me."

"I'll front it; you can pay me back."

Stone had another idea. "While he's at it, I'd like him to take a look at my place."

Dino's eyebrows went up. "Are we still on the *DIRT* thing?"

"We are, and their information is just a little too good. Come to think of it, I'd like him to take a look at Amanda Dart's place, too, but not until he's been to me first."

"His name is Bob Cantor; he'll call you tomorrow."

"Think you can get me a better rate for the three places?"

"I'll see what I can do."

"What's new with you?"

"Mary Ann is apartment-hunting on the East Side."

"Uh-oh."

"You said it."

"How is this going to happen?"

"The old man swears it's going to be straight up. We're going to rent it from a corporation that owns it."

"Doesn't sound straight up to me," Stone said.

"What? That we rent?"

"Dino, make sure it's a corporation that already owns rental units, and that the rent is in line with the market."

"That's what the old man has in mind. The rent will be more than we pay now, but he'll lay some cash on Mary Ann, to make up for it."

"That sounds fairly clean. You're going to need a checkable story that starts right from the beginning—how you find the agent, how you heard about the agent, a proper lease. It's got to look like anybody could find this apartment, you understand?"

"I understand."

"Tell Mary Ann to make sure her daddy understands, too."

"What, you think the old guy doesn't know something about hiding ownership?"

"This isn't like holding a cement company, Dino; if the commission starts looking into this, it's got to be airtight, and you be sure that neither the agent or the head of the corporation has a name that rhymes with a pasta."

"Right, right." Dino looked up and smiled. "Hey, look what's coming in," he said.

Stone turned to see Arrington enter the restaurant. "Not bad," he said offhandedly.

"Not bad? You're losing it. As it happens, I know this one." He waved at Arrington, who waved back and started for the table. "Give us a few minutes, then get lost, okay?"

"Sure, Dino, whatever you say."

Dino was on his feet, taking Arrington's offered hand. "Long time no see," he was saying. "This is my friend...."

Arrington let go of Dino's hand, turned to Stone, and planted a large kiss on his lips. "We've met," she said.

Stone held her chair while Dino stood, dumbfounded. "Sit down, Dino," he said; then he leaned over and whispered, "Give us a few minutes, then get lost, okay?"

When Dino had left, Arrington pulled out a copy of the new *Vanity Fair*. "My first piece for them," she said, opening the magazine. "It's about the mayor's wife."

"That's great, Arrington," Stone said. "That has got to be a tough market for a writer to break into."

"Not if you're a good enough writer," she said.

"Can I have this? I'd like to read it later."

"Later you're going to be busy," she said, "but you can have it for tomorrow."

Stone flipped through the pages of the magazine. "You know any models, by any chance?"

"I have a passing acquaintance with a few," she replied.

Stone found the cologne ad. "How about this guy? Know him?"

Arrington looked at the ad, then back at Stone. Her face was suddenly expressionless. "Why did you have to do it this way?"

"What?" Stone was baffled.

"Why didn't you just...." She turned away, and there were angry tears in her eyes.

"Arrington, I don't understand," Stone said. "I just wanted to know who this guy is. It's a business thing."

She turned back angrily. "You know who it is," she said.

"I swear to you I don't have the slightest idea."

"Are you lying to me?"

"I am not. Arrington, what is going on?"

She pointed at the photograph. "That's him," she said.

"Who?"

"Jonathan."

Chapter 27

Has he got a brother?" Stone asked. She was still looking very angry.

"No, he hasn't," she said. "What's this about, Stone?"

"As you are aware, I saw Dick Hickock's girlfriend, Tiffany, this morning. She called me because somebody was following her, somebody who, as it turns out, answers to this guy's description. She showed me this ad."

"She said Jonathan was following her?"

"No, she was emphatic that the guy was not the man in the photograph, he just looked very much like him."

"Well, he doesn't have a brother."

"Okay, that answers my question. Shall we drop it?"

"I'm sorry I got so angry; I didn't understand." She took a deep breath and let it out. "Stone, do you want to know about Jonathan?"

"Is there any reason why I *should* know about him?"

"No, not really."

"Then I couldn't care less. *You,* I care about; him, pfffft!"

She smiled. "That's the kind of talk I like to hear."

A waiter handed them menus. "I recommend the Caesar salad and the osso bucco," Stone said.

"Sold; I'd like some wine, too."

Stone turned to the waiter. "I'll have the same as the lady, and bring us a bottle of the Dry Creek Merlot and two straws."

Stone let them into the house and followed Arrington up the stairs. Halfway up she began undressing, dropping a trail of garments behind her, which Stone gathered up. "You want to shock my housekeeper? She's a very proper Greek lady."

"I'm sure it won't be the first evidence she's

152

seen of a woman in the house," Arrington replied, lobbing her bra over her shoulder.

"She doesn't come in until ten a.m."

"That may not be long enough." She stepped out of her panties and kicked them backward.

Stone followed a very beautiful backside up the stairs and into his bedroom.

"I'm finished with my clothes," she said, "let's start on yours." She began working on his buttons.

A moment later they were in bed, leaving a large pile of clothing at the foot.

"Do you know," Stone said, kissing her, "this is the first time I've kissed you?"

"I never kiss until the third date," she said. "And I never make love until...."

Stone slid easily into her.

"...now," she breathed.

Sunlight streamed into the rear windows of the house and across the bed. They lay in each other's arms, sweating, breathing hard.

"I thought that went very well," Arrington panted.

"All three times?" Stone asked.

"Don't brag. Oh, all right, all three times." She kissed him noisily on the ear. "I'm hungry; it's your turn to make breakfast."

"Eh?" he shouted, cupping a hand behind his ringing ear.

She got out of bed and headed for the kitchenette in the hall. "And turn on the *Today* show," she called.

"Television? In the morning?"

"I never miss it."

"The honeymoon's over," he grumbled, fumbling in a drawer for the remote control.

She came back with juice, muffins, and coffee. "How'd you know what I wanted?" he asked.

"Easy. That's all there is in your kitchenette."

"Would you like me to lay in a stock of whatever you eat for breakfast?"

"This will do nicely," she said, "as long as I can keep having you as well."

Stone ate his muffin and gazed at the TV. "I don't think I can make love to Bryant Gumbel," he said. "But I might be able to manage something to Katie Couric."

"I told you to stop bragging," she giggled. "Now eat your muffin."

"This muffin is not all I'm going to eat," he replied.

"You never told me you were a sex maniac," she said. "But it's a nice surprise."

The phone rang. Stone unconsciously reached for it. "Hello?"

"My name's Bob," a man's voice said. "Dino said to call."

"Right. I've got some work for you."

"He gave me a couple addresses."

"Why don't you start here, and I'll brief you on the others."

"Okay, half an hour?"

Stone looked at Arrington, sitting cross-legged, naked, in his bed. "Make it an hour," he said.

Bob Cantor had been in the house for two hours when he came down to Stone's office.

154

"Come in, and have a seat."

He closed the door behind him.

"Well?"

"Somebody's very interested in you," Cantor said.

Stone sat up. "How interested?"

"The whole house; top to bottom. Phone lines, too, but not the offices."

"Jesus Christ."

"I don't think He needs to use a wire."

"Bedroom?"

"Yep."

"Shit."

"You want me to yank everything?"

Stone thought for a moment. "Can you disable it in a way that will make them think it's just broken?"

Cantor nodded. "I can create enough static to make them think it's their fault."

"Good, do that."

"Okay."

"How long?"

"Half an hour."

Shortly, Cantor was back. "It's done. You may hear some static on the phone lines, but it'll be manageable. I left the fax machine alone; static there would give you garbled transmissions."

"Fine." Stone handed him a sheet of paper and two envelopes. "These are the other two addresses, and I've written a letter to each woman, telling them what you're going to do."

"If I find something, you want me to do the same thing to it? I mean, whoever's bugging you might think something's up if all three systems go down."

"Good point. Do the same work on Ms. Dart's offices and apartment, but leave the Potts place up and running. Then call me."

"One thing," Cantor said.

"What's that?"

"You got a very nice burglar alarm system in the house; you ever use it?"

"When I go away."

"Start using it all the time. I mean, now that the wire on your place isn't working right, they might come back to fix it."

"I hadn't thought of that," Stone said.

Chapter 29

Amanda got to Stone first. "What the hell is going on?" she demanded. "This man of yours says there are bugs all over my offices."

"What's going on, Amanda, is that there are bugs all over your offices. That's where your leak is, or at least part of it."

"Well, I told him to yank them all out."

Stone groaned. "I told him to create static, but leave them in place. Now whoever planted the bugs is going to know you know."

"That's just fine with me," she said. "I want the bastard to know."

"Amanda, you got the surveillance reports on your people, the ones I sent you?"

"Yes, and they both look innocent enough to me."

"To me, too; that leaves Martha."

"Stone, I've told you, it *couldn't* be Martha."

"We're running out of suspects; there's only the maid and Martha. I want your permission to check out both of them. Oh, and the chauffeur, too."

"I hate paying for work that I know will turn up nothing."

"That's understandable, but anytime you investigate a group of people, you have to investigate them *all*. That's the only way it will work. So, have I your permission to investigate these three people?"

"Oh, all right, but for God's sake, don't let any of them know. It would be so embarrassing for me if they found out."

"Not as embarrassing as what *DIRT* is publishing."

"You have a point. Do it."

"Yes, ma'am."

Her voice changed, became lower. "I thought you were going to call me for a get-together."

Better bite the bullet, Stone thought. "I'm sorry, Amanda, but I have to be frank with you. I'm seeing somebody, and she's taking all my…attention."

"Shit," Amanda said, and hung up.

Tiffany was next.

"I'm calling from a pay phone," she said.

"Good girl."

"That Bob says that *somebody* can hear every word that's spoken in my apartment or on my phone, and that he's not fixing it."

"If we fix it, Tiff, whoever is listening will know that you know."

"Stone, you told me to find a boyfriend, so I did. Now when I bring him home, somebody's going to hear us in bed."

"You're an actress; think of it as a performance."

She was quiet for a moment. "I hadn't thought of that," she said finally. "Come to think of it, that could be a turn-on."

"Whatever works for you, Tiff."

"I wish there was a way I could turn the bug off for a few minutes at a time, though."

"Does the boyfriend have a home?"

"Yeah, but it's way down in the Village."

"The Village is charming; a great place to make love."

"Mmmmm," she said.

"And Tiff, for God's sake, stay away from Dick—no hotels or anything; it's for his own good, tell him that."

"He has been insistent."

"How did you communicate?"

"Pay phone at both ends."

"Do this: Tell him no contact for two weeks." Stone had no idea where he'd be on this investigation in two weeks, but what the hell?

"Okay."

"See you, Tiff."

"Bye."

Bob Cantor called next.

"Boy, that Tiffany is something!" he said.

"Down, Bob. Her boyfriend could buy and sell you, and he would."

"Too bad. Oh, Amanda Dart made me rip out everything."

"She told me. I'll just have to live with it. You ever do any surveillance work?"

"Once in a while."

"I've got two people need checking out; got a pencil?"

"Shoot."

Stone gave him the names and addresses of the maid and chauffeur. He would check out Martha himself. "I need this soonest," he told Cantor.

"Gotcha. Oh, Stone, I almost forgot; I might know who did the wiring job on you and the other two."

"Yeah? Who?"

"Maybe a guy who occasionally hangs out at a bar I go to."

"What makes you think you know?"

"He has a signature; it's the way he wraps a wire around a terminal—he makes a kind of knot. Somebody told me about it. You want me to add this to my list?"

"You do that; I'd like very much to know who he's working for."

"You got it."

Stone had a thought. "Bob, will you wire a place for me? Phone, too?"

"You bet; but it's more expensive if I have to break in and work under pressure."

"Her name is Martha McMahon; she works all day, five days a week; she lives in a small elevator building, no doorman." Stone gave him the address.

"You want to listen live, or have it taped?"

"I don't have time to listen live. Can you tape it

from a remote location, so you don't have to be there?"

"Sure."

"Do it. Make her first on your list."

"You got it."

Stone hung up. It bothered him that he himself was the subject of surveillance. He was going to have to start watching himself. He went into his study, unlocked a cabinet, and took out a Remington riot gun with an eighteen-and-a-half-inch barrel. It was standard police issue; he had bought it at a departmental surplus equipment sale years before. He ignored the double-ought buckshot shells in the cabinet and chose number nine birdshot; he wasn't out to blow a yawning hole in anybody. He inserted four shells into the gun, pumped a round into the chamber, then added one more shell and flipped on the safety. Then he walked upstairs to his bedroom and put the weapon on a small shelf he had built under the bed.

Remembering that he had not relocked the cabinet, he went back downstairs to the study, key in hand. For a moment, he gazed at the nine-millimeter automatic, hanging inside in its shoulder holster, then decided against it and locked the cabinet. No need for that yet.

Chapter 30

Stone stood half a block from Amanda's building and waited for Martha to come out. Martha knew him by sight, and he would have to be careful.

It was nearly six when she left the building, and she walked with great purpose down Lexington Avenue, went into a Gristedes market, stayed twenty minutes, and left with nothing in her hands. Probably having her groceries delivered. She walked on downtown, did some window shopping, and then did something Stone thought odd: She went into an expensive cosmetics shop and spent nearly forty minutes there, allowing a salesgirl to make her up, then leaving with a loaded shopping bag. This seemed strange, because Martha, on the occasions when he had seen her, had never worn makeup at all. There was a new man in her life, Stone figured.

She continued downtown until she reached her building and went inside. Stone intended to wait until she emerged again. If she was still all made up she might have a date later. Then he saw a van parked a few yards down the street from her building; it was gray and had a telephone company logo on the sides. What surprised him was that Bob Cantor was behind the wheel, wearing a hard hat. Stone approached and knocked on a window.

Cantor jumped, then grinned and let Stone in. "Just in time," he whispered, "she's on the phone with a guy." He flipped a switch, and the call was played over a speaker.

"...really sorry, but I've got this meeting," a man's voice was saying.

"Aw..." Martha responded, "and I just made myself look so pretty for you."

"I'll miss that, baby, but there's nothing I can do."

"Tomorrow, then?"

161

"I'll have to call you; it's a rough week."

"Oh, all right," she said, the disappointment heavy in her voice. The call ended.

"How much did I miss?" Stone asked.

"Nothing important."

"Did she make the call?"

"No, he called her."

"Shit. If she makes any calls, can you extract the numbers from the keypad beeps?"

"Sure."

"What about Caller ID? Can you pick up her incoming calls?"

"Nope; that has to be done centrally, at the exchange. Nothing I can do about it."

"What did you find inside her apartment?"

"Nice place; not large, but good furniture—antiques, nice upholstered pieces, a baby grand piano, out of tune. Her clothes are pretty dull, but there was a new black dress in a Saks bag that looked more elegant than her other stuff. I found some credit card bills; she's got a balance on her Visa of six thousand and change, pretty high for a secretary, but she pays on time."

"She makes good money, so the Visa balance isn't out of line," Stone said. "What else? Any photographs of men?"

"Nope, only one photograph; looks like her parents. She reads a lot, almost all hardbacks; there are a lot of bookcases in the place. She buys expensive-looking sheets and towels, there are a couple of good oriental carpets in the place. All in all, a fairly high-end joint, especially for a single woman."

"Anything else?"

"I saved the best for last; her apartment's already wired, and by the same guy who did your job."

"Jesus, that's four residences they've gone after; these people must have some money behind them."

"Either that, or one of them knows his way around electronic surveillance. The equipment isn't very exotic or very expensive, but whoever did it knew what he was doing."

Music suddenly came from the speaker in the van.

"Sounds like WQXR, the classical radio station," Cantor said. "Interesting lady; pity she's not more of a looker."

"Where are you going to park the recorder?" Stone asked.

"Right here; I'm in a legal parking spot, and I don't have to move the van until tomorrow morning, when the alternate side parking rules change. I'll just leave it until then."

"Good. No point in surveilling when she's at work, either. Just check her between quitting time and bedtime; let's see if the guy really calls back or if he's just handing her a line."

"Okay. How long do you want me to keep the recorder going?"

"The rest of the week, if you can check out the other two names I gave you while the recorder listens."

"Sure thing. Tell me, did you set your alarm when you left the house?"

"Damn it, I forgot."

"They'll come back, I promise you."

"How will I know if they do?"

"You won't, unless you know exactly what to look for."

Stone opened the door of the van. "I think I'd better get home."

The phone was ringing when he opened the front door.

"Hi," Arrington said. "How about tonight?"

"I've got to do something tonight," he said, "and I'm afraid you can't help."

"I can be very helpful," she said.

"I know, but this one I need to do alone. How about tomorrow?"

"You're on; see you later." She hung up.

Stone walked around the house and took a good look at things; nothing seemed to have been disturbed in his absence. He switched on the living room lights and left the house by the front door, careful to set the alarm this time, then walked around to the other side of the block and rang the bell of a neighbor of his acquaintance.

"Hi," he said to the woman. "I've forgotten my front door key; could I go out the back door of your house? I've got a kitchen door key hidden."

"Sure," the woman said, then let him into and out the rear of her house.

It was dark now, but the lights in the common garden had not yet come on. Stone stood very still for ten minutes, sweeping the entire garden, looking for any sign of movement. There was none. He walked slowly toward the back door of his own house, as if out for an evening stroll, then stopped again at his back gate. Still no movement in the garden.

He went to his kitchen door and let himself in, then disarmed the burglar alarm. Without turning on any lights, he went upstairs to his bedroom, changed into slippers, got the loaded riot gun, and went back downstairs to his study. He sat himself down in a comfortable chair and began to wait. The only light in the room filtered in from the living room, where a single lamp burned.

It had been a long time since he had been on a stakeout, and he tried to remember how he had dealt with the boredom without falling asleep. Reading was out; so was listening to music or watching television. Instead, he tried to remember things, things from a long time ago; that, he knew from experience, would keep him awake and wouldn't interfere with his hearing. He tried to remember all the names of his high school graduating class, scoring about 80 percent, he reckoned.

The graduation memory done, he started on girls. He tried to remember each of the girls he had slept with from his freshman year at NYU, when he had had his first sexual experience, until he graduated. He began with Susan Bernstein, his first, who had invited him back to her dorm room and brazenly seduced him, cheerfully waiting until he had recovered from his first, premature ejaculation so that they could do it again, this time for a considerably longer period. He had slept with her throughout his freshman year; he tried to remember each experience. She didn't come back his sophomore year; she had quit school to marry a jeweler in the diamond district.

He worked his way through the college years, lingering over the first experience he had had with two girls, at a summer house in East Hampton. The girls, he remembered, had been just as interested in each other as in him, something that had fascinated him no end. Then there had been the assistant professor of English whom he had screwed late at night in the faculty lounge and on three other occasions, always in the same room. For some reason, doing it there had turned her on.

He was somewhere in the middle of his senior year, in the back seat of a Cadillac convertible parked on a dark Greenwich Village street, fucking the beautiful daughter of a New Jersey car dealer, when he was suddenly snapped back to the present. He had heard a noise from somewhere downstairs.

Chapter 31

Stone stood up, retrieved the shotgun leaning against his chair, and checked to be sure the safety was still on. If he had to use the shotgun, he reckoned, he would use it as a club, if at all possible. He had no desire to kill anybody, and he knew, from his experience as a police detective, what a pain in the ass it was to deal with the aftermath of a killing, even a legal one.

The noise had seemed to come from the lower front of the house, so he tiptoed down the hall toward the front stairs, keeping to the edge of the floor to avoid creaking. He went slowly down the stairs the same way. There was another noise, a tiny one, and he was sure it came from the direction of his office. He was in the kitchen dining area, and he moved very carefully toward the door that opened into his office. Arriving there, he put an ear to the door, held his breath, and listened. He was certain he could hear something, but it was so faint that he reckoned it must be coming from his secretary's office or the hallway where the telephone box was located.

Slowly, he turned the knob and opened the door an inch. He could hear the noise better now, and it wasn't coming from inside his office. He opened the door and stepped into the room. The noise stopped. Stone stood silently immobile for perhaps a minute, then the noise began again, this time a series of noises, like tools being taken from or returned to a toolbox. He moved on toward the closed door to the hallway and put an ear against it. Again, the noise had stopped. Stone reckoned that whoever it was was engaged in work that periodically made some noise, then was quiet. He began turning the knob, a quarter-inch at a time; when he had turned it all the way he opened the door an inch and listened. Silence. Then, slowly, an inch at a time, he swung the door open just enough to allow himself through it. He held the shotgun across his chest, ready to swing the butt if he encountered anybody, and stepped into the hallway. The floor made a tiny creak. He could hear nothing else.

As he inched along the hallway he began to be

able to see better, and he realized that the tiny red lights from the alarm system and the telephone box were beginning to light his way; then he saw that the doors to both boxes were open. Bingo, he said to himself, almost at the very moment that something crashed into the back of his neck. It seemed a long time afterward that his head, along with his consciousness, came to an abrupt stop against the hall floor.

The first thing he heard was a ringing in his head. Then the ringing seemed to float out of his body and into another place, while changing pitch upward. Finally it stopped and he heard his own voice: "This is Stone Barrington; please leave a message, and I'll get back to you." There followed an electronic beep, then a familiar voice.

"Stone, are you there? If you're there, pick up." A brief silence. "Please pick up, will you? I've got to talk to you right now!" Another silence. "Goddamnit, if you're in the sack with somebody else, you're in very big trouble!" There was a loud noise of a connection being broken.

Stone didn't feel like moving just yet, since the floor seemed to be doing the moving for him. He lay there, his cheek against the cool oak, and tried to still it. Finally, hours later, it seemed, stillness arrived. He opened his eyes and blinked a few times. There was something inches from his nose, something tubular, and when he could move his head back and focus, he realized that it was the barrel of his own shotgun, lying on the floor in front of him.

He got to his hands and knees, then, using a coat rack for support, struggled to his feet, blinking rapidly to make the dizziness go away. That took a while. After a few more deep breaths to get some oxygen in his system, he turned and, leaning on the wall, went back toward his office. He found the switch that turned on the desk lamp, then moved around the desk and into his chair, resting his head on his hands against the desktop. He thought he had never had such a headache.

He forced himself to sit up and grope in a drawer for some aspirin, then swallowed four with some stale water from a carafe on his desk. That done, he sat up in his chair and tried to think. Somebody had just spoken to him. He looked down at the flashing red light on the answering machine, then pressed the replay button and listened to Arrington's voice, an urgent voice. He struggled to remember her number, pressed the speaker button on the phone, dialed, and laid his head down beside it.

"Hello!" she said, sounding angry.

He tried to speak, cleared his throat, and tried again. "It's Stone."

"You're trying to sound sleepy, aren't you?" she cried. "You were there all the time."

"Listen," he said.

"You son of a bitch, you were there in bed with somebody, weren't you? You got rid of her, and now you're calling me back."

"Arrington," he said, as clearly as he could manage, "if you don't shut up and listen I'm going to hang up."

"All right," she said, "I'm listening!"

"What time is it?"

"It's eleven-thirty; lose your watch?"

"I've been out since, I don't know, ten, ten-thirty."

"Out of the house?"

"Out like a light." He looked at his left wrist. "And, as a matter of fact, I did lose my watch."

"You're not making any sense."

"I know." His head began to swim again. "Will you call an ambulance, please? I think I...." He passed out again.

This time, he came awake in a hurry. Somebody was waving something horrible under his nose, and he pushed it away.

"How're you feeling, pal?" a man's voice asked.

Stone looked up and found a cop and a paramedic standing beside him; just beyond them was Arrington. His head seemed to be resting in a puddle of something.

"Let's ease you back here," the paramedic said, lifting him by the shoulders and sitting him up in the chair.

Stone wiped at his face. "What's this?"

"Vomit. You threw up on the desk. Out, as you were, you're lucky you didn't choke on it."

"Stone," Arrington said, "I'm sorry I yelled at you."

Stone nodded, and it hurt a lot.

"Let's get you onto the stretcher," the paramedic said. His partner appeared from somewhere, and they helped him onto the litter. "Just lie back and relax," the man said. "We'll have you checked out in no time."

Stone drifted off again.

When he woke up he was in a curtained-off area. A woman in a green jacket was bending over him; Dino and Arrington were sitting beside the bed.

"How are you feeling?" the woman asked.

"Not so hot," Stone responded.

"What's your name?"

"Stone Barrington."

"How many fingers do you see?"

"Three."

"Good count."

"How is he?" Arrington asked.

"He's got a pretty good concussion, I think," the doctor answered. She continued with a brief neurological examination. "I think we'll admit him, at least for tonight."

"Can I ask him some questions?" Dino asked.

"Make it brief," the doctor replied, stepping back.

"You remember anything, Stone?" Dino asked.

"I heard a noise downstairs. Went down to check on it. That's about it. My watch is gone." He held up a wrist.

"Did you see the guy who hit you?"

"No; from behind, I think."

"Right. Remember anything else?"

"The doors were open."

"Yeah, the street door to your office was ajar."

"No, the telephone and alarm doors."

"Huh?"

"To the boxes in the hall."

"I gotcha."

"How did I get here?"

"You called Arrington, remember?"

"No. Yes. She's mad at me."

"No, I'm not, darling," she said, bending over him and kissing him on the forehead.

"She called nine-one-one, and an ambulance and a cop showed up. The cop recognized you and called me."

"That's it," the doctor said. "We need to get him to bed now."

"Good idea," Stone said, closing his eyes.

Chapter 32

Amanda looked into the mirror and was horrified at what she saw. God knew she had been under a lot of stress lately, if anger caused stress, but this was the absolute end! High on her left cheek was an irate, fiery-red pimple. A pimple! She had not had a pimple since high school!

She covered the protuberance with makeup as well as she could, then finished dressing and went to her office. Her staff of three was already hard at work as she entered. "Messages," she said to Martha without so much as a good morning.

"Good morning, Amanda," Martha said, handing her a stack of pink slips.

Amanda went into her office without a word and closed the door, tossing the messages onto her desk. Lately she had been operating at a high level of irritation, and at times she had had a very hard time to keep from losing her temper, something she *never* did. This *DIRT* business had gotten under her skin, and nearly two weeks had passed since she had hired Stone Barrington to get to the bottom of it, with no visible results. She picked up the phone and dialed his office number. His secretary answered.

"Good morning, Ms. Dart, how are you?"

"Terrible, thank you. Let me speak to Stone."

"I'm afraid Stone won't be at work today," the woman said, "and possibly not tomorrow."

"He's taking a *vacation?*" Amanda spat. "On *my* time?"

"I beg your pardon?"

Amanda got hold of herself. "What I mean is, is Stone taking some time off?"

"He is ill at the moment."

"Ill? Then I'll call his home number."

"He's not at home, Ms. Dart."

"Where, then, is he? I want to speak to him immediately."

"He's in Lenox Hill Hospital."

"*What?*" She hoped to God he hadn't had a heart attack on her.

"He's at Lenox Hill, but he can take phone calls. I'll give you the direct number for his room."

Amanda scribbled down the number. "Thank you," she said, and hung up. She dialed the other number, and it was answered on the first ring.

"Hello?"

"Stone? It's Amanda. You sound terrible."

"Thanks, Amanda."

"What on earth is wrong?"

"Concussion, they tell me. They want to keep me here and observe me for another day."

"Concussion? How the hell did you get a concussion?" she demanded, as if a concussion were a personal affront to her.

"Amanda, are you quite all right?"

"We're talking about you, Stone."

"I surprised a prowler in my house, right before he surprised me."

"A burglar?"

"Maybe. He took my wristwatch and the cash in my wallet."

"Maybe a burglar?"

"Maybe not."

"What's that supposed to mean?"

"I think he may have been bugging my house and phones again."

"Does that mean he'll try to do my place again?"

"Possibly, although being caught at it might give him pause. I wouldn't count on it, though."

"How can I stop him?"

"Hire a security guard, I suppose. Do you want me to find somebody for you? I might be able to get an off-duty cop to sit on your apartment and offices."

"Oh. Yes, I would like you to find somebody for me."

"I'll make a call or two."

"Stone, does this business mean this person is getting violent?"

"Not necessarily, unless he's caught in the act."

"I do *not* want to catch him in the act."

"That's what the cop will be for. I don't think

you have to worry about violence, Amanda; he hasn't attacked anyone else but me, and I did get in his way."

"I'm relieved to hear it, but I'd still like your policeman to come. How soon can you get somebody?"

"Right after my nap," Stone said. "They want me to take lots of naps."

"Oh, of course, I don't want to interfere with your recovery."

"Don't worry about it; I can still use a phone."

"What kind of watch was it?"

"What?"

"Your wristwatch that was stolen; what kind?"

"A Rolex. It had my name engraved on the back."

"What kind of Rolex?"

"The quartz one; I don't remember what they call it. Why are you worried about my watch?"

"I was just curious. You go back to sleep, and call me when you've found a guard for me."

"I'll do that," Stone said, and hung up.

This was not going well, Amanda thought. She called Richard Hickock and was put through immediately.

"Have you heard?"

"Heard what?" Hickock asked, as if he weren't sure he wanted to know.

"Stone Barrington's in the hospital. Somebody broke into his house and hit him over the head."

"Jesus Christ. Does this have anything to do with our problem?"

"He disconnected the bugging in his house, and he thinks they came back to put it in again. Has he checked your office?"

"I had it done; both the office and the apartment are clean."

"What about…that little friend of yours?"

"That was bugged. Stone's guy figured it out."

"I'm hiring a security guard," Amanda said. "I don't want my place bugged again."

"I don't blame you," Hickock replied. "I'm having my premises checked daily, and I'm not using my cell phone when it counts."

"Good God, can they bug a cellular phone?"

"A cell phone is a radio; people can listen in if they have the right equipment. I know a guy who's got a scanner thing in his car; he listens to other people's phone conversations for entertainment while he's being driven around town."

"That's disgusting!" Amanda jotted a quick note to herself to ask Stone how to get a scanner.

"Well, that's life these days."

"I suppose it is. Do you have anything to report?"

"Nothing. Is Stone okay?"

"Yes, he'll be out of the hospital by tomorrow at the latest, or I'm having a word with his doctors."

"Good, we need him on the job."

"Goodbye, Dickie."

"Bye."

She hung up just as Martha buzzed her. "Yes?"

"Allan Peebles is on line two."

"Peebles? That awful man who edits the *Infiltrator*?"

"That's him; he's called twice this morning already. His message is on top of your stack."

"What could he possibly want to talk to *me* about?"

176

"I've no idea. Do you want me to get rid of him?"

No need to court trouble, she thought. "No, I'll speak to him." She pressed the button. "This is Amanda Dart."

"Amanda, this is Allan Peebles."

"Yes?"

"We don't know each other—not really, I mean, but I thought we should talk."

"Talk? About what?"

"Well, Amanda, you and I are the principal targets of this *DIRT* scandal sheet, aren't we?"

"So?"

"So, I thought perhaps we should compare notes."

"I don't have any notes, I'm afraid," she said. *And if I did have any,* she thought, *you're the last person on Earth I'd share them with.*

"Tell me, have your telephones been bugged?"

She paused. "Why do you ask?"

"I thought so. Where can we meet?"

"I suppose you could come to my office." She certainly was not going to be seen in public with this man.

"Oh, no, I'm not talking anywhere that might be bugged."

"Just what is it, exactly, you want to talk about?" she asked.

"I'm not going to talk about it on the phone."

"How long are you in town for?"

"Until the day after tomorrow."

"I've got somebody working on this; I'll have him get in touch with you."

"Listen to me, Amanda; I probably know more

about this than you do, but I'm not talking to anybody else. It will have to be you and I, face-to-face."

Amanda thought for a moment. "You be on the corner of Madison and Seventy-second Street, outside the Ralph Lauren sports store, on the west side of the street, at four o'clock today. I'll be in a black Mercedes Six Hundred."

"Fine."

She hung up. "God," she said aloud, "some of the people you have to *deal* with in this business!"

Chapter 33

Dino showed up at the hospital as Stone was getting dressed to leave. "Where are *you* going?" he demanded.

"Home. I can't stand it here anymore."

"Are you nuts? You look rotten."

"I'm fine." He didn't really feel all that great, but he thought he would feel better in his own bed.

"Has a doctor discharged you?"

"Yes; I didn't give him any choice. Can you give me a lift?" he asked, holding up his slippers. "I don't have any shoes."

"Yeah, okay. At least I'll know you didn't pass out on the street."

The phone rang, and Stone picked it up.

"It's Arrington; how are you feeling today?"

"Well enough to go home."

"Really?

"Well, I ache all over, but apart from that, I'm fine."

"Want me to come get you?"

"Dino's giving me a lift."

"I'll drop by to see you a little later; maybe feed you some chicken soup."

"Sounds good."

"See you." She hung up.

"That Arrington?" Dino asked.

"Yep."

"Looks like you might have something good going there, pal."

"Maybe. Sometimes she gets a little crazy."

"Only sometimes? You're a lucky man; I could tell you about crazy."

"You found an apartment yet?"

"Yeah, and they've accepted our offer."

"How much?"

Dino lowered his voice. "You ready for this? Seven hundred thou and change."

"*Seven hundred thousand?*"

"And change."

"You have a very generous father-in-law."

Dino shook his head. "He just wants her to shut up about it, like me. He'd pay twice that, if she'd shut up about it."

"Where is the apartment?"

"East Sixty-sixth, between Fifth and Madison."

"Uptown!"

"Yeah. We've still got to go before the co-op board."

"Relax, they'll be delighted to have a cop in the building. You might let drop that you can get the patrol frequency increased on the block."

"Good idea. I can do that, too; I'll have a foot patrolman by there every hour."

"How are you going to dress?"

"In a suit, I guess."

"Want me to loan you one?"

"What's the matter with my suits?" Dino demanded indignantly.

"They're probably a little too Italian for an East Side co-op board. A trip to Brooks Brothers or Ralph Lauren might be a good investment."

"I'll think about it. When this board hears us talk, they might bounce us."

"Use your interrogation English."

"Huh?"

"Talk to them the way you interrogate upscale witnesses."

"Oh, that. That could work, if I don't let Mary Ann talk at all."

Stone laughed. "Come on, get me out of here."

Dino dropped him in front of the house, and Stone climbed the front steps more slowly than he'd planned. Helene met him at the door, fussing, and in five minutes she had him tucked in bed.

"Don't bring food," Stone said. "There's a lady coming whom you haven't met yet, and she'll want that privilege."

Helene went back to her work, chuckling.

An hour later, Arrington showed up. He could hear her and Helene coming up the stairs together, laughing. When they came into the room, Arrington was carrying what looked like a large leather portfolio and a paper bag.

"I take it you two have met," Stone said.

"Yes, we have," Arrington said, handing the paper bag to Helene. "I stopped by the deli for soup; can you warm this up?"

Helene went to the kitchenette and came back in five minutes with a large steaming mug.

Arrington made him drink it. "Good for what ails you," she said. When he had finished the soup, she opened the leather thing, which turned out to be a portable massage table. "A little gift," she said.

"Thanks very much," he replied. "How does it work?"

She took a sheet from the linen closet and spread it over the table. "Get out of that night-shirt, and hop up here; I'll show you." She retrieved a bottle of oil from her large purse.

Stone climbed onto the table and stretched out, his face in an opening provided for breathing.

Arrington started with his neck and shoulders. "You've got a very large bruise right here," she said, poking the back of his neck. "Is that sore?"

"You bet it is; go easy there."

She worked her way slowly down his back and buttocks, letting her hands stray now and then.

"You keep that up, and I'll forget I'm sick," Stone breathed.

"Oh, shut up." She moved down to his legs and feet, then had him turn over.

"What was that angry phone call the other night about?" Stone asked. "The one on the machine."

"Oh, I didn't want to tell you until you were better."

"Tell me what?"

"Somebody broke into my apartment earlier that evening."

Stone sat up, but she pushed him back down. "What was taken?"

"Very little. I had a couple of hundred dollars in a dresser drawer; he passed up my jewelry, thank God."

"That sounds strange."

"Especially when you consider that my jewelry box was in plain sight on the dresser."

"How'd he get into the building?"

"I don't know; the doorman swears nobody got past him."

"There's that side entrance that you and I left by one night."

"I guess that might be how, if he knew about it, and if he could get past the lock."

"Is there something you're not telling me about this break-in?" Stone asked.

"Sort of."

"What do you mean, sort of?"

"I think Jonathan did it."

"Why?"

"He's been calling, and I've refused to talk to him. There've been some messages on my machine."

"I want to hear the tape."

"I'm sorry; I was so annoyed that I erased them immediately."

"Anything threatening?"

"Not exactly."

"What does that mean?"

"Well, I didn't like his tone; it was...well, sort of proprietary." She moved down to his chest and belly.

"I don't think I like the sound of that."

"Neither did I."

"I think I should have a little talk with Jonathan."

"I don't want you two getting into fights over me."

"I don't get into fights."

"Jonathan does."

"Trust me; I can handle this one."

"Whatever you say, sir." She giggled and stroked his penis, which was erect. "Is this the way you say howdy?"

"Can you think of a better way?"

"No, sir, I can't," she said, rubbing oil on it.

"Is my massage over?" he whispered.

"Not by a long shot," she whispered back.

"By the way, what's Jonathan's last name?"

"Dryer."

That rang a bell somewhere with Stone, but at the moment, his mind was elsewhere.

Chapter 34

Amanda rode up Madison Avenue in the back of the Mercedes. "Paul," she said, "we're going to pick up a gentleman at Madison and Seventy-second, lefthand side, near the corner."

"Yes, ma'am," Paul replied.

"I'm going to want to go someplace nearby, park for a few minutes and have a private chat with him. Can you think of a good place?"

"There's a place in the park," Paul said.

"That will be fine; better get in the lefthand lane." Amanda put the armrest down to separate her from her unwanted guest, pressed a switch that put up the sunscreen on the rear window, for privacy, and eyed the corner ahead. "That must be him," she said. "The one in the raincoat." She had no idea what Allan Peebles looked like, but this was the only lone man on the corner. The car rolled to a stop, and Amanda pressed the window button.

The man leaned over and looked into the car. "Amanda?"

"Get in," she replied. The car turned left on 72nd and headed for Central Park.

"I'm Allan Peebles," he said, extending his hand.

She shook it perfunctorily, then held a finger to her lips for silence.

Halfway through the park, Paul pulled off the road into a small lot for maintenance vehicles and stopped.

"Give us a few minutes, Paul," Amanda said.

Paul got out of the car and walked twenty yards to a bench and sat down, still in view of the car.

"Now," said Amanda, "what do we have to talk about?"

"I've always been an admirer of your column," Peebles said.

"I wish I could say the same." She glanced at her watch.

"All right, I'll get to the point: Why do you suppose you and I have been targeted by this scandal sheet?"

"I haven't the faintest idea," she said. "After all, Richard Hickock has been targeted, too, and Stone Barrington has been mentioned more than once, as well as Vance Calder."

"With the possible exception of Calder, who was probably an innocent bystander, everybody is connected."

"Connected? How could I possibly be connected with you?"

"We're both published by the same people, in a manner of speaking."

"What on earth are you talking about? I'm published and syndicated by Dick Hickock's company. Stone isn't published by anybody."

"Barrington doesn't really come into it, except as your surrogate."

"What was that you were saying about 'the same people'?"

Peebles smiled slightly. "You really don't know, do you?"

"Know *what?*" Amanda demanded, irritably.

"About Hickock and us."

"Who is 'us'?"

"The *Infiltrator.*"

"What does Hickock have to do with the *Infiltrator?*"

"My father-in-law owns sixty-five percent of the paper, I own ten, and Hickock owns the other twenty-five percent."

Against her will, Amanda's jaw dropped.

"Surprised, aren't you?" Peebles asked, smiling.

"You are out of your mind," Amanda said. "Dick Hickock is a legitimate publisher with half a dozen companies—newspapers, magazines, book publishing, the whole gamut."

"It's a broader gamut than you know," Peebles said. "Hickock has a corporate entity called Win-

185

dow Seat, Limited; the stock is in the name of his wife's half-brother, Martin Wynne."

"I didn't even know she had a half-brother," Amanda said, interested now.

"Neither does just about anybody else. I doubt if he'll show up in Dickie's obituary. Wynne is British, a friend of my father-in-law. The stock is in his name, but believe me, the money is Hickock's, and Wynne doesn't make a move without his permission."

"How very odd."

"It gets odder; Window Seat owns *Personality*."

"That dreadful rag?"

"Dreadful it may be, but it hauls in the bucks, just as the *Infiltrator* does. There's more: through two other corporations, Window Seat controls three gay porno magazines."

"This is incredible; I don't believe a word of it."

"I'd say ask Hickock, but I don't think he'd appreciate it. Window Seat is an offshore corporation, and the profits go straight into Cayman Island accounts, all tax-free. Hickock spends it in Europe; he never brings a dime into the U.S., unless it's in cash."

"He does spend a lot of time in Europe," Amanda admitted. "So does Glynnis."

"It's profitable for them to do so."

"They spend a lot of time at a friend's château in France."

"Owned by Window Seat, or an offshoot."

"What you're talking about would be a major scandal, if it were known," Amanda said. "Why haven't you printed this? After all, scandal is your business."

"I told you, we're in bed with Hickock. So are you."

"Well, I don't really care about any of this; it's nothing to do with me."

"It will be if it ever gets out, and I think that's what this *DIRT* business is about."

"What if it does get out?"

"There would be a major federal investigation, and the IRS would be all over Hickock. Can you imagine what that sort of investigation—not to mention a trial—would do to Hickock's other interests? The stock in his various companies? He'd be ruined, and he'd take a lot of people down with him. Like you and me."

Amanda was horrified.

"You've just done a new deal with him, haven't you?"

Amanda said nothing; she stared into the middle distance and thought about what a Hickock collapse could do to her.

"I think you can see why it's in our mutual interests to cooperate with each other," Peebles said. "The first crack in the dike has already appeared."

"Crack?"

"Glynnis Hickock's divorce action."

"You think Glynnis knows about this?"

"Do you think Hickock could be involved with her half-brother in something as complex as this and Glynnis not know about it?"

"Surely she wouldn't jeopardize Dick's fortune by some intemperate action," Amanda said. "That wouldn't be in her own best interests."

"A woman scorned doesn't always act in her own best interests," Peebles said. "Anyway,

Glynnis is a wealthy woman in her own right. If Hickock sank it wouldn't cause more than a ripple in her lifestyle. And if she's mad enough, she could sink him very deep. The odds would heavily favor a prison term, and she could plausibly deny all knowledge."

Amanda stared at a squirrel outside the car, her mind racing.

"I think you can see why this *DIRT* thing has to be stopped," Peebles said.

Amanda snapped back to attention. "Yes," she said. "But so far, I don't have a clue who's involved. Stone Barrington is still investigating, but he's been in the hospital."

"Hospital?"

"Someone...this goes no further."

"Of course not."

"Someone broke into his house, and when he investigated, he got hit over the head."

"I must say, I'm not surprised."

"What do you know that I don't know?" Amanda asked.

"You must understand, I'm in a very difficult position. The...allegations about me in the scandal sheet are very, very dangerous to my interests. I'm already persona non grata in London, with my wife and my father-in-law, and if the old man were sufficiently riled, he could, quite literally, destroy me. I'd never hold a job again, anywhere in the world."

"Why is your position any worse than anybody else's in this wretched business?" Amanda asked.

"Because I suspect—although I can't prove it—that one of the people, perhaps the *only* person, behind *DIRT* may be someone I was once... *involved* with."

"A lover?"

"That's too strong a term, I think. No, there was never any love in it."

"Who is this person?"

"His name is Geoffrey."

"Geoffrey what?"

"When I knew him—this was nearly a year ago—he called himself Power, but I doubt that's his name. I went through his wallet once, and I found three driver's licenses, in different names."

Amanda was alert now. "What were the other two names?"

"I don't remember. I didn't have any reason to, at the time; I figured they were aliases, too."

"Geoffrey Power. Is Geoffrey his real first name?"

"I can't swear to it, but I think so. I remember that the initial 'G' appeared in the names on all three licenses."

"What does he have against Dick Hickock?"

"I don't know, but I know what he has against me."

"What?"

"After we stopped...seeing each other, I was very angry with him, and I did something that someone in my position should never do—I used the *Infiltrator* to get back at him."

"How?"

"He was trying to make a career as an actor in L.A., and I assigned a reporter to call a couple of dozen casting directors and studios, and let drop that the *Infiltrator* was investigating him. Of course, no one would have anything to do with him after that. He left town and, I think, came to New York."

"What does he look like?"

"Early to mid-thirties, tall, slender, but well-built, light brown hair, highlighted at the ends. He's quite beautiful, actually." Peebles sounded regretful.

Amanda had produced a notebook and was writing furiously. "Have you had him investigated? Really, I mean?"

"No; I'm afraid to. I'm afraid of what he'll do."

"What do you mean?"

"He has a somewhat unsavory background. He hinted at working for some government agency at one time, something secret. That may have been bragging, of course, but I don't really doubt it. He seems to have all sorts of, well, *skills* that ordinary people never come by. And he has a violent streak." Peebles blinked rapidly. "I'm terribly afraid of violence. Also, I can't be seen by *anyone* to have had an interest in him. I've compromised myself too much already; my whole world is hanging by a slender thread."

"I understand your position," Amanda said. "Why did you come to me?"

"You already have an investigation under way that is not seen as being connected with me. Stone Barrington has a reputation as very bright and discreet; if he can track this thing down and put it out of business—*quietly*—then we're all safe: Hickock, you, and me."

"I see," Amanda said.

"Tell your investigator as much of what I've told you as you feel is necessary, but for God's sake, keep my name out of it, if you possibly can. I don't know any more than I've told you, so there's no point in my speaking directly to Barrington. Will you do that?"

"I'll have to think about this," Amanda said. "About the best way to approach it. Of course, I'll keep your name out of it...if I can."

Peebles's face fell; he obviously knew that his fate was in her hands. "I would be very, *very* grateful," he said.

Amanda lowered her window and waved at Paul. In a moment they were rolling back toward the East Side.

"Where can I drop you?" Amanda asked.

"Anywhere," Peebles said disconsolately. "It really doesn't matter."

Chapter 35

On the morning following his return from the hospital, Stone felt well for the first time since his encounter with the intruder. He was sitting at his desk, trying to make some sense of the work that had accumulated, when his secretary buzzed.

"Yes, Alma?"

"Bob Cantor is here to see you," she said.

"Send him in."

Cantor was, uncharacteristically, wearing a business suit. "How you doing, Stone? Recovered?"

"Much better, thanks."

"This guy is some piece of work, huh?"

"Apparently so. Have you got something for me on the maid and the driver?"

"Right." He got out his notebook. "The maid, Gloria, lives in Queens; she rides in every morning with the driver, Paul, and takes the subway home. She's divorced, lives alone, sees a lot of her sister. The neighborhood storekeepers like her. Most of them give her credit, and she pays on time. She's Hungarian, a devout Catholic, teaches catechism to kids at her church. Hard to imagine a straighter arrow. I got a look at her phone bills; she makes very few calls, none of them long distance. Nine out of ten are to her sister, her priest, and Amanda Dart. I tapped her for three days, she got four calls, all of them from her sister. I honestly think that to do more on her is a dead end."

"I agree. What about the driver?"

"Paul is something of a character in his neighborhood. He's gregarious, plays the ponies in a small way and, on his day off, takes the train into the city and sits in a brokerage office, watching the ticker. He's got a couple of hundred thousand in investments, not bad for a chauffeur, and he deals in used cars, one at a time—buys them, fixes them up, and sells them for a profit. He's good on his bills and maintains a healthy bank balance, in the low five figures, in an interest-bearing checking account. I guess he keeps that much on hand in case he finds a car he wants to buy. He's pretty honest about selling the cars, doesn't lie about their condition, and he gets repeat customers. One little niggling thing, for whatever it tells you: He cheats Amanda when he sells her cars."

"How?"

"She gives him ten percent to sell them, but he takes fifteen to twenty in the end. This was easy to figure out from his recent bank statements. Still, he always gives her book wholesale. I don't want to make too much of this."

Stone laughed. "I can't say that I blame him. Amanda is the kind of woman who has to be annoying to work for a lot of the time, even if he is well-paid. Anything else that troubles you about either of these people?"

"Nope. All in all, I'd say that Amanda Dart has herself first-rate help in every department. Except maybe Martha, who could have a weakness."

"What has the bug turned up?"

"The guy who calls never uses his name; she recognizes his voice. He's giving her a pretty hard time, I think; he could be at the point of dumping her, but he hasn't yet. She hasn't seen him since I've been on this. I get the feeling that he thinks he might still need her for something, so he's keeping his hand in, so to speak. I've got the tapes if you want to hear them, but they're all brief; the guy doesn't like to talk on the phone. Tell you the truth, I think that if there's a leak in Amanda's office, it's got to be Martha."

"I've been resisting that idea myself, because Amanda seems so certain that it's not Martha, but after what you've told me about the others, and about these phone calls, I agree that she has to be our girl. I'm not entirely certain about Barry yet, because he screws so many people, we could never keep track. But it's looking an awful lot like Martha."

"Are you going to tell Amanda that?"

"Not yet. I don't want to ruin their relationship without some hard evidence, and we're not doing very well on coming up with that. Did Amanda talk with you about some guard work?"

"Yeah; a guy I know is going to handle it. He'll come into the office when she closes and sit on it until her people arrive in the morning. I swept the place again, and she's still clean. Maybe I ought to have another look around here, too."

"Okay, go ahead; check back with me when you're finished. There's something else I want to talk with you about."

"See you in half an hour," Cantor said, and left the office.

Stone started dictating correspondence and signing checks; he had just finished when Cantor returned.

"Well, I'll tell you," the ex-cop said, flopping down in a chair, "this guy is some piece of work. He's done the phones again."

"Jesus."

"I guess while you were napping the other evening, he calmly went about his business. It's just the phones, though; I didn't find anything else."

"Did you screw up his work?"

Cantor held up a handful of wires and devices. "I yanked it. No need to be subtle anymore."

"You had any luck with this guy in the bar who has the signature with the wires?"

"I almost forgot; I talked to him for half an hour last night; the signature is something he was trained to do."

"Who taught him?"

"A federal agency, is all I could get out of him; he denied that it was the CIA. Maybe the National Security Agency."

Stone shook his head. "Aren't they more into the wireless sort of surveillance?"

"Yeah. It could be some group we don't know about—maybe even something illegal."

"Do you really think that sort of stuff still goes on?"

Cantor shrugged. "Who knows? There are a lot of guys on the street who used to work for somebody in D.C. Maybe he's that type."

"Maybe. Listen, Bob, there's something else."

"Shoot."

"How good are you on your feet?"

"I'm okay; I used to study karate pretty seriously, and I box once or twice a week at my gym. What is it you need, Stone?"

"There's a guy needs talking to, and to tell you the truth, I'm not sure I'm up to it just yet. He's been harassing a friend of mine, a woman, and I want a stop put to it."

"So is this guy muscle, or something?"

"She says he gets into fights; I have no idea how good he is at it."

"What exactly is it that you want done?"

"I want the fear of God put into him. I'm not talking about leaning hard on him, but if he reacts badly, I don't want him to come out of it with the upper hand."

"You think this guy might be the one wiring all these places?"

Stone shook his head and pushed a copy of *Vanity Fair* across his desk. "This is the guy; he's a male model, at least some of the time. The connection's with this girl, whose name is Arrington; not with the *DIRT* thing."

Cantor looked at the picture. "I can handle it."

"There's something else, something I only just found out."

"Yeah?"

Stone handed him a slip of paper. "His name is Jonathan Dryer; that's where he lives. Arnie Millman got clipped in the alley next to the building."

"You think the two things are connected?"

"I can't see how, but I don't like coincidences. I thought you ought to know about Arnie, though."

"Yeah, I'm glad you told me."

"If your talk with him turns up anything that makes you think he might be connected with Arnie by more than just geography, then we'll bring Dino into it."

Cantor nodded. "When you want this done?"

"The sooner the better."

"You think he might be at home now?"

"Only one way to find out."

Cantor stood up. "I'll check him out."

"If he's not there, maybe you could take a look around his place, see what he's about."

"Sure thing."

"Give your bill for the other work to Alma, and she'll cut you a check. What do you want for the Dryer business?"

"Let's see how it goes," Cantor said. "He might be a pushover."

"As long as you're ready for him, if he isn't."

"Don't worry about me." Cantor left and closed the door behind him.

Chapter 36

Amanda had thought long and hard overnight about what to do, and her first decision, characteristically, was to protect herself. She called her lawyer, Bill Eggers, at home.

"Morning, Amanda."

"Bill, I want to ask you a hypothetical—*very* hypothetical—question."

"Shoot."

"In the unlikely event that I felt I really had to, could I get out of my contract with Dick Hickock?"

"*What?*"

"Now, Bill, I told you this was hypothetical; don't get upset."

"Amanda, you've only just signed the contracts; it's a terrific deal!"

"Bill, you haven't answered my question."

"The answer is no, not unless Hickock were willing to release you."

"Nothing I could do, if I wanted out?"

"It's more about what *he* could do. He could prevent any other newspaper or magazine from publishing you. All you could do would be to beg him to let you go. What's this about, Amanda?"

"Bill, this isn't going to happen; I just like to know where I stand, that's all."

"The only way you could get out would be non-performance on Dick's part. As long as he pays, you're stuck with him."

"Thank you, Bill; just forget I asked, all right?"

"Asked what?"

"Bye, Bill." She hung up. Well, that was bad news; if Dickie started downhill, he could drag her with him, and all the way to the bottom. She was going to have to nail whoever was publishing *DIRT*. She had nailed lots of people in her time, but Amanda was not accustomed to going after faceless people with no fixed address.

She picked up the phone to call Stone, then hung up again. She didn't want to tell him about Hickock's sub rosa business activities; after all, he was also representing Dick in this matter; she had given him permission to do so. Oh, well, she didn't have to tell him everything. She picked up the phone again and got connected.

"Stone, darling, I have some information that might be of help," she said.

"I'm all ears," Stone replied.

"You remember the issue of *DIRT* that featured Peebles, the editor of the *Infiltrator*?"

"Yes."

"Peebles and I had a chat yesterday; he thinks that an old boyfriend of his might have something to do with this, might even be the one behind it."

"What's the old boyfriend's name?"

"Geoffrey, spelled the English way, Power. At any rate, that's what he called himself. Peebles thinks he might use more than one name. He's a failed actor, in L.A. anyway—actually, he failed out there because Peebles screwed him with the studios. He could be in New York."

"You have anything else on him that might help me locate him?"

"A description."

"Shoot."

She read from her notes. "Early to mid-thirties, tall, slender, but strong, sandy hair. Peebles says he's quite beautiful."

"Anything else? An address, a phone number?"

"Afraid not, but Peebles thinks he might be in New York; he pulled out of L.A."

"I'll see what I can come up with."

"Bye."

Stone's immediate thought was that the description fit the man who had been following Tiffany Potts, who looked like the man in the magazine, who had turned out to be Jonathan Dryer. He tried to remember his visit to Dryer's apartment, but there wasn't much there. The man had been backlit, standing behind a partially open door, and he had never gotten a good look at him. All he had was the magazine photo. He turned his attention to Geoffrey Power, starting with his computer telephone directory. That contained a hundred million names, but not a single Geoffrey Power. He called Dino.

"Yeah?" Dino said.

"Will you run a name for me?"

"Sure."

"Last name Power, first name Geoffrey." Stone spelled it for him.

"Hang on."

Stone could hear the computer keys clicking.

"He's never been arrested," Dino said.

"Try the alias database."

More key clicking. "Zip," Dino said.

"Thanks. How's it going with the apartment?"

"We're meeting the board this afternoon; I took your advice and bought a suit. When the meeting's over I'll give it to you."

"You're sweet. See you." He hung up and tried New York telephone information, new listings. If Power had just moved to town, he might be there. Nothing. He called Amanda.

"Yes?"

"He doesn't have a telephone in the United States, or one in New York; he's never been arrested. That's all I can do with a name, especially one that might be an alias. You'll have to get me some more information."

"I don't think I can," she replied.

"Then it's a dead end."

Stone had an idea. "Have you got a copy of the new *Vanity Fair* handy?"

"Of course."

"Call Peebles and tell him to look at the ad for Spirit men's cologne." He gave her the page number. "See if the guy in the ad looks familiar. I'd like to hear his response."

"I'll get back to you." She hung up.

Half an hour later, she called back.

"The resemblance is close, but it's not Power, Peebles says. How did you come up with that picture?"

"It arose in connection with something else. The description seemed to fit."

200

"Oh, good. Keep on this Power person, will you?"

"Amanda, there's nothing more I can do until we get more information on the guy. As it stands, he's nothing more than a wisp of smoke."

She hung up without another word.

Chapter 37

Bob Cantor got out of the cab on Second Avenue and walked down the block until he found the building. "Basement apartment," he mumbled to himself, consulting the address Stone had given him. He walked down the steps to the apartment door and found it ajar; the smell of paint reached him. He pushed the door open. The living room was empty and freshly painted. He heard the rattle of a bucket from a rear room and walked that way.

A middle-aged man in paint-stained jeans and sweatshirt was rapidly rolling paint onto a bedroom wall. He looked at Cantor. "Sorry, I'm not showing the apartment until tomorrow, when the ad runs in the *Times*," he said.

Cantor showed him his badge briefly. "I'm looking for Jonathan Dryer," he said.

"So am I," the man replied. "He owes me four months' rent."

"When did you last see him?"

"Last Friday, when I was going away. When I came back on Wednesday, he was gone, and the place was empty. Four months he owes me; that's how long his lease had to run."

"Mind if I look around?"

"Help yourself." He went back to painting.

Cantor walked slowly around the apartment, looking in closets and drawers. It was a nice place, he thought. Good kitchen, nicely done bathroom. Cantor was living in Chelsea, and he thought he wouldn't mind living uptown. All the closets, drawers, and cabinets were empty. He went back to the bedroom and walked out the rear door, which opened onto a small terrace and a garden area behind. There was nothing in the way of planting, but there was soil; soil was a valuable real estate asset in New York. He went back inside.

"Nice place," he said. "Who's the agent?"

"No agent; I own the building. I live on the top two floors."

"How much you asking?"

The man told him.

"How much less would you take to have a guy with a badge living here?"

The man looked at him narrowly. "You married?"

"Divorced."

"Any kids?"

"None."

"You play any musical instruments?"

"The stereo, softly."

"I'd need a police reference."

"Call Lieutenant Dino Bacchetti, at the Nineteenth, around the corner."

"I'll do that. If you check out, it would be worth a couple hundred off for a cop."

"Retired cop, actually, but that's even better for you. I'd be spending more time in the building than somebody who has to pull duty."

"What's your name?"

"Bob Cantor."

"How long a lease you want?"

"Three years would be good."

"You wait here; I'll be right back." The man left and came back ten minutes later. "Bacchetti says you're okay; give me a check for a month's rent and a security deposit, and the place is yours."

Cantor wrote him a check.

"My name's Jim O'Brian." He stuck out his hand.

Cantor shook it. "Back to this guy Dryer; tell me about him."

"He kept to himself, didn't make any noise. I only saw him coming and going, or when he paid the rent. Always paid in cash, which was okay with me."

"How long was he here?"

"Eight months."

"Anybody room with him?"

"A long string of girls, one night at a time."

"Any guys visiting him?"

"He was straight, believe me."

"I mean friends staying over a few days, that sort of thing."

"Not that I recall."

"When he rented the place, did you take an application from him?"

"No, I don't bother with written applications if the renter looks okay. I never got burned until now."

"What did Dryer do for a living?"

"Said he was a filmmaker."

"You ever see any evidence of that?"

"What kind of evidence?"

"Cameras, film equipment?"

"The only equipment Dryer had here was a computer, a copy machine, and a fax machine. Pretty neat computer, though—Pentium, fast laser printer, big monitor."

"Did Dryer apply for his own phone service?"

"Nah, the phone's on my bill. Shit! I forgot about the phone bill. That's more money out of my pocket."

"Did he make many long distance calls?"

"Yeah, quite a few."

"Could I have a look at your phone bills? I'd like to know who he was calling."

"I've got to go upstairs and get you a lease form; I'll dig them out for you."

"One more thing; did Dryer leave anything here?"

"Nothing but trash."

"Has it been picked up yet?"

"No, it'll still be out in the alley next to the building. There's two plastic bags in the first can. It has a 'B' on it, for basement."

"Thanks, Jim, I'll take a look at that while you get the lease and the phone bills—all eight months, if you've got them."

"I'll be back in five minutes."

Cantor followed him outside, walked into the alley, and found the garbage cans. There were three bags; one of them contained uninteresting kitchen garbage, the others a lot of paper and magazines. He pulled out the two bags of paper and walked back to the front of the building. O'Brian was coming down the front steps.

"Standard lease; I've already signed it," he said, handing Cantor the document.

"What about subleasing?"

"No problem, if I approve the tenant."

Cantor signed the lease, kept a copy, and handed it back. "Jim, you really ought to start taking a written application from your tenants; there are a lot of bad people out there."

"You're probably right; was Dryer one of them? Why are you checking up on him?"

"He did something impolite to a friend of a friend of mine. I was just going to talk to him and tell him not to do it again. Don't worry about him; if he walked out on his lease, you won't be seeing him again."

O'Brian nodded and handed Cantor a manila envelope. "Here are the phone bills. The basement number is 1232."

"Can I borrow these for a day?"

"Sure, but I need them back for my taxes."

"I'll get them back to you. Thanks, Jim; I'll probably move in at the weekend, if that's okay."

"Fine with me. Glad to have you aboard."

Cantor tucked the manila envelope under his arm, grabbed the two trash bags, and started looking for a cab.

Chapter 38

Stone was working at his desk when he heard the street door open, and a moment later Bob Cantor walked into his office carrying two garbage bags.

"Never say I didn't give you anything," Cantor said, dropping the two bags on the floor and depositing a manila envelope on Stone's desk. "Dryer jumped his lease and moved out of the apartment last weekend." He grinned. "Nice place; I rented it."

"Did he leave anything in the apartment?" Stone asked.

Cantor pointed at the garbage bags. "If he did, it's in there. His phone bills are in the envelope; the landlord says he made a lot of long distance calls." He pulled up a chair.

Stone opened the envelope and shook out the phone bills.

"The phone was in the landlord's name; last four digits are 1232."

Stone began going through the bills. "L.A., L.A., L.A. Jesus, he lived there for what....?"

"Eight months."

"And he never called anywhere but L.A.? Hard to believe."

"Yeah."

"And only one number," Stone said. He turned to his computer, inserted a CD-ROM, and brought up his national telephone directory. He typed in the L.A. phone number and waited while the computer searched. "Here we go," he said, "the Santa Fe Residential Apartments, in West Hollywood. When did you say that Dryer moved out?"

"Sometime between last Friday and Wednesday."

"Look, he's called this number virtually every day, sometimes three or four times a day."

Stone picked up the phone and dialed the L.A. number.

"Santa Fe," a man's voice said.

"Hello," Stone said, "this is Detective Cantor of the New York City Police Department."

"Thanks a lot," Cantor whispered.

"Yes?"

"Do you have a regular apartment building there, or what?"

"Short-term furnished apartments, by the week or month."

"I'm trying to reach someone who may have moved out last Wednesday or Thursday; could you check your records and tell me who that might be? I don't have a name."

"Don't need a name," the man said. The sound of pages turning came over the phone "Only one person has moved out in the past couple of weeks. We stay pretty full."

"Who would that be?"

"A Mr. G. Gable."

"Can you tell me what he looks like?"

"Early thirties, dirty blond hair, kinda long, fairly tall. Nice-looking guy."

"Have you got a forwarding address?"

"Nope, nothing. You looking for this guy or something?"

"Not yet."

"Well, if you find him, will you let me know? He owes a month's rent. He left here by the back way, very early in the morning."

"Has his place been cleaned out?"

"Oh, yeah; I rented it right away. We always have a waiting list."

"Thanks very much; I appreciate your help." He hung up and turned to Cantor. "He was using the name of G. Gable."

"And we're looking for G. Power. It's gotta be our guy."

"Right. Let's see what his trash looks like." Stone cleared off his desk and, a handful at a time, they began going through all the paper.

"Okay," Cantor said, "we got a lot of very real trash—newspapers, magazines."

"*Vanity Fair, New York, People, Us.* He seems to be celebrity-oriented."

"Here's a receipt from Saks, from the Armani shop," Cantor said. "He paid cash. The landlord said he paid his rent in cash, too."

"What's the date of the receipt?"

"Let's see, nearly a month ago."

"He would have already picked it up after the alterations, then. Too bad."

"More receipts; one from a limo service; here's one from the Four Seasons—Jesus, nearly three hundred bucks for dinner!"

"He's living well, isn't he? And he doesn't seem to use credit cards or write checks for things that most people would. I wonder where he's getting all this cash?"

"I don't see any old bank statements in all this stuff," Cantor said, dropping another double handful onto the desktop. "Look at this, another limo receipt, more clothes—Alan Flusser, this time, who's that?"

"High-end tailor and ready-made clothes."

"Here's one from Ferragamo for six hundred and change."

"That's two pair of shoes."

"Every one of them is marked cash. Oh, he told the landlord he was a filmmaker. Where does a filmmaker get this much cash? A bookie doesn't have this much cash!"

Stone had a thought; he called Dino.

"Yeah, Bacchetti," Dino said.

"It's Stone."

"Hey, you must be making Bob Cantor rich. I got a call from somebody who wanted a reference for renting an apartment up here somewhere."

"Yeah, he's moving up in the world. Listen, Dino, have you had any burglaries reported recently where just about the only thing taken was cash?"

"Burglaries? How the fuck would I know; I don't mess with that kind of shit."

"Yeah, but your guys do. Would you talk to somebody on the burglary detail and ask about it?"

"I'll have to get back to you."

"Thanks, friend." He hung up.

"What makes you think he's doing burglaries?" Cantor asked.

"Just a hunch. Whoever burgled Arrington's place took only cash; the guy who hit me over the head took cash—and my Rolex. Whoever capped Arnie Millman in the alley outside Dryer's—pardon me, your apartment—took cash."

"You think all of those are the same guy, then?"

"Maybe. Maybe two guys."

"Two? One of 'em's Power, then?"

"One of my clients was being followed by a guy who looked like Dryer, but she said wasn't Dryer, judging from the photograph, and yet they fit the same description. I got a tip that a guy from L.A. who might be behind the *DIRT* thing fits the description. Now we've got Dryer repeatedly calling a guy in L.A. who fits the description, and who left L.A. recently. Maybe he's in New York now."

"Brothers?"

"Could be."

The phone rang.

"It's Dino. What do you know about these burglaries?"

"What burglaries, Dino?"

"The burglaries you called me about."

"I called to *ask* you about burglaries. You find some?"

"Eight in the Nineteenth where only cash was taken, or cash and men's' jewelry, watches, that kind of stuff, all of them in high-end buildings. What do you know about this?"

"I'm just chasing a wild hunch. Find a copy of *Vanity Fair*, the new issue, and look for an ad for Spirit men's cologne. There's a guy's picture in it; he's been calling himself Jonathan Dryer. Get one of your burglary detail to show it to the eight victims and see if anybody recognizes him. If they do, I'd love to have a name and address."

"Why do you think this guy's connected to these burglaries?"

"Because I think he went into Arrington's place and took cash, and he may have been the guy who did me, who also took cash. He's an old boyfriend of Arrington's."

"Well, she must know where to find him."

"He moved out and didn't leave a forwarding address, and get this: He lived in the apartment next to the alley where Arnie Millman bought it. Interesting?"

"Very."

"One of your guys must have interviewed him that night. When I went around there he said he'd been talking to the cops. Will you find out who it was and what notes he took?"

"I'll do that."

"And I'd like to hear about it."

"You will." Dino hung up.

"Bob, you call the cologne manufacturer, and see if you can track down Dryer through his modeling agency."

"Okay, Stone; sounds like you're putting something together here," Cantor said.

"Maybe," Stone said. "We'll see."

"I forget," Cantor said, "did I mention that Dryer had a hotshot computer, a laser printer, and a fax machine? Maybe this is *DIRT*?"

"Maybe paydirt," Stone said.

Chapter 39

The following morning, Stone and Arrington lay in his bed, watching the *Today* show and eating breakfast.

"I checked out Dryer," Stone said. "He's bolted from his apartment."

"I hope he's bolted from the planet," Arrington said.

"Do you mind telling me a little more about

him?" He was treading carefully; he knew this was a sensitive subject.

"What do you want to know?"

"How'd you meet him?"

"At somebody's house in East Hampton, in August."

"Whose house?"

"A photographer's."

"A friend of Dryer's?"

"No, Jonathan didn't know the host; he came with somebody else, I think. I can't remember who."

"How many times did you see him after that?"

"Two or three times a week, I guess; we both had a lot else going on."

"What did Dryer have going on?"

"I assume he was hustling for some sort of living, although he always seemed to have money."

"When you went out somewhere, how did Dryer pay?"

"On the occasions when I didn't pay, he always paid in cash."

"Never with a credit card or check?"

"No, always cash. I asked him once why he always carried so much cash, and he said he played poker a couple of times a week and always won."

"Did he say who he played with?"

"No."

"Did you ever know, specifically, what he was doing on any night when he wasn't seeing you?"

She sipped her orange juice and shook her head. "Never; I always had the feeling that he had at least one other complete life going, maybe more than one."

"Did you ever see him with other people, or always alone?"

"Usually just the two of us, but I took him to a few parties."

"Did he know people at these parties?"

"Never; I was always introducing him to people I knew."

"Were you ever in the apartment on East Ninety-first?"

"A couple of times. More often we were at my place."

"Can you describe the furnishings of the apartment for me?"

She frowned. "I guess you'd say it was the typical single-guy place, but of a younger guy than Jonathan."

"How so?"

"Well, the furnishings were inexpensive, off-the-shelf things, the sort of stuff you could pick up at the Door Store or Crate and Barrel. There were posters, but no pictures—original art, I mean. There was a cheap stereo and a small TV and a computer; he had sort of a home office. Nothing to speak of in the kitchen, just the bare minimum of plates and glasses and pots and pans. Nothing much ever in the fridge, except breakfast stuff and beer. Jonathan said he was thirty-four, and usually a guy of that age would have accumulated a few more permanent possessions."

"What about clothes?"

"Lots of clothes; he was always shopping. Most of his stuff seemed quite new."

"Jewelry?"

"Watches; he had three or four."

"Do you remember what kind?"

"A couple of Rolexes and one or two dressier things. One from Tiffany's, I remember."

"Did you ever know him to leave town for any reason?"

"No, except for the time in East Hampton. He never said anything about traveling."

"Did he ever tell you anything about where he was from, or his family?"

"I asked him once where he was from; he said nowhere, really, that his family moved around a lot. Something he said—I can't remember exactly what—led me to believe that his father might have been in the military."

"Which branch?"

"I don't know; I'm not really sure of the military thing; it was just an impression. He also gave me the feeling that he and his family didn't talk. Believe me, he's the perfect candidate for black sheep."

"Any brothers or sisters?"

"Not that he mentioned."

"What about school or college?"

"He said he went to a small Eastern college; I asked him which one, but he said I would have never heard of it."

"Do you know if he ever lived in other cities?"

"Washington. He said he was there for several years."

"Did he say what he did there?"

"Something about selling some kind of equipment to the government. I don't know what."

"Did he have any hangouts in the city? Bars? Restaurants?"

"We always went to restaurants, and do you know, I don't think we ever went to the same one twice. He liked to order elaborate meals, liked expensive wines."

"Any bar hangouts?"

"Not when he was with me, but he gave you the impression of knowing every place in town. He liked to stay up very late, later than I did, anyway. I had the feeling that when he left me he usually went someplace else, but I never knew where."

"When you were at his place did he ever get phone calls?"

"Often."

"Did you ever know from who?"

"No, but most of them were probably women. He never called anybody by name on the phone. I only ever saw him make one phone call—it was long distance, but I don't know to whom. Is this helping at all?"

"You've told me a lot, but nothing that would help me find him."

"Now that he's gone, why would you want to find him?"

"It's possible that he might be involved in this *DIRT* business. Would that surprise you?"

"Nothing about Jonathan would surprise me. If you told me he was a Russian spy I wouldn't be bowled over."

"Anything else you can remember about him?"

"He wasn't the kind to be very forthcoming; if anything, he always seemed to have something to hide."

The phone rang, and Stone picked it up.

"Hi, it's Cantor."

"Hi."

"I checked out things at the Spirit cologne office. Turns out Dryer wasn't hired through a modeling agency. A girl who works there met him at a party and thought he looked right; she got her boss to hire him as a one-shot thing."

"Can you find out how they paid him? I'd love to have a Social Security number."

"He insisted on cash. The phone number she had for him was the East Ninety-first apartment."

"Does she know anybody else who knows him?"

"Not a soul; it's a dead end."

"What's happening on your tape stakeout?"

"What's happening is, she comes home at night, fixes dinner, and cries. He hasn't called again."

"Sounds like she's been dumped; you can pull the plug on that one."

"Will do. What else can I do for you?"

"Why don't you drop by here in, say, an hour; we'll see where we are."

"See you then."

Stone hung up.

"We've only got an hour?" she asked with mock sadness.

"Let's use it well," he replied, rolling toward her. Then the phone rang again.

"Hello?"

"It's Dino. I want you to come over here and go over some stuff with me."

"When?"

"This morning."

"Around eleven?"

"That's good; you can buy me lunch."

"Can I bring Cantor?"

"Why not? Maybe he'll have some sort of a take on this."

"On what?"

"I'll tell you when you get here." Dino hung up.

Stone hung up and rolled toward Arrington again. "Sorry about that," he said.

"Don't let it happen again," she said.

He reached over and took the phone off the hook.

"Good boy," she said, reaching for him.

Chapter 40

Stone and Bob Cantor arrived at the 19th Precinct on time and were sent to Dino's office right away. Both men still knew detectives working there, and they said a few hellos along the way. Stone hadn't often been back to the 19th since he'd taken retirement, and he'd never been really close to anybody there but Dino, so his reception was on the cool side. Once they were in Dino's office, the reception got hostile.

"You remember Ernie Martinez, Stone," Dino said.

"Sure. Hi, Ernie."

Martinez nodded. He was a portly detective of Puerto Rican extraction who didn't like anybody who wasn't Puerto Rican. He didn't like Dino much, and he certainly didn't like Stone.

"Ernie's the lead detective on the burglaries."

Stone and Cantor took chairs, and Dino moved

a stack of files to the middle of his desk, not a high stack, because each of them was thin, containing only a sheet or two of paper.

"Stone," Dino said, "three of the eight burglary victims made the Dryer guy. Turns out they all met him at the same party, which took place in one of the burgled residences."

Stone nodded; he wasn't surprised.

Dino continued. "He was with Arrington Carter on that occasion; she introduced him around."

"Were any of the other victims at the same party?"

"No. But we're going to have to talk to Arrington. You want to bring her in?"

"I don't think that'll be necessary," Stone said.

Martinez sat up, bristling. "You don't think it'll be necessary! Since when does anybody give a shit what you think is necessary, Barrington?"

"Shut the fuck up, Ernie," Dino said. "For starters, I care what he thinks. I'll get to you in a minute." He turned to Stone. "Talk to me about Arrington."

"I talked to her at length this morning about Dryer, so right now I know what she knows; that's why it won't be necessary to get her in here."

"So what does she know?"

"Not a whole lot; this Dryer character is real good at not letting anybody know anything about him that counts. Arrington did take him to some parties, though; several of them."

"Could you ask her which parties, in which apartments?"

"I'll get a list, and we can compare them to the files. My hunch is they'll match up."

"Okay, I want you and Bob to take a look at

each of these files, and I will, too." Dino passed out the files, and they all read each of them, which didn't take long, since each consisted of a burglary report and a list of stolen items.

"Money and men's jewelry," Cantor said. "Three watches out of eight hits."

"Arrington says he likes watches, that he had three or four," Stone said.

"He could be wearing yours on his charm bracelet right now," Martinez said.

"Probably not," Stone said. "It had my name engraved on the back, so he's probably tossed it. He's too smart to get caught with that. Same thing with Arnie's watch; he didn't take that either."

"Arnie's watch?" Martinez asked.

"That's another case," Dino said. "Don't you worry about it; stick to burglary."

"All the entries were through the front door," Cantor said, "and alarms didn't stop him, so the guy's a mechanic."

"Not much doubt about that," Martinez said.

"Did you dust anything, Ernie?" Stone asked.

Martinez grimaced. "You know we don't have time for fingerprinting at small-time jobs like this."

"One of them wasn't so small time," Stone said. "He lifted thirty-five thousand dollars in cash from a wall safe."

"That, I dusted," Martinez said. "Nothing there but the owner's prints."

"The watches were all Cartiers," Cantor said. "Two Tank models and a Panther. The guy's got taste."

Dino spoke up. "Anything else to ask Ernie, Stone? Bob?"

"Not right now," Stone said.

Cantor shook his head.

"That's all for now, Ernie; I'll get back to you." Dino waited until Martinez left, then he turned to Stone. "What's this about Arnie?"

Stone nodded. "There's something I'd like Ernie to ask the victims about, but I think it's better if the suggestion comes from you."

"Right," Dino agreed. "What is it?"

"I'd like to know if any of the victims lost a twenty-five automatic in the burglaries."

Dino nodded slowly.

Cantor spoke up. "There's nothing in any of the reports about a stolen gun."

Stone shrugged. "Maybe it didn't happen, but if the gun was unregistered, the victim would be reluctant to mention it; it wouldn't be a big loss. If Ernie could let each of them know he's not interested in pursuing the lack of registration, somebody might admit to it."

"Good point," Cantor said.

"In fact, Dino, I think it might be best if you called each of these people. Ernie just might not be the kind of guy these people would feel comfortable talking to about this. Rank would impress them."

Dino shrugged. "Okay, I'll phone them."

Cantor spoke up. "Are we talking about Arnie Millman here?"

"Possibly," Stone said. "Dino, can we talk to the cop who interviewed Dryer?"

Dino got up, opened his door, and shouted, "Gleason! In here!" A moment later a fit-looking fifty-year-old detective came into the office. "Kevin, you know Stone, Bob."

Gleason shook hands cordially with both men.

"You got your notes on the Dryer interview at Arnie's scene?" Dino asked. "Give us your impressions."

Gleason produced a notebook. "Looked to me like Dryer was in the rack with somebody when I rang the bell. He was still getting dressed when he came to the door, and he made a point of closing the bedroom door after I got in. He seemed willing to be helpful, but said he didn't hear anything, didn't know anything. Said he'd been in the house all evening and had a witness to that effect, if I really needed it, but he obviously didn't want to involve the girl, so I let it go. I bought his story."

"You think we might pull up a print or two in that apartment?" Dino asked.

Cantor spoke up. "I doubt it very seriously; the place has been cleaned and painted."

"Stone, you got any questions?" Dino asked.

"This was what time, Kevin?"

Gleason looked at his notebook. "I talked to him around eight-thirty."

"And what time did Arnie buy it?"

"ME says between seven and eight."

"That's a pretty tight fix."

"It was body temperature. We reckon we got there pretty quick; a neighbor who was taking out his garbage found Arnie's body."

"Did you get any kind of look at all at the woman in the bedroom?" Stone asked.

"No, nothing."

"Was there anything in the living room that looked like it belonged to a woman?"

Gleason closed his eyes and thought for half a minute. "Yeah, there was a woman's brown tweed overcoat on a chair. I didn't note that at the time; I just remembered it now."

"How about a scarf?"

"Yeah, a yellow one."

"Thanks, Kevin, that's all I've got."

"Okay, Kevin," Dino said, "that'll do it."

"Did I miss anything, boss?"

"No, you didn't," Dino said. "Good job; the coat was good." When Gleason had left, Dino turned to Stone. "What?" he asked.

"It may be nothing; I want to check something out first."

"Stone, don't you hold out on me."

"I promise I won't; I just think I can learn more about this by treading softly than you can with a standard interview."

"Okay, I'll trust you on that," Dino said. "But the minute you've got something, I want to know."

"I promise. I assume you ran a check on the Jonathan Dryer name?"

"Yeah; nothing."

"That's what I figured."

"Well," Dino said, "we've made a start, I guess, but I don't have enough evidence to arrest Dryer for the burglaries."

"Assuming you could find him," Stone said.

"Right. I don't even have enough evidence to start looking for him. This all sounds good, but it's very tenuous."

"You're right, Dino," Stone said. "I'll stay on it and see if I can come up with something else. And I'll get that list from Arrington. You'll let me know about the gun?"

"Sure. We having lunch?"

"You're on. Bob, join us?"

"Okay."

Dino stood up. "I got to go to the can; I'll meet you guys outside."

Stone and Cantor left Dino's office and walked through the squad room and out the front door.

"Stone," Cantor said.

"Yeah?"

"The other night when I clocked Martha going into her apartment building, she was wearing a brown tweed coat and a yellow scarf."

"I know," Stone said. "Don't bring it up at lunch."

Chapter 41

When Stone got back to his desk there was a small package waiting for him.

"It was hand-delivered," Alma said.

Stone opened the package and found a new Rolex Oyster-quartz, with his name engraved on the back. He picked up the phone and dialed.

"Hello, Amanda."

"Hello, Stone."

"You shouldn't have bought me a watch; really, you shouldn't have."

"You lost your old one in my service," Amanda said. "It was the very least I could do. I hope you won't upset me by trying to return it."

"No, I won't do that. Thank you very much for the watch."

"Is it identical to yours?"

"The face is different, but I like it better."

"I'm so glad."

Stone took a deep breath. "Amanda, we've come to the point in this investigation where I've got to question Martha."

"Stone, I've told you, I don't want her bothered."

"This is how it is," Stone said. "She's been seeing someone, a man who calls himself Jonathan Dryer."

"The name doesn't ring a bell," Amanda replied.

"It may not even be his name, but that's what he's been using. Dryer may very well be connected with the man in California who told Allan Peebles his name was Geoffrey Power, so the two of them may be behind the *DIRT* business."

"I see," Amanda said.

"What's more, Dryer may have burgled a number of apartments around town, and he could even be mixed up in a murder."

"If that's true, why haven't you had him arrested?" Amanda asked.

"Two reasons: right now, this is all just supposition; we don't have any hard evidence. Also, we don't know where Dryer is; he moved out of his apartment. Martha may know him better than anyone else we're aware of, so it's crucial that we get as much evidence as possible from her about Dryer. She may even know his whereabouts." Stone knew this was probably not true, but he needed to push Amanda on this. "I think it would be better for Martha if I talked to her rather than the police doing it."

"Well, I *certainly* don't want the police grilling her," Amanda said. "She'd go to pieces."

"I'll be gentle with her, I promise."

"No."

"Amanda...."

"I'll talk to her myself."

"Amanda...."

"I'll get more out of her than you can; I've been a journalist all my adult life, and I know how to conduct an interview. Also, Martha is afraid of me."

"Amanda, I really think it would be better if I talked to her."

"No, Stone; I will do it, and that's final. Is there anything in particular you want me to ask her?"

"We want as much information about Dryer as possible—present whereabouts, friends, relatives, family background, personal history. We need to know everything she knows. If she tries to deny knowledge of him, tell her she was seen going into Dryer's apartment, and that we have taped conversations between the two of them."

"Don't worry, I'll get everything out of her."

Stone sighed. "All right; when will you do it?"

"I'll spend some time with her, and I'll call you on Monday."

"All right, Amanda, but it can't wait any longer than that."

"Goodbye, darling; I'm so glad you liked the watch." She hung up.

Dino walked into P.J. Clark's at four o'clock. It was too early for the after-work trade, and the place was deserted, except for a man at the opposite end of the bar. He was wearing a cashmere overcoat, and an expensive briefcase was parked on the bar next to him. There was also a large whiskey in front of him. Dino walked over. "Mr. Elliot?"

"Lieutenant Bacchetti?" He stuck out his hand. "Take a pew."

Dino pulled up a stool.

"Something to drink?"

"I'll have a beer," Dino said to the bartender. He waited until the beer had been served and the bartender had retreated before continuing. "Now," he said to Elliot, "a few general questions."

"All right. I hope you understand that I didn't want to talk about this on the phone."

"Of course. Now, Arrington Carter brought a man named Jonathan Dryer to your party, is that correct?"

"She brought a young man; I didn't get his name."

"During the party did you notice whether this young man might have visited some part of your apartment that a party guest might not ordinarily visit?"

"He used the bathroom in the master suite," Elliot said.

"Is that bathroom near where you kept the pistol?"

"Only a few feet away."

"What about the control panel for your burglar alarm? Where is that located in your apartment?"

"In a linen closet just outside the master suite."

"So Dryer might have had access to that?"

"Very possibly."

"All right, let's talk about the twenty-five automatic."

"Before we do," Elliot said, "you have to understand something."

"Okay, what is it?"

"I'm a lawyer, and I can't afford to lose my license over something like this."

"I understand."

"Whatever passes between us in this conversation is just between you and me. If it ever comes up again, in any context, I'll deny everything."

"All right, Mr. Elliot, I understand you; now you have to understand me. Your gun may have been used to murder a police officer. When we make an arrest, you're going to have to identify the gun, and if we can't find it, testify to the type and how it might have left your possession. As a lawyer, you certainly understand that."

Elliot went to his next negotiating position. "All right, but I won't testify unless I have complete immunity."

"I think I can probably arrange that," Dino replied.

"That's not good enough. I want your personal word that you won't ask me to testify unless you can get me immunity."

"I'm not sure I can do that."

"Come on, Bacchetti, it's a murder case, a murdered cop. They're going to want the perpetrator, not me."

"All right, I give you my word that I won't ask you to testify, unless I can get you immunity."

"Understand, if you don't get me the immunity I'll take the Fifth."

"That's not going to be necessary, Mr. Elliot; you have my word."

"Okay."

"Now, how did you come into possession of the weapon?"

"I bought it from a guy on the street."

"What guy? Who was he?"

"I don't know his name."

"Come on, Mr. Elliot, you're not cutting it, here."

"I mean, his real name. His street name is Lowrider."

"And how did you come to know Lowrider?"

"I fell into conversation with him in Central Park; he was selling drugs. I told him I was interested in something for personal protection, and he said he could have something for me the next day."

"And did he?"

"Yes, a twenty-five Beretta, nickel-plated."

"How much did you pay him for it?"

"Twenty-five hundred dollars."

Dino knew immediately that something was wrong here. "That's an awful lot of money for a street gun, especially small caliber," he said slowly. His gaze let the lawyer know that he was suspicious.

"Yeah, well, maybe so, but I don't buy all that many guns on the street, you know?"

"Mr. Elliot, you'd better tell me all of it, and right now."

Elliot began to look very uncomfortable. He looked around the bar, checked the position of the bartender, and drained his glass of whiskey. "All right, it had a silencer."

Dino's eyebrows went up. "I see," he said. "Well, that would certainly put the price up. Now why...."

Elliot held up a hand. "That's it; I told you what I said I would; I'm not answering any more questions." He rose to leave.

Dino put a hand on his shoulder and shoved him back onto the barstool. "We're not finished," he said.

Elliot sat down but said nothing.

"And you kept the weapon in your safe?" Dino asked.

"Yes."

"The same safe that held the thirty-five thousand dollars that you reported stolen?"

"That's right."

"Where is the safe located?"

"In my dressing room. It's one of those that fits between the studs in the wall."

"And what else was in the safe besides the pistol and the cash?"

"A jewelry box."

"Was the stolen watch in the jewelry box?"

"Yes, a Cartier Panther with a gold bracelet."

"Was there anything else of value in the jewelry box?"

"About fifty thousand dollars' worth of assorted jewelry—diamond cuff links, things like that."

"Mr. Elliot, why did you have thirty-five thousand dollars in cash in your safe?"

Elliot glared at him. "I can't always get to the ATM when I need cash," he said. "And that's all I have to say on that subject."

Dino nodded. "Did you make a record of the serial number on the pistol?"

"As a matter of fact, I did," Elliot said, handing Dino a scrap of paper.

"Very good," Dino said. "Why? I mean, you weren't exactly going to register the warranty, were you?"

"Habit," Elliot said.

"Well, I'm very grateful to you for all this information," Dino said, slipping the serial number into his pocket. "It may very well help capture a murderer."

"Good." Elliot looked at his watch.

"I'm so grateful that I'm going to give you a very valuable piece of advice, Mr. Elliot."

"Yeah?"

"The combination of a lot of cash in a safe with a silenced pistol raises a very large warning flag," Dino said. "So I'm going to advise you right now that if any loved one of yours, say your wife, were to meet a sudden end; if something awful should happen to a business associate of yours; in fact, if your name should arise in any investigation of a death by any cause, then I'm coming to see you. Do you get my drift?"

Elliot looked him in the eye. "I do."

"Good, because dealing with that kind of event in your life would be so much more painful than whatever is causing you concern now."

Elliot nodded.

Dino shook his hand and walked out of the bar.

Martha looked into Amanda's office. "Anything else before I'm off?"

"No, dear. Listen, why don't you come up to the country with me tomorrow? Just for the day. Unless you have some plans, of course."

Martha sighed. "No, I don't have any plans. I'd love to."

Amanda smiled a disarming smile. "It'll be just the two of us, dear."

Chapter 42

Driving Amanda's car, Martha turned onto the dirt road, as directed. "It's so lovely up here," she said. "I've never been to Connecticut before."

"Yes, it is lovely, isn't it?" Amanda replied. "The leaves are just a bit past their peak, but still glorious. Make your next left up ahead, dear."

Martha followed her instructions and drew up before Amanda's house. "Oh, it's too perfect! What a wonderful place!"

"Thank you, dear," Amanda said. "Let's go inside." She got the shopping basket from the rear seat, unlocked the door, and strode off toward the kitchen. "Don't even take your coat off," she called over her shoulder. "I'll just get a bottle of wine, and we'll have a picnic up at Steep Rock."

"Where?" Martha asked.

"Steep Rock is a beautiful land preserve that borders my property. You'll love it."

"How far is it? I'm not much of a walker."

"Oh, not far, and believe me, it's worth the effort."

"I'll take your word for it."

Amanda put a bottle of wine and a corkscrew into her basket, locked the door, and led the way at a brisk pace. "Come on, Martha!" she called out. "Let's get that heart pumping!"

Martha hurried along behind her, already beginning to pant. "How much farther?"

"Not far; hurry up."

At the top of the long hill Amanda spread out a tablecloth and opened the bottle of wine. She had already drunk half a glass when Martha came lumbering up the hill and flopped down beside her, completely out of breath.

"Take that heavy coat off," Amanda said. "You'll cool down much quicker. And here, have some wine."

"Do you have any water?"

"I'm sorry, dear, I only brought the wine."

Martha accepted the glass and drank it greedily. "I'm so thirsty," she puffed.

Amanda refilled her glass. "Of course you are. It's a very nice Chardonnay, isn't it?"

"Yes." Martha was beginning to catch her breath now.

"Have some bread and cheese," Amanda said. "It will fortify you for the walk back."

"Thank God it will be downhill," Martha said, digging into the food.

Amanda kept her glass full.

When they had finished their lunch, Amanda leaned back against a tree. "Now," she said. "We're all alone, just the two of us. Time for some frank girl-to-girl talk."

Martha worried, but didn't say anything.

"Why don't we start with Jonathan Dryer," Amanda said. "Tell me about him."

Martha seemed to hold her breath for a moment, then answered, "Who?"

"Why, the young man you've been sleeping with," Amanda said. "Did you think you could keep a secret from me?"

"I'm afraid I don't know who you mean," Martha said. She was blushing now.

"Martha, darling, it's useless to play this game. I've had detectives following you, listening in on your telephone conversations. You were seen going into Dryer's apartment and your phone conversations were taped. I think you'll feel a lot better when you've told me everything." In that part of the brain that deals with fury and revenge, Amanda felt a small explosion, but she kept her temper. "How did you meet him, Martha?"

Martha's shoulders slumped. "At the grocery store," she said. "We talked about food; he knows a lot about food and wine."

"I'm sure he does, dear. When did you start talking about *my* business? Before or after you began fucking him?"

Martha blushed even redder. "I don't really think that's your business...."

"Martha, my darling," Amanda interrupted, "let's remember whose business you and Mr. Dryer talked about."

A tear ran down Martha's cheek.

"You're going to feel so much better when you've told me everything."

"You're going to fire me, aren't you?"

"Why, Martha, of course not. You're absolutely indispensable to me; I could never do without you. I just have to know what you told him and what he told you, and then all will be well. Start at the beginning, now."

Martha slumped. "We went out to dinner, and we talked about everything in the world. Everything! Then we went back to his place and...."

"And he fucked you, didn't he?"

Martha nodded. "I had to go to confession," she said.

"Confession is good for the soul, dear. Go on."

"It wasn't until our second date that your name came up. He didn't even know where I worked until then."

"Didn't he, dear?"

"He just seemed so very interested in you; he wanted to know everything."

"Everything?"

"Where you came from, who your friends were, who you were...."

"Who I was fucking, dear?"

Martha nodded. "He seemed especially interested in your sex life. I just wanted the evening to last forever, so I kept talking."

"And you just poured out everything, didn't you?"

Martha nodded again. "I'm afraid so."

"You told him about my plans for that weekend, didn't you? And where I'd be meeting my friend."

Martha continued to nod. "I didn't realize what I'd done until the first *DIRT* arrived."

"And then you knew you'd betrayed a confidence, didn't you?"

"Yes," Martha said, bursting into tears. "I'm sorry, Amanda; I didn't know he'd do that."

"But you didn't stop seeing him, did you? You went on and on, didn't you?"

"I couldn't help myself. He was so beautiful;

234

I've never known such a beautiful man. He taught me so much about love."

"I'm sure he did, dear, in between screwing sessions."

Martha looked up sharply. "I didn't think of it that way," she said. "I was in love with him."

"And now? Aren't you still in love?"

Martha nodded. "But he won't see me. I called his apartment, but there was no answer. I went by there, and all his things were gone. He'd left."

"And where did he go, dear?"

"I don't know," Martha wailed. "I want to know, but I don't. I kept hoping that he would call, but he didn't."

"What did he tell you about himself, dear?"

"Well, he said he went to Harvard, and that he worked for the State Department in Washington for a long time."

"What else?"

"I don't think he sees his family; there was some kind of argument with them. They're very wealthy, though, and Jonathan always had a lot of money. He paid cash for everything."

"I'm sure he did. Did he say how he knew about Allan Peebles's, ah, predilection?"

"He said something about having friends in Los Angeles, but he didn't mention any names."

"Who are his friends in New York?"

"I don't know; I never met any of them. We spent all our time...alone."

"What else can you tell me about him, Martha?"

"I don't know anything else, Amanda, believe me. I've told you everything." She began to cry again.

"There, there, darling," Amanda said, rising to

her feet and looking around. They were alone in the dense forest. "Come over here; you haven't seen the best part of the view."

"What?"

"Come over here, dear," Amanda said, holding out a hand.

Martha took her hand and struggled to her feet. They walked a few yards farther along through the fallen leaves. A distant roar filtered through the trees, like the sound of heavy traffic.

Amanda led her along, thinking about the humiliation this little bitch had caused her, and after all she had done to make her life comfortable and secure. "Just a little farther, dear," Amanda said soothingly, her brain on fire with anger.

"What's that noise?" Martha asked. "It sounds like...."

"It's the Shepaug River, dear," Amanda replied as she took hold of Martha's wrist with her other hand. "Just ahead is where it goes over the rapids." Amanda took a step, turned, and with both hands swung Martha ahead of her, just as the ground fell away. Martha teetered on one foot on the brink of the rock, and for a moment it appeared that she would recover her balance. Then, without a sound, she went backward over the edge and, looking wide-eyed back toward Amanda, fell ninety feet onto the river-washed boulders below.

Amanda watched for a moment as Martha's limp form traveled through the rocks and downstream, out of sight in the rushing waters. Then she returned to where she'd spread the tablecloth, sat down, poured herself the last of the wine, and sipped it. When she was again completely composed, she took her portable cellular phone from her pocket and punched in a number.

Chapter 43

Stone and Arrington were having brunch at the Brasserie, which had become a weekend hangout for them. Stone had his notebook out and was writing as quickly as Arrington could talk.

"So that's five parties I took Jonathan to, one of them a dinner party," she was saying.

Stone checked his notes against the list of burglaries. "He hit all five, plus three more—Berman, Charleson, and White."

"They were all at one or more of the parties I took him to."

"Plus your apartment and my house."

"Ten burglaries in all?"

"That we know about. Jonathan has been a busy fellow."

"What about women?"

"Beg pardon?"

"How many other women was he seeing when he was seeing me?"

"Two that I know of. His landlord said there were a lot of women coming to his apartment."

"Figures," she said. "I can really pick 'em, can't I?"

"Your record is improving."

She reached across and squeezed his hand. "It certainly is," she said.

Stone's pocket telephone rang. He dug it out and pressed a button. "Yes?"

"Stone, it's Amanda." Her voice was shaky.

"Hi, are you all right?"

"I'm afraid something awful has happened."

"Tell me."

"I'm up at the Connecticut house. Martha and I went for a walk and a picnic, and I'm afraid she strayed too close to a bluff called Steep Rock."

"Go on."

"She fell, and I couldn't stop her."

"Is she badly hurt?"

"It was a long fall, and there were rocks at the bottom."

"I see," he said. "Where are you now?"

"I'm still at Steep Rock; this happened only a moment ago."

"Have you called the police?"

"No; I wanted to talk to you first. After all, you're my lawyer."

Stone noted the emphasis on those words. "Amanda, I want you to call nine-one-one right this minute and report what happened."

"All right. Can you come up here?"

"I'll have to rent a car, so it's going to take at least two and a half, three hours."

"All right."

"After you've talked to the police, ask them to take you back to your house; I'll meet you there. If anything else comes up, call me on this number."

"All right. Goodbye."

Stone hung up. "Jesus Christ," he said.

"What's happened to her?" Arrington asked.

"Not to her, to her secretary, Martha. She's had what sounds like a fatal accident." Stone began to wonder if "accident" was accurate.

"You're going to Connecticut, then?"

"Right now; I've got to rent a car first."

"I've got a car; I'll drive you."

"You don't have to do that."

"I *want* to drive you."

"Then let's go." He waved for the check, paid the bill, and they took a cab uptown to Arrington's garage. Twenty minutes later they were in Arrington's Jeep Grand Cherokee, on their way.

When they arrived at Amanda's country house, a state police car was parked out front, and two uniformed troopers were leaving.

Stone got out of the car and handed them his card. "I'm Stone Barrington; I'm Mrs. Dart's attorney."

"I'm Captain Quentin," one of them said. "This is Sergeant Travis."

Stone shook their hands. "Can you tell me what's happened?"

"Mrs. Dart said she phoned you."

"That's right, but she was pretty shaken up, and I'd like to know what you've learned."

"The two women went for a walk up to Steep Rock, took a picnic lunch. According to Mrs. Dart they had lunch, drank a bottle of wine between the two of them. Miss McMahon got up to stretch her legs, wandered too close to the edge of the bluff, and fell."

"Is she dead?"

"Yes. Her body finished up a couple of miles downriver, at a weir. It's being taken to the state morgue in Hartford for an autopsy, but I don't think there's much doubt about the cause of death.

For now we're calling it an alcohol-related accident."

"Is it absolutely necessary to report alcohol-related on this? Mrs. Dart is a very well-known person, and her reputation might suffer. From what you've told me she has no culpability; it was an accident, after all."

"I can leave it out of my initial written report, but the final determination will be made by the medical examiner. It will depend on the blood alcohol level."

"Thank you, I appreciate that," Stone said. He shook the men's hands. "Is there any reason why Mrs. Dart can't return to New York when she's ready?"

"None at all; we have her phone number in the city if we need to get in touch with her."

"If you need to speak with her, I'd appreciate it if you'd call me," Stone said.

"Sure. Good afternoon."

The two men left, and Stone opened the front door. "Amanda?" he called out.

"I'm in the kitchen," she called back.

They left their coats in a hall closet and went to the kitchen, where Amanda was washing and putting away dishes, apparently from the picnic. She showed only a trace of surprise at seeing Arrington.

"You remember Arrington," Stone said. "We were having lunch when you called, and she offered to drive me up here."

Amanda shook her hand. "How very kind of you, Arrington."

"How are you feeling?" Stone asked.

"Still shocked, and very sad, of course. Would either of you like a drink? I'm having one."

Everybody took a drink into the living room.

"I talked with the troopers as they were leaving," Stone said. "It doesn't sound as though there's going to be any kind of problem. What might get into the papers is that the accident was alcohol-related. They've agreed not to report it that way, but the medical examiner in Hartford will have the final say, and we can't influence him."

"I understand," Amanda said.

"Do you want me to notify Martha's family?" Stone asked.

"I have already done so. Her parents live in Westchester; they're arranging for a local funeral director to pick up the body as soon as it's released. I'm paying the funeral expenses, of course."

"Have you mentioned that to her parents yet?"

"No. I thought I'd wait until they were over the initial shock."

"If I may sound like a lawyer for a moment, be sure that when you make the offer you be clear that it's an act of friendship toward a valued colleague. Don't say anything that might imply any sense of guilt or liability for what happened. From what you've told me and from what the trooper said, you've no reason to feel badly about the accident."

"Thank you, Stone, that's good advice."

"Would you like me to drive you back to the city?"

"No, thank you. I'll stay the night and drive

myself back tomorrow. I'd really like to be alone, unless, of course, you and Arrington would like to stay."

"Thanks, but I think we'll go back today. Is there anything else I can do for you?"

"I don't believe so, Stone; thank you for coming, though, and please drive carefully going back to town." She saw them to the door.

On the way back, Arrington spoke up. "Do you believe her?"

Stone didn't want to answer that question directly. "I don't have any real evidence to make me disbelieve her," he said.

"I thought it was an act," Arrington said.

"What?"

"Her grief. Her composure wasn't an act, though; that lady is in perfect control."

"Are you saying you think Amanda murdered Martha?"

"Let's just say that I don't think she's terribly upset about it."

"I can't disagree with that," Stone said, then changed the subject. After all, Amanda was still his client.

Amanda picked up the phone and called one of her two assistants. "Helen?"

"Yes, Amanda?"

"I'm afraid I have some very bad news. Martha has been killed in an accidental fall."

"Oh, my God!"

"Yes, it's terrible, isn't it?"

"That's just awful!"

"Of course it is. We're going to have to learn very quickly to get along without her help. I'd like you to take Martha's job; there'll be a substantial raise, of course."

"I'll be happy to, if it will help," Helen said.

"I'm in the country now. Can you meet me at the office at one o'clock tomorrow? We have to get you started in your new position."

"Of course."

"See you then, darling. Oh, and would you call Barry and tell him what's happened? I'm really too stricken to talk anymore now."

"I'll do that. You try and get a good night's sleep, and I'll see you at the office tomorrow."

"Thank you, dear. Goodbye." Amanda threw another log on the fire and sat, staring into the flames, making mental notes on what had to be done the following day.

Chapter 44

Dino and Mary Ann Bacchetti got out of a cab on Sixty-sixth Street. Mary Ann had spent the morning having her hair cut by Frederic Fekkai at Bergdorf's and having virtually every other part of her body attended to. She was wearing a newly purchased Chanel suit and matching black alligator shoes and handbag from Ferragamo. Dino was wearing a three-piece gray flannel suit from Ralph Lauren, a Turnbull & Asser shirt, and a polka-dot bow tie. A cream-colored silk square peeked from his breast pocket. His shoes were from Ferragamo, too, but they were only black calf. His hair had been cut at Bergdorf's men's store by a Fekkai disciple.

"I like the suit," Mary Ann said to Dino. "You should get some more like it."

"Stone made me buy it; the other stuff, too. I'm giving it all to him after this meeting. Listen, let me do the talking, will you?"

"What's the matter, you think I can't talk?"

"Stone tells me these people like to hear mostly from the men, and he knows about this stuff."

"Stone can go fuck himself," Mary Ann said pleasantly.

As they approached the building the doorman placed himself between them and the front door. "May I help you, sir?" he asked Dino, only slightly officiously.

"Thank you, I have an appointment with Mr. Whitfield; my name is Bacchetti."

The doorman opened the door and allowed them into the lobby, then stepped inside and announced them to a man at a desk. "Mr. Bacchetti for Mr. Whitfield," he said to the man, then backed out into the street. The man at the desk murmured something into a telephone, then hung up. "Mr. Whitfield is expecting you," he said. "Charles will take you up in the elevator." He indicated a uniformed man standing beside the lift. "Mr. Bacchetti for Mr. Whitfield."

Dino couldn't remember the last time he'd ridden in an elevator with an operator. The car was equipped for self-service but had an operator anyway; he wondered how much the guy got paid. The elevator stopped, and they emerged into a small foyer. The elevator operator locked the car, stepped out, and rapped on the double front doors. A maid opened the door. "Mr. and Mrs. Bacchetti for Mr. Whitfield," he said to her.

The woman admitted them. "They're in the library," the woman said in an English accent. "Please come this way."

"I'll come any way I want to," Dino muttered under his breath, earning a sharp glance from his wife.

The maid led them into a paneled room where a sixtyish man in a pinstriped suit stood, his back to a merry little fire. A woman in an expensive-looking wool dress sat in a chair beside him.

"Mr. and Mrs. Bacchetti," the maid said, then left.

"Ah, the Bacchettis," the man said, approaching them. "I am Charles Greenleaf Whitfield, and this is my wife, Eleanor." He offered his hand.

"I'm Dino Bacchetti," Dino said in a voice and accent he could muster when it suited him, "and this is my wife, Mary Ann; good to meet you." They both shook hands with Whitfield and his wife.

"Won't you come and sit by the fire?" Whitfield asked, showing them to a sofa facing a pair of chairs, in one of which Eleanor Whitfield was seated. "May I get you a sherry?"

"Thank you," Dino said. "Mary Ann?"

"Thank you, yes," Mary Ann said.

Dino was surprised that Brooklyn seemed to have left her voice, as well.

When everyone had a sherry and was seated, Whitfield picked up a file on the table next to his chair. "Is it nice outside? I haven't been out today."

"A beautiful day," Dino replied, crossing his legs and sipping his sherry.

That was it for small talk. "Now, Mr. Bacchetti, Mrs. Bacchetti, I hope you will forgive us for the formality of this meeting, but as you know, the board of a cooperative building has a responsibility to meet and interview prospective purchasers of apartments in the building to try and render some judgment of the suitability of applicants both as purchasers and as neighbors."

"Of course," Dino said.

"I am the president of the building, and, as such, my board members have asked me to represent them. There are one or two questions with regard to your answers on the application; perhaps I could ask you to expand on them just a bit."

"Of course," Dino said.

"You understand that it is the policy of the board not to allow the apartment to be used as collateral for a mortgage or other loan, which means, of course, that the price of purchase must be paid in cash."

"I understand," Dino replied.

"It's not exactly clear to us from your financial statement just where the cash is coming from."

Mary Ann spoke up. "The cash is a gift from my father," she said.

"I see; how very generous. You have one child, as I understand it."

"A son," Dino said. "He's four years old."

"And where will he be attending school?"

"He'll be going to Collegiate," Mary Ann said, surprising her husband, who had never heard of Collegiate.

"Ah, yes; fine school. Do you have any pets?"

"No," Dino said.

"And you are of Italian extraction?"

"I am."

"Can you tell me a bit about your family background?"

"My family seat is Venice, where my ancestors have been Doges for twelve hundred years," Dino lied.

"Ah, Doges, yes," Whitfield said. The thought seemed to excite him. "And when did your family come to this country?"

"I am a tenth-generation American." Minus nine.

"And Mrs. Bacchetti, are you of Italian extraction as well?"

"Yes. My people have always had lands in Sicily, from time immemorial." There was only the tiniest trace of sarcasm in her voice.

"I see. And your family name?"

"Bianchi."

"Ah." Whitfield seemed to have heard this name before, somewhere, but he apparently didn't remember where.

"Mr. Bacchetti, I see your father is deceased; may I ask what work he did before his death?"

"He was curator of a private art collection. His specialty was Renaissance drawings." The closest Dino's father had ever been to a Renaissance drawing had been the pictures in the girlie magazines in his candy store.

"How very interesting. And Mrs. Bacchetti, what does your father do?"

Dino felt Mary Ann shift; irritation was boiling

247

off her in waves. He squeezed her hand, and she seemed to relax a bit.

"My people have always been in the revenge business," she said sweetly.

Dino, unable to control himself, burst out laughing. To his amazement, Whitfield and his wife were laughing, too, as if Mary Ann had made some very clever joke.

"Just one more question," Whitfield said when he had composed himself. "Mr. Bacchetti, I see that you are employed by the city of New York."

"I am."

"In what capacity?"

"I am a lieutenant with the New York Police Department; I command the detective division of the Nineteenth Precinct."

"I see," Whitfield said, not at all certain that he did. "And how did you come to choose that particular line of work?"

"My family has always been drawn to public service," Dino replied.

"Very commendable," Whitfield mused. "We had a burglary in our building recently, I'm afraid. Never happened before."

"And if I come to live here, it will never happen again," Dino said smoothly.

"Ah, yes!" Whitfield cried, his tumblers working. "I quite see your point! One watches *NYPD Blue*."

"Excellent program," Dino said. "Utterly realistic. By the way, I should mention that I am aware of the burglary, and I have doubled the police patrol on this block."

"Wonderful! Have you caught the perpetrator yet?"

248

"I can reveal, in confidence, of course, that we now know his identity. We expect an arrest at any moment."

"Excellent! Well, Mr. and Mrs. Bacchetti, I believe that tells us all we need to know. You will be hearing from the board very soon, and I think I can intimate that the answer will be a favorable one."

The Bacchettis made their goodbyes and departed. Once in the street again Dino said, "You sure you want to live in that place?"

"Very sure."

"I mean, couldn't you find a building with at least some Jews or something?"

"Get used to it," Mary Ann said.

Chapter 45

Arrington, Dino, and Mary Ann sat at Stone's kitchen table drinking wine while Stone cooked linguine with white clam sauce. The television was on NFL football, muted, and the men occasionally stole glances at the set.

"Anyway," Dino was saying, "you shoulda been there to hear my wife tell these people that her family is in the revenge business."

Everybody laughed.

"I always tell the truth," Mary Ann said.

"Yeah? Then what was that about the Collegiate School?" Dino asked.

"That was almost the truth."

"I never even heard of the Collegiate School, and my wife is telling these people that our kid is going there."

"How old is he?" Arrington asked.

"Four," Mary Ann replied.

"Apply now," Arrington advised. "It may already be too late."

"There's not a public school in that neighborhood?" Dino asked innocently.

"Forget about it," Mary Ann said. "He's going to Collegiate."

"Sounds like it's tough to get in," Dino said hopefully.

"We'll have help," Mary Ann said.

"Mary Ann, there are some things your old man can't help with."

"Name three."

"Well, the Collegiate School is probably one of them."

"Wanta bet?"

"I don't think so," Dino said resignedly.

"Good move," Stone chipped in.

Arrington moved over to the stove and pretended to watch Stone work on the clam sauce. "Who is Mary Ann's father?" she whispered.

"Why?" Stone whispered back. "You want somebody in cement shoes?"

"Oh." She went back and sat down at the table. "Smells wonderful," she said.

"I'm having a hard time with this," Mary Ann said.

"With what?"

"With this extremely white-bread person over there making me Italian food."

"I'm pretending to be a guinea," Stone said.

"I hope it works."

"We're about to find out," Stone said. He

drained the pasta and dumped it in with the sauce, moving it around with a fork and spoon. He set the steaming platter on the table, where a salad and garlic bread already rested.

Everybody watched as Mary Ann expertly twirled some linguine around her fork and popped it into her mouth, chewing thoughtfully. "Not enough garlic," she said.

"There's twelve cloves in there," Stone said, sounding hurt.

"Just kidding," Mary Ann said, "my mother couldn't have done it better. Well, not much better."

Everybody pitched into the pasta. A commercial interrupted the game, and Dino switched to New York One, the all-news local channel.

"Don't do that," Mary Ann said.

"Why not? There was a commercial on the game."

She turned to Stone and Arrington. "He turns on New York One in the hope that he'll learn about a recently committed crime and he can leave his dinner and rush out to solve it." She turned back to her husband. "You can do that at home, but not when you're at somebody else's house." She picked up the remote control and switched back to the game.

"Wait!" Arrington cried. "Turn it back!" She grabbed at the remote control and started changing channels desperately.

"Channel ten," Dino said helpfully.

She found it.

"What's going on, Arrington?" Stone asked.

"I saw him."

"Saw who?"

"He's there, look for him!"

"Look for who?"

"Shut up."

Stone shut up and watched. Arrington turned on the sound.

"...the biggest benefit of the year," a woman reporter was saying as a crowd swirled around her. "The Shubert Theatre is completely sold out at prices of up to a thousand dollars a seat, and some of the biggest stars on Broadway will be performing tonight."

"There," Arrington said, pointing. "The man just behind the reporter. You can see the back of his head."

"So?" Dino asked.

"That's Jonathan Dryer," she said. "I'm sure of it."

The crowd was moving slowly toward the doors of the theater. Just as the head was about to move off the top of the screen, it turned.

"There, it's him!"

There was a brief glimpse of a face before the camera zoomed in on the reporter. "The crowd is just returning from intermission, and there's been a rumor circulating that Barbra Streisand is going to make a surprise appearance. We'll let you know." There was a cut to the studio, and the anchorman began to talk about a fire in Queens.

"Are you sure?" Stone asked.

"That's him."

"Could you tell who he was with?"

"No, but that was Jonathan."

"Who's Jonathan?" Mary Ann asked.

"A guy Stone is interested in," Dino said.

"You're not interested?" Stone asked him.

"Yeah, sure, but I'm not going to worry too much about him until we have some more evidence."

"And you'd like *me* to come up with it?"

Dino shrugged. "I wouldn't mind."

"Dino, he may be involved in a cop killing; doesn't that mean anything anymore?"

"It does, if there's any evidence tying him to it. All you've got right now is a lot of supposition. Okay, he went to parties at some people's apartments that later got burgled. So did a lot of other people, including Arrington here. Should we take her to the precinct and beat a confession out of her?"

"Come on, Dino; for the first time we actually know where the guy is."

"What do you want me to do? Send a SWAT team into a theater crowded with a black-tie audience of celebrities and people who can afford to pay a thousand bucks a seat? The mayor's probably there; my *chief* is probably there."

"Then have him picked up on the way out."

"Stone, maybe you don't read the papers anymore, but there are four cops in the city under indictment right now for arresting and, in some cases, leaning on people with no evidence, and two of them are uniforms at the Nineteenth. You think I'm going to wade into *that* crowd and create yet another incident at a time when we've got a full-blown commission investigating the department?"

"You can't ever find a cop when you need one," Mary Ann said. "Especially when he's stuffing his face with linguine."

"Thanks, sweetheart," Dino said. "That's all I need, is you weighing in."

"Any time," she said sweetly.

"I got an idea," Dino said. "Why don't you call your daddy and have him send a couple guys over to the Shubert and blow the guy away? Then we won't even have to think about this anymore."

"I've heard worse ideas," Arrington said.

"Eat your dinner, Arrington," Dino said. "*Please,* everybody just eat the white-bread pasta and forget about it just for tonight. We're celebrating getting this apartment, which, believe me, may not be worth celebrating."

"It's worth it," Mary Ann said.

"You're trying to turn us into Wasps, aren't you?" Dino demanded. "I can't even wear my own clothes to meet these people; neither can you, come to think of it."

"Dino," Mary Ann said, "don't look a gift horse, you know? We're taking the apartment; we're getting out of Brooklyn. Try and be happy about it."

"I'm trying, I'm trying," Dino said.

"Try harder."

"Tell you what," Stone said. "Dryer is going to be in that theater for at least another hour. Let's finish our pasta, eat our dessert, drink our coffee, and then wander over to the Shubert and tail this guy home. I'd really like to know where he lives, wouldn't you, Dino?"

"Fuggeddaboudit!" Dino screamed.

Chapter 46

By the time they got out of the cab it had started raining, and the two women ran into the theater lobby. Dino turned up his collar. "This is just great," he said. "I might as well be back on the beat."

"A little beat work will do you good," Stone said. The four of them huddled in the lobby until Stone could find an usher.

"Should be over any minute now," the man said.

"You planning to do this on foot?" Dino asked Stone.

"Ah, maybe not. You want to get us a cab?"

"We just gave up a cab, and it's raining. It's a known fact that all New York City cabs go off duty the minute it starts to rain, and on top of that, a couple of thousand people are going to come pouring out of this theater in a minute, and they're all going to be trying to hail the same cab."

Arrington spoke up. "There are two entrances to this theater," she said. "This one and one in Shubert Alley. We'd better cover both, don't you think?"

"I don't want Dryer to see you," Stone said. "Do you think you could try hailing a cab for us and just wait in it until we come out?"

"You're sweet."

"Here, take my hat." He placed his fedora on her head; it came down over her ears. "Best get one going east on Forty-fourth."

Arrington took a deep breath and ran into the street, waving her arms. Mary Ann stood her ground. "This guy doesn't know me; I'm staying right here."

"Could you keep an eye on Arrington, so we'll know where she is if we have to move in a hurry?"

"That I can do."

"I'll take the alley," Stone said. "Holler if you see him."

"Right," Dino said. "I hope he looks like his picture."

"Me, too." Stone left the lobby and walked up Shubert Alley, which ran between 44th and 45th Streets. The alley offered no shelter, and he stood there, getting wet. Shortly, a door opened and a trickle of people began leaving the theater, followed by a flood. Stone tried to search the faces without turning head on to them. After all, Dryer knew what he looked like. The theater was half empty when he heard Dino's voice.

"Stone!"

He looked toward the corner of 45th and saw Dino waving for him. He hurried toward him.

"He just got into a limo with some other people," Dino said, pointing at a line of limousines lining the curb.

"Where's Arrington? Did she find a cab?"

"I don't know; she went off toward Eighth Avenue."

The line of limos started to move.

"Shit," Dino said. "Where is she?"

"I'm getting wet," Mary Ann said.

"Don't melt," Dino replied.

"There!" Stone pointed. Arrington was waving at them from the window of a cab. They all ran for it, and as they did, the limos began picking up speed. "Which car is he in?"

"That one," Dino said nodding.

Stone tried to see inside, but the windows were tinted too darkly. Then he wondered if Dryer could be looking back at him through the opaque windows.

They piled into the cab with Arrington; Stone took the front seat. "Follow the third limo ahead," he said to the driver.

"Oh, great," the driver muttered. "How far we going? Queens? Montauk?"

"Shut up and drive," Dino said, shoving his badge under the driver's nose.

"Awright, awright," the driver moaned.

"He's crossing Seventh Avenue," Dino said. "Keep up, and don't let any more traffic get between him and us."

"Yeah, yeah," the driver said.

They moved slowly toward 6th Avenue; then, as they approached the corner, the light turned red, trapping them while Dryer's limo turned left.

"Shit," Stone said.

"Look, what can I do?" the driver whined. "There's two cars in front of me. You want me to drive over them?"

"He's stopped at the next corner; we can still catch up."

A raft of traffic moved past them on 6th Avenue. Now they were ten or twelve cars back. Finally the light changed and they were able to turn left, but the light at the next corner changed and they were stopped again.

"Have you got him in sight?" Dino asked.

"I think so."

They struggled up 6th Avenue in heavy traffic, getting no closer to the limo, then they were stopped again.

"Uh-oh," Dino said, pointing. A hundred yards ahead of them, Dryer was getting out of the limo.

"He's heading for the subway," Dino said.

Stone turned to Dino. "I'm going after him; you pull up at the subway entrance. If I'm not back in five minutes, will you take Arrington to my house?"

"Sure; you better get going."

Stone got out of the cab and ran toward the subway entrance. The rain was pounding down now, and the steps were slippery as he clambered down them. As he descended into the station he saw Dryer going through the turnstiles, and at the same moment, he remembered that he had no tokens; he rarely took the subway. He hurried down the stairs, and he could hear a train coming into the station.

"The hell with the token," he said to himself. He ran at the turnstile, planted a hand on it, and vaulted over. As he did, his raincoat caught on something, and he was jerked to a halt.

"Hold it right there!" somebody yelled, and before he could get his coat untangled a cop had him by the elbow.

"I'm on the job," Stone lied.

"Yeah? Let's see some ID, pal."

Stone groped for his wallet, flashed the badge, and tried to go after Dryer, who was getting onto the subway train three cars from where he stood.

"Let's see that," the cop said, grabbing the wallet. "Retired, huh? What's going on, fella?"

"I've got to catch up with a guy," Stone said.

"Okay, but start buying tokens, okay?" He let go of Stone's arm.

Stone sprinted up the platform toward an open car door and hurled himself at it. The doors closed on him. He struggled, pushed on the doors, and fell into the car, banging a knee. He got to his feet in time to look out the window and see Dryer standing on the platform, looking at him as the train pulled out. Dryer gave him a little smile.

Stone watched him for as long as he could; then the train was in the tunnel. He sat down, hoping to God that Dryer would go back up to 6th Avenue and be spotted by Dino. His raincoat, a new one, was torn from his leap over the turnstile, and there was a hole in his trousers' knee where he had fallen. It was one hell of an expensive subway ride, he thought.

He got off the train at the next stop; then, unable to find a cab, he limped home.

Chapter 47

Amanda dialed Stone's number and waited, tapping her perfect nails on the desktop while the secretary put her through. She had been standing at Martha's graveside the day before when her thoughts about the *DIRT* business had begun to fall into place, and she had begun to fully realize how dangerous her position was. Amanda had always made a habit of turning danger into opportunity, but first she had to know exactly where she stood, which meant knowing exactly where Stone stood.

"Hello, Amanda; I'm sorry to have kept you waiting."

"Not to worry, darling. Look, I'd like to know exactly where you are in this investigation. Can you bring me up to date, and as concisely as possible?"

"Of course. Most of this you already know, of course, but I think we've identified the person or, perhaps, persons who are publishing the newsletter. One of them calls himself Jonathan Dryer and the other, Geoffrey Power or G. Gable. They appear to be working together. Dryer has abandoned his apartment, and we haven't been able to locate him yet. Last night we got a look at him at a benefit at the Shubert Theatre, but he managed to elude us."

"Who's us?"

"Dino Bacchetti, my old detective partner."

"Are the police involved in this?" she asked, alarmed.

"No, this was completely unofficial. We think Dryer has been pulling off burglaries to support himself, and a gun that was stolen from one of the apartments may have been used to kill a retired cop, but we can't prove anything yet."

"I see," she said, relieved. "And where do you intend to go from here?"

"I intend to find Dryer," Stone replied. "He's the key to this whole thing."

"And that's it? That's everything?"

"That's everything."

"Thank you, darling; see you soon." She hung up and dialed Richard Hickock's private office number.

"Hello?"

"Dick, it's Amanda. Break your lunch date today; we have to meet."

"Is this really important?"

"I think you could call it vital. Twelve-thirty at Twenty-One?"

"See you then."

When they had settled into a banquette in the inner horseshoe of the bar at '21,' and after Hickock had ordered his steak and baked potato and Amanda her grilled salmon, no butter, and after Hickock had been served a double vodka martini and Amanda her San Pellegrino, she got down to business.

"Dick, darling," Amanda said, "I'm afraid that, through no fault of your own, you have been placed in a very dangerous position." She did not mention the danger to herself.

"Oh?" he said, not particularly alarmed, "How so?"

She gave him a brief rundown on what Stone Barrington had learned about the *DIRT* business.

"Well, at least he's making progress," Hickock said, taking a sip of his huge martini.

"Dick, my dearest, he may be making too much progress."

Hickock frowned. "Too much progress?"

"Yes. You see, while Stone has been conducting

261

his investigation, I have been conducting one of my own, and, as is my wont, I have been looking into more than who is doing this; I have been learning *why*."

"And just *why* have this Dryer and Power, or whatever their names are, been doing this?"

"It seems, my darling, that they harbor some grudge against you."

"Me? You mean only me?"

Amanda nodded gravely. "Apparently they've gone after me only because of my connection with you."

"What did *I* ever do to these guys? I don't even know who they are."

"Who knows? What's important is, they seem to know a very great deal about you and your business affairs."

Hickock put down his martini. "Just what the hell is that supposed to mean, Amanda?"

"It means, Dick, that they seem to have unearthed information about your connection with an entity called Window Seat."

All expression left Hickock's face. "That's impossible," he said. "I mean, I never heard of anything like that."

"Dick, my dear, you don't have to worry about me; I'm on your side."

"Amanda, how did you find out about this?"

"About what, darling?"

"About Window Seat, goddamnit!"

"Dick, keep your voice down," she said, looking around them. "You know that I have a great many sources for all sorts of information."

"Yeah, well, how the hell did you hear about Window Seat? And don't you think for a moment

262

you can plead the confidentiality of a journalist's sources. I want to know *now.*"

"Well, your Glynnis is in possession of this knowledge, and she's a pretty unhappy woman at the moment, isn't she?"

"Don't try that with me, Amanda; Glynnis and I have reconciled our differences, and she would *never* mention this to *anybody.*"

Amanda had misjudged Hickock; she was not going to be able to play him quite as she had imagined. Inwardly, she shrugged; well, that little vermin Peebles would just have to be sacrificed. "From Allan Peebles," she said.

"He *told* you about Window Seat?" Hickock asked, unbelieving.

"Everything. About the *Infiltrator* and the porno magazines. The gay porno magazines."

Hickock blanched. "I'll have his balls by close of business," he said.

"Well, now, Dick, that might not be the wisest move; not just yet, anyway."

"Why not?"

"Well, these two little creeps Dryer and Power are still out there. If you do something so public as sacking Peebles, it's bound to cause a new round of faxing, reporting the whole business, and I don't think you want that to happen, do you?"

"I see your point," Hickock said, returning to his martini. "I'll have to be more subtle."

"Oh, Dick, I'm sure you can deal with Allan Peebles at any moment you wish, after this *DIRT* thing has blown over."

"Yes, I can *certainly* do that, but when is this going to blow over?"

"Well, clearly it won't blow over if we leave Stone Barrington to his devices. Eventually he'll unearth the whole thing."

"Yes, I suppose he will," Hickock agreed.

"I think it might be best if we terminated his investigation and turned to, shall we say, other means."

Hickock turned and looked her in the eye. "Just what means did you have in mind, Amanda?"

"Consider this, Dick: More than the *DIRT* business is involved. Dryer, or perhaps Power, or both, may have caused the death of a police officer—a retired one, but nevertheless...."

"Jesus Christ."

"So far the police are not officially involved in the investigation of these two men, but if Stone— or anyone else, for that matter—should come up with evidence linking the two to the murder, then the whole can of worms—*DIRT,* Window Seat, everything—will be opened up."

"Yes, I see that. So Dryer and Power are the immediate problem."

"Yes. Surely you have connections with people who make a business of solving troublesome problems by more direct means."

"Such as who?"

"Well, you did have some help in solving your labor problems last year, didn't you? A *consultant,* so to speak?"

Hickock looked around him. "I think we've talked enough about this, Amanda."

"Probably."

"I understand the parameters of the problem now. Will you call off Stone Barrington?"

"Of course, darling, if you think that's best."

"I do."

Amanda looked up. "Oh, here comes your steak, darling." She watched as the perfectly grilled slab of meat was set down before him. "Why ever haven't you already had a coronary?" She tested her salmon with a fork.

"I give other people coronaries," Hickock replied, sawing off a hunk of beef and stuffing it into his mouth.

Amanda tucked into her salmon, secure in the knowledge that, while she had probably solved the *DIRT* problem, she had also ingratiated herself with Richard Hickock, at the same time letting him know that she *knew*. That knowledge would certainly be useful at some later date. The salmon was delicious.

Chapter 48

Richard Hickock got out of his car and tapped on the driver's window. "I'm going to take a little walk," he said. "You wait here."

"Around here, Mr. Hickock?" the driver asked, surprised. They were in a desolate area of the Long Island City section of Queens, amid empty, run-down industrial buildings.

"I'll be back soon," Hickock said. He trudged off into a misty rain, down an empty street. Following the directions that had been faxed to him that afternoon, he turned left and crossed the street. The number "19" had been spray-painted on the door of a building, but it looked locked.

He tried it, and it wasn't. Inside, he went to a huge freight elevator, pulled a cord that closed the doors from the top and bottom, and pressed the number for the fourth floor. The thing actually worked.

When it stopped he pushed open the door and walked out of the elevator into a large, empty factory area. Daylight was waning, and the low light threw into relief holes in the floor where machinery had once been bolted down. There was no place to sit, so he walked slowly around the floor, wondering at what he was about to do. Suddenly he heard an electric motor running, and a moment later another freight elevator at the opposite end of the floor stopped, and Enrico Bianchi stepped out.

The two men walked from their opposite ends to the middle of the huge floor and embraced.

"Hello, Ricky," Hickock said. "Thank you so much for coming." Bianchi was, as always, tanned and slim, and his finely barbered hair had gone snow white.

"Dickie," Bianchi said, holding him at arm's length and looking at him. "You lost some weight."

"Yeah, well, Glynnis made me buy a treadmill."

Bianchi laughed heartily. "My wife will never get me on one of those."

"How is she? And your daughter?"

"The wife is the same, maybe a little fatter. Mary Ann is married to the law, you will remember."

"That must be a little touchy," Hickock said.

"We manage to get along, mostly by not talking. He's not a bad fellow, for a cop. I bought them an apartment on the East Side; Mary Ann has never liked Brooklyn."

"That's very generous of you."

"Well, she's my only daughter, you know, and she's a tough one, like me. She gets what she wants, always." He tucked Hickock's arm into his. "Let's walk."

Hickock moved with him and, arm in arm, they promenaded slowly around the empty floor.

"I'm sorry we have to meet like this, but the feds are everywhere these days, have everything bugged. I can't even talk in my car anymore, and we had to lose a carload of them before coming here today."

"It's all right; I understand. I'm just glad you could take the time."

"Something's wrong, eh?" Bianchi asked.

"I'm afraid so."

"Tell me about it."

"There are two young men who have been circulating rumors about me; they have almost cost me my marriage."

Bianchi made a noise. "That is awful, to attack a man's personal life. Is this a business thing?"

"They seem to know more than they should about my business. An employee has talked out of turn."

"And you want me to, ah, speak to this employee?"

Hickock shook his head. "No; I can take care of him when-ever I like. But the two young men are out of my reach."

"But, perhaps, not out of mine?" Bianchi said, chuckling.

"I hope you are right. They have been very elusive; I have names, but they may be false; I have no address, but they are circulating around the fashionable quarters of Manhattan." Hickock pulled a copy of *Vanity Fair* from his overcoat pocket and opened it. "But I have a very good photograph of one of them. He calls himself Jonathan Dryer."

Bianchi stopped walking, fished a lighter out of his jacket pocket, and struck it, studying the photograph. "A good-looking boy," he said. He closed the magazine and tucked it into his own overcoat pocket.

"Yes, he seems to do well with the ladies. The other one has used the name Geoffrey Power, and maybe G. Gable."

"What else can you tell me about these young men?"

"They resemble each other—so much so that they may be brothers. One of them has recently arrived from L.A. One or both of them has some considerable skill as a burglar; he has broken into several large apartments and stolen cash, jewelry—always men's wristwatches—and a pistol with a silencer attached. One of them may have killed a retired police officer with the stolen pistol."

"So the police are already looking for them?"

"No, not yet; there hasn't been enough evidence to connect them to the murder. I have no hard information whatever about these two; everything I have told you is just guessing."

"How did you come by what you have already told me?"

"I hired an investigator."

"His name?"

"Stone Barrington. You know him?"

"I know of him; he is a friend of my son-in-law, the cop."

"He's very good."

"Is he still working on this?"

"He's being called off today. I'm afraid that if he finds them and the police start talking to them, too much of this will get into the papers."

Bianchi nodded. "I see. Is there anything else you can tell me about these two?"

"No, that's all Barrington has been able to find out."

"And it's only these two you wish me to deal with?"

"There's a third." He handed Bianchi a slip of paper. "I haven't decided what to do about that one yet. If we move, it will have to be an accident; I'll let you know later about that."

"I see. So you wish me to find these two young men and then…."

"I want a permanent solution; I don't want to hear about them again," Hickock said. "Ever."

Bianchi nodded. "I don't blame you; it is what I would do, in the circumstances."

"I apologize for bringing up money, but I know this will be expensive."

"You are very kind, Dickie."

Hickock removed a thick envelope from his other overcoat pocket and handed it to Bianchi. "There's fifty thousand in there," he said. "I hope that will cover it."

"I believe so," Bianchi said, "unless there are unusual complications."

"I'm very grateful to you, Ricky," Hickock said.

Bianchi shrugged. "It is at times like this that one must come to one's old friends. I am sorry that circumstances prevent us from meeting more often, when there is no business to discuss."

"I'm sorry for that, too, old friend. Do you know that we have seen each other only a half-dozen times since Yale? I feel badly that I only come to you when I have problems."

"Do not concern yourself," Bianchi said. "I know your heart."

"You are a good friend, Ricky."

Bianchi embraced Hickock again. "I must go; there is always business to do. I will be in touch through the usual channels when this business of yours has been completed."

"Goodbye, Ricky."

"Goodbye, Dickie."

The two men parted, and each walked to his own elevator.

There was a man waiting for Bianchi on the ground floor, and he handed him the magazine. On the way back to the car he imparted the information he had just learned. "Make copies of this photograph, small ones; put the word out on the street, especially in the good bars and restaurants, that we want to locate both of them. There will be a two-thousand-dollar reward for this information. When they have both—not one, but both—been found, they should die in a way that will seem to be an ordinary crime—a mugging, a robbery. There will be five thousand each for this work, but for the money to be paid, they must both be killed, you understand?"

The man nodded. "*Si, padrone,*" he said.

They had reached the car. Bianchi held a finger to his lips for silence, then they got in.

"Stone?"

"Yes, Amanda, what's up?"

"I had lunch with Dick Hickock today, and we've decided to call off the *DIRT* investigation."

"Really?" Stone asked, surprised. "Why?"

"We talked about it, and we decided it's just not important enough to continue devoting all this effort and money to it, so will you send me a final bill?"

"Of course. There isn't much; you've already paid most of it."

"Good, just send it, then. Hope I'll see you and Arrington soon."

"Thanks, Amanda."

"Bye." She hung up.

Stone turned to Arrington. "Amanda and Hickock are calling off the investigation."

"Good God! Why?"

"I don't know. She said something about it not being worth the trouble, but I don't buy that. They've both been very avid about it up to now."

"This is very strange."

"I think there's something going on that we don't know about," he said.

"Are you going to stop looking for Jonathan, then?"

"Certainly not. I still have a couple of personal things to talk with Mr. Dryer about."

"Maybe you should just let it go, Stone. The whole thing is a little too scary."

"No, I won't let it go," he said.

Chapter 49

Stone got out of the cab at the Washington Square Arch and walked along the north rim of the park, enjoying the clear, cold morning and looking at the small children playing in the new-fallen snow, their mothers or nannies watching over them like mother hens. He crossed the street to a row of elegant townhouses that were occupied by senior faculty and administrators of New York University, then climbed the steps to a highly varnished front door and rang the bell.

A uniformed maid answered the door. "Yes?"

"My name is Barrington; I have an appointment with Dr. Bernard."

"Oh, yes, he's expecting you; please follow me." She led him up the stairs to the second floor, to a set of double doors on the south side of the house, and knocked briefly.

"Come!" a muffled voice cried.

She opened the door. "Dr. Bernard, your visitor is here."

"Ah, yes; show him in, please."

The maid admitted Stone, then closed the door behind him. He was in a good-sized library, which could not contain the books that had been stuffed into it. They were everywhere, on every surface, on chairs and on the floor. A row of high windows afforded a fine view of Washington Square Park.

"Mr. Barrington," the old man said, rising and extending his hand.

"Dr. Bernard," Stone said, shaking his hand. "It's been a very long time." About twenty years.

Bernard waved him to a chair before the fireplace, opposite his own. "Just dump those books on the floor. Yes, it has been a long time, though I've read of you in the papers once or twice. You were injured, weren't you?"

"Yes, sir, a bullet in the knee; occupational hazard. It's in pretty good shape now."

"Ah, yes, the occupation you chose. I admit, I never understood it."

"With hindsight, perhaps it wasn't the best choice," Stone said. "But it's been an interesting life."

"I see you've gained wisdom with age," Bernard said, a trace of a smile crossing his plump face.

The maid entered with a tray bearing a Thermos, some cups, and a plate of cookies.

"Some coffee?" Bernard asked.

"Thank you; black, please." He watched as his old professor poured. He hadn't changed much; a little heavier, maybe; he still wore very fine suits, hadn't let himself go the way many old men do. He was freshly barbered and shaved, and when he crossed his legs, his most visible foot wore a very expensive shoe.

"You left the police department, I believe."

"Yes; I was given the boot, really, on medical grounds, with a full salary."

"And what have you been doing since your retirement?"

273

"I'm of counsel to Woodman and Weld."

"An estimable firm. I've known Woodman all his life. You said 'of counsel.' Not a partner?"

"No. I'm rather a special case there; I work out of my home, which is not far from their offices, handling cases for their clients that don't quite fit the Woodman & Weld profile."

"Ah, I see; dirty laundry."

"In a manner of speaking."

"Are you happy doing this work?"

"I suppose I'd rather be arguing cases before the Supreme Court, but I'm content with my lot."

Bernard nodded. "Contentment is devoutly to be wished, perhaps more than glory."

"Perhaps."

"I always saw you as a very fine trial lawyer."

"I do some trial work, but maybe not the kind you saw me doing. As a matter of fact, I recall that you saw quite a different calling for me."

"Ah, yes. Is that what you've come to see me about? A little late in life for that sort of thing, isn't it?"

"Probably so."

"They're in such a mess now, after that Aldrich Ames business. Makes me regret that I steered young men their way. Still, some of them have served honorably. As for the rest, well…the Company always finds *somebody* to do that kind of work, much as Woodman and Weld have found you."

That stung. "Well, what you describe as Woodman and Weld's 'dirty laundry' is still honorable work," Stone replied.

"Of course, and I know you've conducted yourself honorably. I apologize for what must have seemed a slur."

"Not at all, sir."

"So, why *have* you come to see me?"

Stone took the ad from *Vanity Fair* from his pocket and handed it to Bernard. "I want to find this man," he said, "and there's some indication that he may have picked up certain unsavory skills while working for some federal agency."

"This is not at all in my line," Bernard said. "Why do you want to find him?"

"He may have been involved in some very serious criminal matters."

"How serious?"

"He may have committed a number of burglaries in New York, including one at my house, during which I was attacked. The burglaries exhibited certain skills that are not possessed by your garden-variety burglar. He may have an accomplice, who may be his brother."

"What else?"

"He may be implicated in the murder of a retired police officer, a man who sometimes worked for me."

"That's very serious indeed," Bernard said. "What exactly is it you wish me to do?"

"If you still have contacts in place, I would be very grateful if you could make some inquiries for me. Any background information on this man would be very helpful. I don't even know his real name."

"What aliases has he been using?"

"Jonathan Dryer."

Bernard burst out laughing.

"What is it?" Stone asked, puzzled.

"That is the name of a man who ran some of the training courses at a place called 'The Farm.' He was not terribly well liked by many of his students."

"What did he teach, if I may ask?"

"The sort of skills that might be useful in a burglary."

"I see."

Bernard picked up the telephone at his side, pressed a single button, and waited. "Hello, this is Samuel Bernard," he said. "Is he in?" He waited a moment for his party to come on the line. "Good morning, Ben," he said. "I'd like to fax you a photograph and see if you can come up with anything on the subject. He may have had some training at The Farm; he's been using the alias Jonathan Dryer." He smiled. "Yes, I thought that would amuse you. I'll send it along now, shall I? Good, see you soon, I hope." He hung and turned to Stone. "Will you excuse me for a few minutes, Mr. Barrington?" He rose and went into an adjoining room and, through the open door, Stone could see him using a fax machine. While it was working, he came back to the door and closed it.

Stone poured himself some more coffee and gazed idly out the window at the children in the park. Perhaps twenty minutes had passed and he had nearly dozed off when the telephone rang and was answered in another room. Then it rang again; Stone could see two lighted buttons on the instrument next to Bernard's chair.

Another few minutes passed, and Bernard returned, holding two sheets of paper. When he had settled himself in his chair and poured himself some more coffee, he looked up at Stone. "Now. You and I must understand each other; what I am about to impart to you goes no further, and I include the police in that admonition. In fact, you may not even say to anyone that we met. Is that understood?"

"Completely."

"Your man's name is Thomas Bruce; he is thirty-four years old. His father was a career naval officer who rose to the rank of captain; his parents are both dead. He has an electronics engineering degree from Rennselaer Polytechnic Institute; he has a brother, Charles, thirty-three, and a sister, Lucille, thirty-seven. He was recruited out of college, probably by someone very like me, and underwent a year's training before being assigned overseas. He served in half a dozen countries and returned to this country four years ago. He was separated from the service involuntarily during a period of cutbacks. His last known address was in northern Virginia, but that was three years ago."

"Is there an address for his brother or sister?"

Bernard scribbled down something on a pad and handed it to Stone. "A New Jersey housewife, apparently—Mrs. Randall Burch—but that address is three years old, too."

"Thanks, I'll check that out."

"The brother is quite something else," Bernard continued. "His last known address was the California correctional institution at Chino. He was serving five to seven years for—you'll like this—burglary. He went in four years ago, and I should think it's quite likely that he has been paroled by now. I suppose you could locate his parole officer and get his last address, but from what you've told me it sounds very much as though he might have left California, doesn't it?"

"It does. Anything else?"

"Thomas Bruce was rated very highly for his technical skills, but his psychological evaluation showed a propensity for violence. He was in trouble a couple of times; had to leave one Central American country after an incident with a woman." He looked up. "That's it," he said. He went to the fireplace and fed the two sheets of paper into the flames.

Stone stood up. "Dr. Bernard, I can't thank you enough. I know that what I asked you to do was irregular, and I'm very grateful to you."

"Not at all," Bernard said. "I hope it will help you find this man. He sounds as though he shouldn't be on the streets." He held up a finger. "Oh, one more thing; the sort of training he had would have included establishing false identities."

"That doesn't surprise me, sir. Thank you again." The two men shook hands, and Stone found his way downstairs and out of the house. Back on the street, he looked at the slip of paper in his hand. Rahway, New Jersey. He'd have to rent a car.

Chapter 50

By the time Stone had rented a car it was snowing steadily, and he was already across the George

278

Washington Bridge before he realized he shouldn't have come. The car was a small one—the only thing available—and he felt unsafe in it, sliding on patches of ice. The snowplows were doing their work, though, removing the accumulation and depositing grit, so he made it to Rahway. He asked a policeman for directions, and he found the house easily enough, in a pleasantly posh neighborhood, the kinds of houses owned by commuters who held executive positions in the city. Louise Bruce Burch lived in a two-story red brick Georgian revival house with slender columns in front; there was a BMW under the carport. He parked in front of the house, made his way up some snowy steps, wishing he'd brought galoshes, and rang the bell. Louise was, somehow, a surprise.

She was of medium height, with sandy blonde hair and a particularly taut body for a suburbanite. Lots of tennis and treadmill, he thought. She did not appear displeased to see him. "Good morning," she said pleasantly.

"Mrs. Burch?"

"Louise Burch."

"My name is Stone Barrington; I'm an attorney. I wonder if I might speak to you for a few minutes."

"Why not?" she said gaily. "Come on back to the kitchen."

He caught a whiff of alcohol as he followed her down a hallway, past a quite formal living room and a small library, to the kitchen, which turned out to be a very large room, with a comfortable seating area before a fireplace. There was a fire going, and a half-empty glass of some brown liquor on the coffee table. There was a stack of house design magazines on the table as well; she had obviously been going through them.

"Please have a seat," she said, indicating the sofa. "I know it's a little early, but I'm having a drink; can I get you one?"

Thinking that having a drink in his hand might make it a bit harder for her to throw him out when she learned why he was there, he accepted. "Bourbon, if you have it."

"Wild Turkey okay?"

"That would be splendid; on the rocks, please." He looked out the window at the snow. "It's becoming a nasty day out there."

She returned shortly with a large drink for him, then sat next to him on the sofa, turned toward him, and drew her knees up, revealing fine legs under a short skirt. "Now, whatever can I do for you, Mr....."

"Barrington. Stone."

"Stone," she said. "I'm Lou. You said you're a lawyer?"

"Yes, in New York."

"And what brings you all the way from the city on a day like today?"

"I wanted to talk to you about your brothers."

She gave a short, sharp laugh. "You're a policeman, aren't you?"

"I used to be."

"And now you practice at the bar?"

"Yes. Why did you laugh when I said I was here about your brothers?"

"Well, Stone, you aren't exactly the first," she said. "There have been a parade of policemen

280

through my house over the years, usually looking for Charlie. But you said 'brothers,' in the plural, didn't you?"

"Yes."

"Funny, no one has ever come looking for Tommy before."

Stone sipped his drink. "I was wondering if you know how I could get in touch with them? Either or both?"

"Now, why would a lawyer want to get in touch with my brothers? A cop, I could understand, but a lawyer? Do you want to sue one of them?"

"No, as a matter of fact, although I am a lawyer, I'm not here in that capacity. It's more of a personal matter."

"How did you get my name and address?" she asked.

"From someone in Washington who used to know Tommy." That was technically correct. "He didn't have a current address."

"Washington, huh? Yes, Tommy used to live there; Tommy has lived in lots of places, lots of countries. He was something in the diplomatic corps, I believe. He was always hazy about exactly what he did."

"Have you...." He was interrupted by the telephone ringing.

"Excuse me," she said, then got up and went to a counter where the phone rested. "Hello? Oh, yes, honey, how are you? Everything going well?"

Stone sipped his drink and looked idly around the room. He felt that in a couple of minutes he was going to know how to find Dryer, or Bruce. He still thought of him as Dryer.

"How much do you need, honey?" she was asking. "Good God, we sent you down there with enough spending money for the whole semester! You were supposed to discipline your own spending, remember?"

Stone, who had not eaten for five hours, was starting to feel the bourbon.

"Well, if it's an emergency, I'll send it, but I am not going down to Western Union; I'll just mail you a check. And if I have this kind of call again, I'm going to let your father handle it! Now you...." She swore and hung up the phone.

Stone looked over at her, then away.

She came back to the couch, downed the last third of her drink, and went back toward the kitchen. "My daughter," she said. "She's in her first year at the University of Virginia. Doesn't know the meaning of money." She came back to the sofa carrying a fresh drink. "You have any kids?"

"No, I'm a bachelor."

"A bachelor," she said. She allowed her hand to brush the back of his. "An interesting one, too. How is it you never married, Stone?"

Stone shrugged and gave her his stock answer. "Just lucky, I guess."

She laughed as if this were *really* funny. "Yes, I'm all alone now, I guess. Husband ran off with a twenty-two-year-old, if you can believe it; daughter in college. It's just me now." She waved a hand. "All alone in this big house."

"I shouldn't think a woman as attractive as you are would be alone for very long."

She raised her glass. "Thank you, kind sir. You really know what to say to a girl."

Stone felt a need to change the subject. "Have you seen either of your brothers lately?"

She set her drink down. "Why don't we change the subject for a while?"

"What did you have in mind for a subject?" he asked mildly.

"Oh, if you knew what I had in mind," she said, smiling.

He believed he did know, and he wasn't sure how he was going to handle it. He certainly didn't want to annoy her and get thrown out before he had found out what he came for, and she was extremely attractive, except for the booze, and he was feeling just a little boozy himself. What canon of ethics covered this situation? None, he decided; he was on his own. Then he saw her nipples rise under her sweater. He had never seen that happen before. He was lost. "Your nipples are hard," he said.

"How can you tell?" she asked, "when you haven't touched them?"

He reached out and rubbed the back of his fingers lightly against her breasts. "Confirmed," he said.

"Not really," she said. She pulled her sweater over her head, released her bra from behind, and dropped it on the floor.

"Reconfirmed," he said, reaching for her.

He got out of the shower and went to find his clothes in the kitchen seating area. Once dressed, he decided to look around. There was a phone book on the kitchen counter, and under "Tommy" was scribbled "Chelsea Hotel." He wondered how old that address was. He went into the living room and found nothing of interest, then tried the library. On a bookcase were a lot of silver-framed family photographs. One of them had been taken in some tropical place; there were palms and a beach. A man dressed in the uniform of a navy lieutenant was standing next to a handsome blonde woman. Arrayed at their feet were two little boys and an older girl of maybe twelve—pretty, straw-haired, smiling.

"Better days," she said from behind him. She was tying a robe around her.

"I thought you were sound asleep," he said.

"So you just thought you'd have a look around."

"Yes, I did."

"Did you find what you were looking for?"

"Beg pardon?"

"Did you find Tommy and Charlie?"

"No. Would you like to tell me where they are?"

"Why do you want to find them?"

"I told you, it's a personal matter. One of them—Tommy, I think—has my wristwatch; it has a lot of sentimental value."

She smiled. "Tommy always loved watches. Strange thing."

"Where is he?"

"In New York; but you know that already."

"Yes. Do you have an address for him?"

"Last I heard, Tommy had an apartment on Ninety-first Street."

"Not any more; he's moved. Do you know where?"

She crossed her arms. "He may be a bastard," she said, "but he's my little brother."

"If you tell me where to find him, I may be able to keep him from getting into more trouble than he's already in."

"What kind of trouble?"

"Stealing, mostly."

"From you?"

"Among others."

"I talked to him last night, for the first time in more than a year; he said he was about to strike it rich."

"Did he say how?"

"He said that he possessed very valuable knowledge. That's all he said."

"And you don't know where he's living?"

She looked at the floor and shook her head.

He couldn't blame her. He walked to where she stood, kissed her on the cheek, and left.

Chapter 51

Stone drove slowly back toward the city, through slush, ice, and fresh snow, which had turned into a blizzard. In spite of his recent shower he felt somehow dirty. His sex life had always been serendipitous, and he liked it that way; in the normal course of his life he would have enjoyed his encounter with Lou Burch and reflected pleasantly on it, but his life had taken a new course with Arrington, and it troubled him that he had not once thought of her until he was back in the car. Guilt was new to him, and he didn't like it.

Just short of the George Washington Bridge traffic came to a complete halt, and he began to fear that it might be permanent. He got out his pocket phone and called Dino.

"Afternoon," Dino said.

"Already?" Stone looked at his watch; it was nearly two.

"Happens every day."

"Dino, I've finally got something on our boys."

"Shoot."

"An old acquaintance did some checking for me with what I believe was Central Intelligence. Turns out our boy, Jonathan, who has an electronics degree, underwent some training by those people and spent several years in their employ. He eventually got bounced. His real name is Thomas Bruce, and his brother's name is Charles. Charlie is probably out of jail recently; he was doing five to seven at Chino, in California, and my guess is he's jumped parole. That ought to be enough to pick him up on."

"It would be if we got a request from California," Dino said. "Hang on, let me check the computer."

Stone heard some keystrokes, then some more.

"Okay, I've got his record; his sheet is short but sordid. Picked up for male prostitution when he was nineteen, suspended sentence; suspect in a dozen burglaries; finally got nailed in somebody else's house, went up to Chino. No mention of parole; according to this, he's still inside."

"Maybe they're slow to update records," Stone said.

"Maybe. Oh, his picture looks a lot like his brother."

"So there's not enough to pick him up?"

"Not when he's still in Chino, Stone," Dino said drily.

"Can you check with California and see if he's out, and if he's been reporting to his parole officer? If he's bolted, you'd have an excuse to arrest him."

"My superiors wouldn't think it was a very good use of manpower to start hunting down parole violators from California, when California doesn't care enough to send out a bulletin."

"Oh, come on, Dino, you're not trying! I may even know where he is."

"Where?"

"At the Chelsea Hotel, maybe."

"Under what name?"

That stopped Stone; he hadn't thought to ask Lou Burch about a new alias, and she was certainly not going to volunteer it. "I don't know. Try Dryer, try Power, try Gable, try Bruce. Maybe he's dumb enough to use his own name."

"First, let me see what I can do with the state of California. I know a guy who might be of some help. Where are you?"

"Somewhere in New Jersey."

"Oh, shit; in this weather?"

"I'm standing still just short of the Bridge, while snow is relentlessly rising around me."

"Lotsa luck, pal. I hope I don't read in the papers that you were one of hundreds who froze to death in their cars."

"I'm moved by your concern. Get back to me." Stone broke the connection.

Miraculously, traffic began to move, or rather to inch forward. Twenty minutes later, the road had been squeezed down to one lane, past a rear-ender that was blocking the other two. Once past the wreck, Stone was back up to thirty miles an hour, which, in the current conditions, felt like sixty. Shortly he was in Manhattan again. His pocket phone rang.

"Yeah?"

"Okay, he's out of Chino, but he hasn't busted parole."

"You mean he's still in California? I don't believe it."

"He's not due to check in with his parole officer until day after tomorrow. If he doesn't show up, my friend has got him flagged to go into the computer immediately as a runner, and he's promised to fax me a request to pick him up."

"But not until day after tomorrow?"

"Not until the day after that, at the earliest. Sorry, it's the best I can do. Oh, I've got an address for him: the Santa Fe Residential Apartments, on Melrose, should you want to go looking for him."

"Nah, he moved out of there a week or so ago. I think I'm going to go looking for him at the Chelsea Hotel."

"You watch your ass, Stone. Remember Arnie; next time I see you I don't want to see a tag on your toe. Are you carrying?"

"No."

"Me, I wouldn't go after these guys without a piece. You shouldn't either."

"See you, Dino." Stone punched out, put away the phone, got off the West Side Highway at 48th

Street, drove over to 9th Avenue, and headed downtown, trying to stay in the bus tracks.

"Gee, I'm not sure," the man behind the desk said, looking at the ad Stone had ripped out of *Vanity Fair*.

Stone flashed the badge. "You don't want to be thought of as harboring a fugitive, do you?"

The man shook his head and checked his guest list. "He's in ten-oh-one."

"Under what name?"

"Jeremy Spencer."

"Is there somebody bunking with him?"

"No, he checked in alone last week, and I haven't seen him with anybody else, except a girl or two. They always leave in the morning."

"Passkey," Stone said.

"Not a chance," the desk clerk replied. "Not without a search warrant. I'm not getting into that kind of shit with my boss."

Stone glared at him. "Okay, I'm going up there, and if you call up and tell him I'm coming, you're going to find yourself in more shit than you would have ever believed possible."

The man held up his hands. "Okay, okay."

Stone took the elevator to the tenth floor, trembling with anticipation. He was looking forward to meeting Mr. Thomas Bruce. The door was at the end of the hall, at the back of the building. The Chelsea was an old hotel with a reputation for harboring rebels, literary and rock. It had been fixed up yet again, and the carpet was new. The hallway wasn't very wide, though; that was good.

Noting that there was no peephole, Stone rapped at the door.

"Yeah, who is it?" a muffled voice replied.

"Bellman. Got a Federal Express for you."

"You sure you got the right room? Who's it for?"

"Jeremy Spencer; from somebody named Burch, in Rahway, New Jersey." Stone braced himself against the opposite wall as he heard the door chain rattle. As soon as he saw the knob turn, he pushed off the wall and threw all his weight behind a kick at the door.

His timing was perfect. The door caught the man in the face and sent him flying backward across the room, and Stone was right on top of him. He held a forearm against the man's neck. "Mr. Dryer, I presume," he said, applying more pressure. "Or maybe I should say Mr. Bruce."

Something hard hit Stone on the back of the head, but he didn't pass out. Somebody grabbed him from behind and yanked him to his feet, pinning his arms behind him. Stone struggled to stay conscious as he watched Tommy Bruce get to his feet.

"You son of a bitch," Bruce said, throwing a right to Stone's gut.

"And I always thought I was such a nice guy," Stone managed to say between gasps for breath.

Bruce hit him high on his cheekbone, snapping his head around.

Still, Stone remained conscious.

Bruce cupped a hand under his chin and raised his head. "How'd you find me?" he demanded.

"Phone book," Stone said.

Bruce looked past him and said, "Hey, Charlie, meet Stone Barrington, the comic." He hit Stone on the other side of the head. "Did I ever tell you I fucked his girlfriend?"

"Oh, yeah, the lovely Arrington," Charles Bruce said from somewhere behind Stone's swimming head.

"And I fucked your sister," Stone said.

"What did you say?"

"Oh, yeah; the lovely Lou."

Bruce hit him again, and this time Stone started to go dark. His last memory was Tommy Bruce's shoe, coming at his head.

He came to in an ambulance, hurting everywhere. He tried to raise a hand to his face and discovered that his arms were strapped down. A paramedic was taking his blood pressure, and a cop dozed on a bench beside the litter. "Hey," Stone said.

The cop's head snapped around. "Huh?"

"Where we going?"

"Bellevue," the cop said.

Stone winced as they hit a bump. "Let's make it Lenox Hill," he said. "They know me there."

Chapter 52

Tommy and Charlie Bruce checked into the Mansfield Hotel on West 44th Street. It was a small hostelry, originally designed as an apartment hotel for well-to-do bachelors, as was its larger counterpart, the Royalton, farther down the block toward 6th Avenue, and it had recently been remodeled.

"I just don't get it," Charlie said. "How the fuck could he find us? How could he know who we are?"

This annoyed Tommy, who was accustomed to knowing everything. "He knows Louise, too."

"You should have let me kill him, talking like that about Louise."

Tommy whipped out a cell phone and called Rahway.

"Hello?" Sleepy voice.

"Hi, Sis," Tommy said. "You sound as though you've been well fucked."

"What?" She was awake now.

"You told him where to find us."

"I most certainly did not. I told him nothing."

"Tell me the truth."

"I am telling you the truth. He asked; I didn't tell him."

Tommy thought for a minute. "Did you write anything down?"

Her silence answered the question.

"Did you fall asleep after he fucked you?"

More silence.

"He looked around the house, didn't he?"

Still silence.

"You still meticulously keep your address book, don't you?"

"All right," she said, "he looked around the house; I caught him at it."

"How did he find you?"

"I have no idea."

"Come on, Louise, *think*. He must have said something about why he was there."

"He said he was a lawyer, but he wasn't there as a lawyer. He was looking for you for personal reasons."

"Did he say what he meant about that?"

"He said you stole his watch. Also, that you'd stolen things from other people. Is that true, Tommy?"

Tommy's turn to be silent.

"Speak to me."

"I had reasons to do what I did," he said finally. "We're right on the verge of something really big."

"What is it? What are you up to?"

"Let's just say that Charlie and I possess some very valuable information, and it's going to make us a *lot* of money."

"You're going to end up in jail, Tommy, just like Charlie. You two are more alike than I ever knew."

"Listen, if he turns up there again, I want you to call me."

"Where are you?"

"I'm going to give you a telephone number, and I don't want you to write it down; memorize it. It's a cellular phone."

"All right."

He gave her the number. "Have you got that?"

She repeated it to him. "Listen, I want you to understand something."

"What's that?"

"I live on alimony and child support; I have no other funds."

"So?"

"So I don't want you to expect me to raise bail or money for lawyers for either of you. I did that once, when I was married, and it was thrown up to me for years by my husband, who had to come up with the money. I'm *not* going to do it again. So if you two get yourselves arrested, I'll read about it in the papers, but I don't want to hear from you. Got that?"

"I got it, Louise. You're a great sister."

"Better than you deserve," she said, then she hung up.

"I'm hungry," Charlie said. "We didn't get any lunch."

"There's an Italian place down the block," Tommy replied. "I saw it from the cab. Come on."

Gaetano Calabrese checked his tie in the mirror, then turned to his boss. "Take a picture of me, okay?" He fished the Instamatic out of his locker and handed it to his headwaiter, who laughed and took his picture.

Gaetano had been in the country for seven months, and he had worked every day of it as a busboy. This was his first day as a waiter, and he was enjoying the tips. He worked days, and in the evenings, he ran numbers for a guy in his neighborhood. Gaetano fished a photograph out of his wallet and looked at it again; his boss had given it to him the night before. Five hundred bucks, that was what it was worth; he memorized the face and put it back in his wallet.

"Let's go, Gaetano," his boss said. "Break's over; customers in the restaurant."

Gaetano strode into the dining room, a smile on his face.

Tommy and Charlie Bruce walked into Figaro and asked for a table. It was late for lunch, and there were plenty. A waiter brought them a menu.

"Did you see that?" Charlie asked.

"What?"

"That waiter."

"What about him?"

"The way he looked at me. At you, too."

"Charlie, don't get paranoid on me."

"Tommy, a guy just busted into our hotel room that nobody was supposed to know about, looking for two guys whose names he didn't know, but he knew about the hotel, and he knew our names. Now you're telling me I'm paranoid?"

"Okay, now we're in another hotel under new names, and we've got ID to back them up, right?"

"Right."

"So how could anybody know about us?"

"I still think he looked at us funny."

"Shut up and order." The waiter was coming back.

"Gentlemen," he said in a heavy accent, "what is your pleasure?"

"I'll have the spaghetti bolognese, Tommy said.

"Pizza margharita," Charlie said.

"And a bottle of the chianti classico."

"Of course, sirs, and welcome to our restaurant."

"Thanks," Tommy said as the man walked away. "He's new on the job; he's just trying too hard, that's all."

"Maybe."

The waiter was back in a moment, and he was holding a camera. "Excuse me, gentlemen," he said, "but I have a new camera, and I wonder if I could take your pictures, you are both so very handsome."

Tommy started to speak, and then the flash-bulb went off in his face. When he could see again, the waiter was gone.

"Jesus," Charlie said. "What the hell is going on?"

"I'll admit, this is very screwy," Tommy mumbled. "I think we ought to get out of here."

Gaetano was on the phone to his night boss. "I got them," he said.

"What are you talking about, Gaetano?" the boss asked. "You're not on until tonight."

"The two men you want for five hundred dollars. I got them."

"Where?"

"At Figaro, where I work, on West Forty-fourth Street."

"Keep an eye on those guys, Gaetano. Somebody'll be there very quickly."

"Don't worry, I took their photograph, too."

"You *what?*"

"I took their picture with my camera."

"Did they see you do it?"

"Of course. My camera has a flash."

"Holy shit, are they still there?"

"Hold on, please, I'll see." Gaetano let the receiver fall, then stepped into the dining room again. The two men had vanished. He ran back to the phone. "They are gone!" he screamed.

"No fucking kidding!" his boss yelled. "Go after them; don't let them out of your sight! We're on the way!"

Gaetano hung up the phone and sprinted for

the street. He ran out the door, nearly knocking down two customers, and looked left and right. Nothing, nothing but traffic. He ran to the corner of 6th Avenue and looked up and down. Still nothing. He ran back to 5th Avenue. Still nothing. His heart sank. Not only was he not going to get the five hundred dollars, he was, as his boss liked to say, going to get his ass kicked.

Tommy and Charlie Bruce burst out of the Mansfield Hotel less than a minute after the waiter had disappeared back into his restaurant and dove into a cab.

"What now?" Charlie asked.

"We've got to find a hole long enough to get the computer out of storage and get off one more issue of *DIRT*. That's all it's going to take; the groundwork has been done."

"But where? I don't want anybody else taking pictures of us."

"I know just the place," Tommy said. "It belongs to a friend who's not using it at the moment." He gave the driver an address, then sat back in the seat. "Just one more issue," he said, "delivered to just one customer."

Chapter 53

Stone looked up at the resident, who was stitching the cut above his eye. "Where's the cop who was with me when I came in?" he asked.

"He's out in the hall."

"Could somebody ask him to come in, please?"

"You just lie quietly, and let me do my work; you can talk to him later."

"It's very important."

"Shut up."

"Are you going to call the cop in here, or am I going to have to do it myself?"

"Oh, all right. Nurse, will you get the cop in here, please?"

"Thank you."

"Will you *please* shut up? We're getting tired of seeing you in here, you know. What was it last time, a concussion?"

"Careful how you talk to me; I'll take my business elsewhere."

The cop walked in. "Somebody ask for me?"

"I did," Stone said. "Will you call Lieutenant Bacchetti at the Nineteenth and tell him I'm here, please?"

"Sure thing." The cop left.

"See how easy that was?" Stone said to the resident.

"Are you a cop, Mr. Barrington?"

"Used to be."

"You look too young to be retired."

"That's what I told them, but they retired me anyway."

"There," the resident said. "What with your scalp wound and this one, you have seventeen stitches in your head."

"A record," he replied.

"I sincerely hope so." She turned to the nurse. "Dress these two wounds, and let's get him admitted."

298

"I don't want to be admitted," Stone said.

The resident paused at the door. "Put restraints on him if he gives you a hard time."

Dino walked into the hospital room. "Now what?" he demanded.

Stone had the bed cranked to a sitting position. "I want to make a complaint," he said.

"A complaint? You look very happy to me."

"I want to file aggravated battery charges against Thomas and Charles Bruce."

"It's already been done. When the cop called me I got it in the computer and onto the street."

"So now you can arrest them."

"Their photographs are being printed up as we speak; the next shift will be carrying them."

"Check hotels," Stone said. "I don't think they're going apartment hunting now."

"Right," Dino said. "You really look like shit, you know?"

"Thanks."

"By tomorrow morning you're going to look like you fought for the championship and lost."

Stone shifted the ice pack on his face. "They're looking to make some kind of a big score, Dino, but I don't know what."

"Another burglary?"

"Doesn't sound like that; they're talking big money. That's what Tommy told his sister, anyway."

"What I don't understand is why they beat you up so bad."

"I told them I fucked their sister."

"Oh, you *wanted* them to kick the shit out of you."

299

"You ought to see the other guy. He should have a door sticking out of his forehead; I kicked it in on him."

"Great, that'll really help nail them for battery, you kicking in the door of their room."

The door opened and Arrington walked in, carrying two large suitcases. She dropped them and rushed over to the bed. "Is he dead?" she asked Dino.

"Not yet."

"I'm just fine," Stone said.

"Oh, sure."

"It was just some bruising and a couple of cuts." He tried to sit up, but winced with pain. "And a couple of ribs. What are the bags for? Are you going somewhere?"

"I'm moving in with you," Arrington said.

"I thought you already had, pretty much."

"The difference between 'pretty much' and moving in is two suitcases."

"Oh."

"If it were Mary Ann," Dino said, "it would be two moving vans. That's what it's going to take to cart our stuff up to Sixty-sixth Street."

"The doctor says you're going to need two or three days in the hospital," Arrington said.

"Fat chance."

"You're not going to get out of here talking like that. They said they'd let me take you home tomorrow, if I promised to keep you in bed."

"Promise them anything."

"Well," said Dino, "I think my work here is done."

"Thanks, Dino," Stone said. "You'd better find those guys before I do."

Dino threw up his hands. "I didn't hear that," he said, walking out of the room.

Arrington pulled a chair up to the bed. "What am I going to do with you?" she said.

"Take me home at the earliest possible moment, that's what."

"I'm so sorry I got you involved with Jonathan."

"His name is Tommy Bruce, and you didn't get me involved; Amanda Dart did."

"And I'm very sorry, too," Amanda said from the door.

"Not your fault, Amanda," Stone said. "Take a pew. How did you know I was here?"

"I have a source in the emergency room," she replied. "Arrington, I know this is a terrible imposition, but may I speak to Stone alone for just a moment?"

"Sure, I need some coffee, anyway," Arrington replied, then left.

Amanda settled herself in the bedside chair. "How badly are you hurt?"

"Only superficially. I plan to get back on the horse tomorrow."

"Stone, I asked you to drop this investigation."

"Don't worry, Amanda, it's not costing you a dime."

"I resent that."

"Sorry, I guess I'm a little irritable today."

"Dick Hickock and I don't want anything else done on this, do you understand?"

"Quite frankly, no; would you explain that to me? A couple of weeks ago you were both nuts to find these guys."

"We got over it."

"Amanda, don't you think it's a little out of character for you to get over something like this?"

"I know when to cut my losses."

"I'm afraid I don't."

"You're going to keep looking for these people, then?"

"As soon as I can walk upright and make a fist. In the meantime, the police are looking for them."

Amanda made a small noise.

"What?"

"Is there anything I can get you?" she asked.

"I'm fine, thanks."

"I hope you won't continue this," she said, standing.

"You can always hope."

"Believe me, it's not in your interests to do so."

"Amanda, do you know what these guys want?"

"No, I don't."

"Does Hickock?"

"Not to my knowledge."

"They're looking to make some big money; are you buying them off?"

"No."

"Is Hickock?"

"He's said nothing to me about it. Look, Stone, Dick has dropped the girlfriend, and he and his wife have managed to patch things up. Don't go pulling the scabs off their wounds."

"I'll be as discreet as I possibly can," Stone said.

"Thanks for that, anyway."

"Thanks for coming to see me."

"Goodbye, Stone."

From her car, Amanda called Dick Hickock. "He's not going to give it up," she said.

"That's his misfortune," Hickock replied, then hung up.

Chapter 54

Tommy and Charlie Bruce spent the afternoon and evening in the movies, seeing four features in three theaters, their luggage on the seats beside them, not venturing onto the streets until after dark. They ate a late dinner at the back of a Chinese restaurant, lingering until long after midnight, then found a cab and got out a block from their destination.

"How are we going to get in?" Charlie asked as they walked quickly down the street.

"I've got a key to the apartment, but it's a doorman building, and we have to get in the back way. Stop a minute."

They put down their bags and looked up and down the block. It was after one o'clock, and there was no traffic.

"Down here," Tommy said, trotting down a flight of dark stairs to a door. He switched on a penlight, clenched it between his teeth, and from his wallet took a set of lock picks. In less than thirty seconds they were inside. "We can't use the elevator," he said. "The doorman will know if we do. We'll have to walk up."

"How many floors?"

"Nine."

"Shit."

"Shut up, and let's get moving." They stopped twice to rest and finally stepped into the ninth-floor hallway. They tiptoed to the door, and Tommy let them in and switched on a light.

"Not bad," Charlie said.

"There's only one bed; one of us will have to sleep on the sofa."

"Toss you for it."

"Fuck you. And keep the noise down; we don't want to attract attention from the neighbors." They busied themselves with getting settled, and Tommy plugged in his laptop computer, connecting it to the laser printer already on a desk in the apartment.

"I'm whipped," Charlie said, flopping down on the sofa.

"Let's get some sleep, then. Tomorrow's going to be a busy day."

The following morning Stone walked stiffly out of the hospital and rode home in a cab with Arrington.

"You need some help with the steps?" she asked.

"I'll manage," he said, but the climbing made his ribs hurt. While Arrington went to consult Helene about lunch, he took the elevator upstairs and went to the safe in his dressing room. He took out a German .765 caliber automatic pistol, a small but damaging weapon, then he dressed in pajamas and a robe and put the pistol into a robe pocket. Finally, and with some difficulty, he knelt next to his bed, retrieved the shotgun from its hiding place under the bed, and set it where he could easily reach it. Only then did he prop himself up in bed. When he next met the Messrs. Bruce, he intended to be ready.

Enrico Bianchi got out of his car on a narrow street in Little Italy and walked into the La Bohéme Coffee House. He nodded to several people at tables, then went straight through to a rear room, where a nattily dressed young man awaited him.

"Good morning, *padrone*," the young man said.

Bianchi tapped his ear with a finger and made a circular motion in the air.

"It was swept ten minutes ago," the young man said. "We're all right."

"What happened yesterday?" Bianchi asked, taking a chair.

"A waiter who runs numbers spotted them on West Forty-fourth Street. He got excited and took their photograph, and they ran. He tried to follow them, but they were gone. We checked the block and found out they had checked in at the Mansfield Hotel less than half an hour before. They returned there, got their bags, and left in a hurry."

"And now?"

"They've gone to ground. As soon as they hit the streets, we'll have them."

"Let me see the photograph," Bianchi said.

The young man handed him a snapshot.

"Yes, that's our boys."

"Don't worry, we'll find them."

"We have a new problem. I had a call this morning; the police are now looking for them, and they've got photographs, too, although we managed to slow the prints down a little."

305

"That's not good."

"It means that we will just have to find them first, and if we do, we won't have as much time as I'd hoped to fake a crime. The important thing, though, is that they are dead."

"I understand."

"I want a dozen men on the streets on the Upper East Side, ready to do the work at a moment's notice. Give them stolen cellular telephones, and tell them to be brief when they use them."

"No problem."

"Be sure each man has a silenced weapon, too, and tell them to use knives if at all possible. This will have to be done quickly and with little fuss."

"What about bystanders?"

"Leave no one alive who could identify our people. I don't want this to come back to us."

"Yes, *padrone*."

"Get to me the minute you have news." Bianchi left the coffeehouse and went back to his car.

Dino stood in the squad room handing out photographs. "Sorry these took so long, but we had problems with the photo lab. We're looking for these two for aggravated battery, but the thing is, we think one or both of them may have capped Arnie Millman, so this is an all-out push. Those of you on a beat, I want every doorman in a hotel or apartment building to see these pictures. If you glom onto these guys, don't try to take them; call for backup. I don't want no dead heroes. Got that?"

There was a murmur of assent from the gathering.

"Okay, get on it," Dino said, then went back to his office and called Stone. "How you feeling, pal?"

"A lot better, thanks."

"The pictures of the Bruces are on the street; we're doing a full-court press."

"That's good to hear."

"Stone, I hope you won't go looking for these guys."

"You can always hope."

"It's better to let us find them. You can be the star witness at the trial. Stay home and get well."

"I'll think about it."

"You got a piece?"

"I have."

"Well, that's something."

"I never fail to take your advice twice, Dino."

Stone hung up the phone, got undressed, shaved, and showered. Arrington rewound the Ace bandage around his sore ribs.

"How's that?" she asked.

"It's okay; I'm really feeling a lot better."

"I'm going out for a while; will you be okay?"

"Sure. Where you going?"

"I've got to see somebody at The New Yorker, and then I want to run by my place for a minute. In my rush to get to you I forgot half my makeup."

"You wear makeup?"

"You're sweet."

Chapter 55

Richard Hickock had just finished a sandwich at

his desk when he heard the fax machine ring in the outer office. His secretary was at lunch, so he got up and walked through the large double doors that separated him from his four office workers and checked the machine. As he watched, a single sheet of paper was fed into the bin. He picked it up.

DIRT

Greetings, earthlings! Time for the *BIG story!*

Those of you who have followed the riches-to-riches career of Richard Hickock, and who may have admired the taste and style of his many publications, might like to know about the underside of Dickie's paper empire.

Our Dickie owns a corporation you never heard of, one called WINDOW SEAT. Remember that name, because you're going to be reading a lot about it, though maybe not in Dickie's papers. WINDOW SEAT, which is operated on a day-to-day basis by Dickie's brother-in-law, Martin Wynne, is a holding company based in Zurich that holds interests in publications as diverse as *The Infiltrator* and two equally lascivious European tabloids, one in London, one in Dusseldorf. So while spouting off about journalistic integrity, Dickie is licking the cream off a pie that also contains three gay porn magazines, and an Internet business that sends out photos of charmingly posed, quite beautiful children in the arms of less charming grownups.

These "organs" are pumping cash, at the

current rate of $70,000,000 a year, straight into bank accounts in the Caymans and in Zurich. (We have the account numbers, for those who are really interested.) What we know will shock you to the core is that our own dear Internal Revenue Service has never seen so much as a sawbuck in taxes on these swill-gotten gains! (Admit it, aren't you shocked?)

Just in case there are any doubters among you, we've prepared a dozen packets containing chapter and verse and addressed them to some of our nation's leading newspapers and television networks, not to mention the boys and girls at the IRS. Once these are sent, we predict that less than twenty-four hours will pass before Dickie is in either a federal lockup or Brazil! Stay tuned for more!

P.S. Dickie, the above copy is for your eyes only. To prevent those packets from going out, call the number below before five today, which is when Federal Express is due to pick them up. It's a cellular phone, so don't try to trace its location.

Before Hickock was halfway through this bulletin, his bowels were turning to water. He finished reading it in his private john, and when he read the postscript, his relief was palpable. He finished up in the john, locked the door to his office, and called the number.

"Good afternoon, Mr. Hickock," a pleasant voice said.

"Who else did you send this to?" Hickock demanded.

"Just you, just this once, *if* you follow instructions. Got a pencil?"

"Yes."

"Write this down very carefully," the voice said, "because it would not react to your benefit if you made a mistake."

"Go ahead."

"Before the close of business today you are to wire-transfer the sum of two million dollars from the Window Seat Zurich account to the Bank of Europe in Luxembourg, account number 353-67-6381. Got that?"

Hickock repeated the information.

"You've got just this one chance to get it right," the voice said. "If you don't make a mistake, the funds will be in Luxembourg tomorrow morning. If you do make a mistake, those packets of information will be at their destinations by three P.M. tomorrow, and you will spend the rest of your life either in prison or running."

"Look, I'm not sure I can raise that much today."

"You're not listening, Mr. Hickock. And by the way, if you make any attempt to find us, or any attempt to bring pressure to bear on the Luxembourg Bank to find out who we are, it will be over for you instantly. We can still make a very nice buck by hawking the story, but we'd rather keep it clean and simple. Since this is the last time we'll ever speak, Mr. Hickock, is there anything else you'd like to say?"

"Yes. I know who you are, Mr. Bruce, you and your brother, and I have your photographs."

"Big mistake, Mr. Hickock; that little outburst cost you one million dollars. So that's *three* million dollars to the Luxembourg account by the close of business. And if either of us should ever meet with an unfortunate accident, you may be sure that the packets will automatically be sent by our designated representatives. Goodbye, Mr. Hickock. I hope you make the right decision." The connection was broken.

Hickock sat at his desk for half an hour, his face in his hands, sweat dripping onto the desktop. His mind raced like that of a cornered rat looking for escape. But there was no escape. Finally he turned to the computer on his desk and opened a fax file to his Zurich bank. He typed in the instructions for the wire transfer to Luxembourg, followed by the code known only to him and his banker. With a sob, he pressed the send key, then he sat back in his chair and wept. Less than a minute later, he sat bolt upright. Enrico Bianchi's people were out looking for those two men now, he remembered, and if they found them....

"Oh, my God," he said aloud. He picked up the telephone and dialed a number. The phone rang twice and an electronic voice said, "Leave...your... message...at...the...tone," followed by a short beep.

"Message for Mr. Crown," he said into the phone. "Contact Mr. Gold at the earliest possible moment, utmost urgency."

"Thank...you," the voice said.

Hickock hoped to God Bianchi was wearing his beeper. He sat back to wait for the call. A moment later, his pocket phone rang. "Yes?" he said.

"Dick, it's Amanda. I've been doing some thinking and believe that before this business goes any further, you and I should sit down and talk about a new contract."

"Amanda, we've just signed a contract," he said, astonished. Then he began to see.

"Yes, but I think the circumstances call for something much more substantial, don't you? After all, you and I have become something like partners, haven't we?"

"Tomorrow," he said, resignedly.

"Lunch? Twenty-One? Twelve-thirty?"

"I'll be there." He hung up. The phone rang again.

"Hello?"

"This is Mr. Crown. Do you wish to meet?"

"There isn't time," Hickock said. "Listen to me...."

"Stop, don't talk. Same place as last time. One hour."

"Yes," Hickock said. The connection was broken.

Hickock struggled into his coat, headed for the door, then stopped and went back to his desk. He dialed a London number.

"Hello?" a familiar voice said.

"It's Dick," Hickock said. "Your son-in-law in L.A. has talked too much; he may have blown the lid off everything."

There was much swearing at the other end of the line.

"Yes, I feel pretty much the same way. I may be able to head this off, but I thought you should know about Peebles. I'll leave it to you how to handle him."

"I know exactly how to handle him," the man said.

Hickock hung up and ran for his meeting with Bianchi.

Chapter 56

Arrington saw her editor at *The New Yorker*, and they had lunch at the Royalton Hotel; then she did some shopping at Bloomingdale's. It was growing dark when she got out of a cab in front of her apartment building.

"Good afternoon, Miss Carter," the doorman said, holding the cab door for her. "We haven't seen you for a while."

"I've been staying with a friend, Jimmy; I just came by to pick up some things."

"I've been keeping your mail for you," Jimmy said. "You want it now?"

"I'll pick it up on the way out," she said. "I'll be down in a few minutes."

"Very good, Miss."

Arrington took the elevator to her floor, rummaging in her bag for the key. She kept a key in each of her bags, and today she had taken the big one. The key was at the very bottom, as usual.

She inserted the key into the lock and opened the door. To her astonishment, there was someone sitting at her desk. Then something struck her on the side of the head, and she fell to the floor, only half-conscious.

"Jesus Christ, Tommy!" she heard somebody say. "You never said she might come home!"

"I didn't think she would," Jonathan Dryer's voice replied. "There's a roll of duct tape in my bag, Charlie; hand it to me, will you?"

She was rolled onto her back, and before she could focus on the face above her, a wide strip of tape was slapped across her eyes, and another across her mouth.

"What are we going to do with her, Tommy?" the first voice said. "We can't leave her here alive."

"I guess not," Tommy replied, "but we're going to be here until tomorrow. Wouldn't you like to fuck her while we wait to hear from the bank?"

Arrington was rolled roughly onto her stomach, and her hands were taped behind her back. She was blind and dumb, but her head was beginning to clear, and she digested what she had just heard.

"Sure," Charlie said, and he sounded greedy.

"She's hot stuff; take it from me," Tommy said. "I won't tape her feet." He hauled her to her feet and dumped her on the sofa. "You'll want to be able to spread her legs, won't you?"

"Right," Charlie said, chuckling. "Just let me finish this fax to the Luxembourg bank."

Out on Fifth Avenue, Detective Ernie Martinez was on foot, doing a patrolman's job. It was beneath him, but Martinez had his own reasons for working so hard that day. He saw a doorman standing outside an apartment building, at least the fiftieth he had talked to that day. "How y'doing?" he asked the man, flashing his badge.

"Pretty good, officer. Can I help you?"

Martinez produced the two photographs. "You ever seen either one of these guys before?"

The doorman looked carefully at the two photographs, then glanced back at Martinez. "Maybe, one of them," he said.

"There's twenty in it for you, if you do me some good here," Martinez said.

"Yeah, I know this guy," the doorman said, holding up one of the photographs. "He's spent a lot of time with the lady in Nine-A, Miss Carter."

"That's Nine-A?" Martinez asked.

"Yeah. Pretty lady, Miss Carter."

"You think he might be up there right now?"

The doorman hadn't seen any money yet, so he played the detective along. "Could be," he said.

"Thanks," Martinez said, turning away.

"Hey, what about my twenty?"

Martinez stopped, produced a twenty, but snatched it back when the doorman grabbed for it. "You don't say nothing to nobody about this, right? I was never here."

"Right," the doorman said, "you were never here." This time he was allowed to grab the twenty.

Martinez hoofed it around the corner and found a pay phone.

"Yeah?" a voice said.

"This is Ernie Martinez. You know those two guys you're looking for?"

"Yeah."

"I just might have them for you."

"Yeah? Where?"

"You'll tell the big guy that Ernie Martinez phoned it in?"

"Yeah, sure, Ernie."

"Ten-eleven Fifth Avenue, Apartment Nine-A. Doorman says they might be up there right now."

"Thanks, Ernie; we'll be in touch."

"I'll have to phone this in, but I'll wait an hour, okay?"

"Yeah, that's good, Ernie."

"Don't forget to tell him."

But the man had already hung up.

Martinez found a coffee shop on Madison and settled himself on a stool with his paper, a cup of coffee, and a doughnut.

It was dark now, and Arrington hadn't returned. Stone was getting worried. He found her diary with the name of her appointment at the magazine, and he called the editor.

"This is Stone Barrington; I'm a friend of Arrington Carter. I believe she had an appointment with you this morning."

"That's right," the woman said. "We had lunch after that."

"What time did she leave you?"

"Sometime after three. She said she was going to Blooming-dale's."

"Thanks very much," Stone said, then hung up. He looked at his watch. Bloomingdale's had been closed for forty-five minutes. She had said she was going to her old apartment, hadn't she? He dialed the number, but only got her answering machine. He heard the beep. "Hello, Arrington? Are you there? If you're there, pick up." He waited a moment, but she didn't answer. "If you get this message, call me at home." He hung up. He'd wait a few minutes, then call again.

Richard Hickock rode up in the freight elevator, and when he emerged onto the empty factory floor it was dark. A moment later, half a dozen low-wattage bulbs came on, and Enrico Bianchi stepped from behind a column.

"You're late, Dick," Bianchi said. "I've been waiting over an hour." He did not sound happy.

"I'm sorry, Ricky, we were stuck in the Midtown Tunnel the whole damned time; there was a big pileup. When we got out I called your beeper, but there was no answer."

Bianchi ran a hand over his hair. "I don't like to wait, Dick."

"I apologize, Ricky; there was nothing I could do."

Bianchi did not seem mollified. "So what's the big emergency?"

"I want to call off the search for those two men," Hickock said. "Something has happened, and it would be very bad for me if anything happened to them."

"Dick, what is this on-again, off-again thing? You should know I don't do business that way. What has happened?"

"They're blackmailing me, that's what. They've threatened to turn me in to the IRS and to send incriminating information to the media."

"How much do they want?"

"Three million dollars. I've already wire-transferred the money."

Bianchi looked astonished. "Dick, you shouldn't have done that; you should have come to me and let me handle it."

"I only had until close of business, Ricky, and they said that they had left the documents with other parties, and if anything happened to them it would be sent out. That's why you have to call off the search; I can't afford for anything to happen to them now."

"Dick, don't you know that's what all blackmailers say? That they've left the pictures or the documents or whatever with a lawyer who has instructions if anything happens to them? They never do it; they never believe anything will happen to them. I think it would be best if we just leave things as they are. I've already had a tip that they might be in an East Side apartment. Someone is on the way there now."

"Ricky, you've got to stop them; I can't afford to find out the hard way if they're lying. I'd rather pay them the money."

"Then they'll want more, Dick, don't you know that? If you're willing to pay them three million dollars on the basis of an unsubstantiated threat, they'll bleed you again and again for years to come, until there's nothing left. You just let me handle these two guys."

"*I can't do that,* Ricky. You've got to call off your men."

Bianchi shrugged. "I'm afraid that's impossible, Dick; it's too late. You'll just have to take your chances."

Hickock slumped. "I hope to God you're right about their bluff."

"Trust me, I'm right. Is there anything else?"

"There is one more thing; the third name I gave you."

"I remember." He patted his pocket. "It's right here. You want me to push the button?"

Hickock took a deep breath. "Push the button. I don't care whether it looks like an accident, just do it."

"It will be done," Bianchi said. "But this is going to cost more money. This search has turned into an expensive operation."

"Of course," Hickock said. "Anything you want, just name the amount."

Bianchi smiled for the first time that day. "That's the way I like to hear you talk," he said.

Stone phoned again, got the answering machine again. He had the awful feeling that something was very wrong. He'd go over there; maybe the doorman would let him in. Then he remembered. He found her handbag in the bedroom, opened it, and shook the contents out onto the bed. There was the key. He put it in his pocket, got a coat, and left the house.

Chapter 57

Allan Peebles had worked a long day. It was only midafternoon in L.A., but it seemed later to him. He was tired, and his editorial meeting was nearly over. He had only a story or two to clear, and he could close the paper for the week and go home. Then, through the glass wall of the boardroom, he saw a strange sight. A man named Harold Purvis, who was head of security for the *Infiltrator*'s building, was striding through the newsroom, followed by two uniformed security guards. Purvis walked up to the boardroom door, rapped sharply, and opened the door.

"Mr. Peebles, I must see you immediately," he said. "Just as soon as you close the paper. It's very urgent."

"I'll be with you in just a couple of minutes, Harold," Peebles said, wondering if another lunatic had gotten into the building. He ran through the remaining stories, gave his approval, and wound up the meeting, then he walked down the corridor to his corner office. Harold Purvis and his two men were in the room, as was his secretary. "What's up, Harold? More crazies with alien abduction stories?" This was a regular feature of life at the *Infiltrator*.

Purvis walked behind him, closed the door, and took an envelope from his inside pocket. "I have been instructed to read you a letter," he said, "which will explain everything."

"All right," Peebles replied, wondering what the hell was going on.

Purvis held up the letter and read aloud. "'Dear Mr. Peebles,'" he began. "'You are herewith and with immediate effect dismissed from your position as editor and publisher of the *Infiltrator*.'"

Peebles blinked. He had not seen this coming.

"You are to vacate your office and depart the

premises at once. Your secretary will send along any personal effects in your office."

Amanda Dart, he thought. *She has betrayed me. I told her everything to save myself, but she has betrayed me.*

"'Your pension plan, medical insurance, and profit-sharing are canceled with immediate effect; your stock options are withdrawn; your signature is no longer valid on any *Infiltrator* bank account; all *Infiltrator* employees will immediately be informed that your instructions are no longer to be followed. Two weeks' severance pay will be wire-transferred to your personal bank account after, and only after, possession of all *Infiltrator* property has been surrendered.'" Purvis handed him the letter. "It's signed by the chairman of the board," he said.

"I don't believe it," Peebles mumbled, starting to read the letter.

"Give me your keys to the building and your office, your medical insurance card, and your credit cards," Purvis said.

"How dare you speak to me that way!" Peebles sputtered. "I am your superior...." He faltered.

"Not any more," Purvis said. He turned to the two security guards. "Gentlemen, clean out his pockets."

One of the guards grabbed Peebles and pinned his arms behind his back while the other went through his pockets and emptied the contents onto the desktop. Purvis stepped forward, removed the cards from Peebles's wallet, and looked through the other items. He detached two keys from a ring, then stepped back. "The rest of this junk is yours; put it back in your pockets."

Peebles obeyed. "There has been some mistake here, and I will remember your conduct," he said to Purvis through clenched teeth.

"Get his coat," Purvis said to the secretary. The woman obeyed, and Purvis handed the coat to Peebles. Peebles put it on. "Tell his deputy that he is in charge until further notice," Purvis said to the secretary, then he turned back to the two guards. "Escort Mr. Peebles from the building."

The two guards frog-marched Peebles through the newsroom, down two flights of stairs, and out of the building. A moment later, he found himself standing alone in the parking lot.

Still unable to believe what had just happened and trying to preserve some semblance of dignity, Peebles got into his Bentley and drove home to Beverly Hills. As he pulled into his driveway and got out of his car, a man suddenly appeared, along with another uniformed security guard.

"I'm from the *Infiltrator*'s leasing company," he said, snatching Peebles's keys from his hand. "The lease on the Bentley has been canceled." The man detached the car key and returned the ring, which now held only a house key, to its owner. As Peebles watched, aghast, the man drove away in the Bentley.

Peebles turned to the security guard. "What do you want?" he said.

"I'm to escort you from the company's house when you have retrieved your belongings," he said.

Cursing under his breath, Peebles opened the

front door of the house and walked in. The place was empty. All furnishings, draperies, and pictures had been removed. He walked down the hallway to his bedroom, his heels echoing on the bare tile floors. In the middle of the otherwise empty bedroom sat half a dozen suitcases, packed.

"I'll give you a hand," the guard said.

Shortly, Peebles was standing on the sidewalk, his luggage stacked beside him.

"Your house key," the guard said.

Peebles handed it to him.

"I've been told to give you a message from your father-in-law: If you ever return to Britain he will make it his business to see that you regret it for the rest of your life." He got into a car parked at the curb. "Do you want me to radio my office to call you a cab?" he asked.

"Thank you, yes," Peebles said.

"Consider it done," the guard said, and drove away.

Peebles stood on the sidewalk and tried to organize his thoughts, but it wasn't working.

Finally the cab came, and the driver loaded his luggage.

He didn't bother holding the door for Peebles, who let himself into the cab. "Where to, Mister?"

"I haven't the slightest idea," Peebles said, staring out the window into the middle distance.

Chapter 58

The tape was suddenly ripped from Arrington's mouth. "Ow, you son of a bitch!" she screamed.

A blow caught the side of her head and knocked her off the sofa. Her eyes were still taped, and she couldn't see it coming.

"Shut up until you're spoken to," Tommy Bruce said. "Does Barrington know where you are?"

"Yes," she said. "He'll be here any minute." She took another blow, to the other side of her head.

"Don't lie to me," he said.

"What do you think, Tommy?" Charlie asked. "Are we going to have a visit from Barrington?"

"Nah," Tommy said. "She just stopped by here for a minute to pick up something; she's been living at his place. Isn't that right, Arrington?"

Arrington said nothing. She hunched up her shoulders, hoping to avoid another blow.

"What are you doing now, Charlie?" Tommy asked. "I thought you wanted to fuck her."

"I'm just addressing Federal Express packets to the *New York Times* and the IRS," Charlie replied. "As soon as we confirm the money's in the bank, I'm going to ship them. I'm sending one to the cops, too, just for the hell of it."

Tommy laughed. "Why not? It'll give us something to read about in the papers for months to come. I wish I could see Hickock's face the first time the IRS calls."

"There," Charlie said, "all done. Now, let's have a look at Miss Arrington."

Arrington heard him coming toward her and she flinched in anticipation of another blow, but instead something clicked loudly, he grabbed her clothing, and she felt her blouse and bra being cut away.

"Not bad," Charlie said, pushing her prone on the couch. "Now let's see the rest."

Arrington aimed a kick at his voice, but Tommy grabbed her ankles and held them while Charlie went to work on her skirt with his knife.

A car pulled up around the corner from Arrington's apartment building and two young men got out. They were sharply dressed and finely barbered, and they moved with complete confidence. They walked around the corner and into the building.

Jimmy, the doorman, who was resting in a lobby chair, sprang to his feet. These men didn't look as though they belonged in his building.

"How ya doin'?" one of the men said as he swung a pistol at Jimmy's head. He stepped over to the prone doorman and held the pistol to Jimmy's forehead. "Answer me fast, or I'll spread your brains all over this nice floor. Where's the passkey for Nine-A?"

"Desk drawer," Jimmy managed to say. "There's a tag on it."

The other man opened the drawer. "Got it," he said. "We better take this guy with us." He grabbed Jimmy by the collar, hustled him across the room, and dumped him into the elevator.

"Nine, please," his friend said, grinning. He hit Jimmy with his gun again, rendering him unconscious. Soon the elevator stopped on the ninth floor. He dragged the doorman so that his head lay in the path of the door. "That'll hold the car for us," he said, stepping over Jimmy and into the hall. Quickly, silently, the two men walked toward the apartment door.

Jimmy began to come to. He got an arm under him and pushed himself back into the elevator. Painfully, he reached up and pushed the button for the lobby.

Arrington was putting up the best fight she could with her hands taped behind her. She was naked now, and she struggled to get a foot free so that she could kick, but Tommy held them fast.

"Why don't you just relax," Charlie's voice said softly. He was close enough that she could feel his breath on her face. Quickly she pulled her head back and aimed her forehead at the voice. There was a cry of pain as she connected, and something warm splashed onto her face. She managed to get a foot loose and kicked with all her might, connecting with something, she wasn't sure what.

"The bitch broke my nose!" Charlie wailed. "I'm going to fuck her with the knife!"

Arrington continued to struggle, but she was losing. Then she heard the door open, and suddenly she was released.

"How ya doin'?" a strange voice said, followed by two dull thumps. She had seen enough movies to know what a silenced pistol sounded like.

Arrington rolled off the sofa and ran blindly in the direction of the bedroom; she knew she was there when she felt carpeting under her feet. She got behind the door and kicked it shut, then turned around and found the lock. One turn, and she was locked in. She ran into the bathroom, knocking a knee painfully against the toilet. There was a pair of scissors in the top drawer of the vanity; she got them out and began trying awkwardly to aim them at the tape holding her wrists. From the living room she heard two more thumps.

The first man straightened up. "Okay, that piece of business is taken care of. What about the girl?"

"We were told to take out any witnesses," the second man said.

"Yeah, but didn't you see? Her eyes had duct tape on them."

"You've got a point."

The first man walked to the bedroom door and tried it. "Locked. We'll have to break it down."

"That's gonna be noisy," the second man said. "These old buildings have solid doors."

"You're right," the first man said.

"We've been here too long already; let's get out now."

Then someone spoke from the front door of the apartment. "Freeze!" the voice said.

Stone stood in a crouch, the .765 pistol fully extended in front of him. He saw, as if in slow motion, the man at the bedroom door start to turn, saw the gun in his hand. He fired once, knocking the man against the bedroom door, then immediately turned and got off another round at the second man, who was pointing a pistol at him. Simultaneously, the man jerked and spun, and

Stone felt the breeze and hum of a bullet go past his ear.

Arrington heard the shots and a loud thump against the bedroom door, and she redoubled her efforts with the scissors. The tape was tearing now, and she forced her wrists apart until she could get a hand free. She ripped the tape off her eyes.

Still holding the pistol out in front of him, Stone stepped over the man closest to him and kicked his gun away from him. He performed the same operation with the man lying in front of the bedroom door, then felt for a pulse at the neck. Nothing. He turned to the other man, who was clutching his side with one hand and struggling to get to his feet. "Lie down," Stone said. When the man continued to get up, Stone hit him with the gun. He went down and lay quiet. "Arrington!" he yelled. He looked around for her. The two Bruce brothers lay near the sofa, bullet wounds in the back of both heads. There was blood all over the floor. "Arrington!" he yelled again, and went into the kitchen. Nothing there.

He went to the bedroom door and tried it. Locked. He stood back, pivoted off his right foot, and drove the left into the door, just below the lock. The door burst open, and he rushed in, the pistol out in front of him. Something was coming at him from his left side, and he hit the floor to get away from it, struggling to get the gun up. Something struck the floor near his head.

Then he saw he was aiming at a naked woman holding a baseball bat. "Arrington!" he shouted, throwing up an arm to ward off the blow.

She froze. "Stone? *Where the hell have you been?*"

He got to his feet, stuck the gun into his pocket, and took her in his arms. "I'm sorry I took so long," he said.

She sagged into his arms. "It's okay," she replied. "As long as you made it."

He laid her across the bed and pulled the bedspread over her. She seemed to have fainted. When he was sure she had a pulse and no wounds, he went back into the living room. The man he had hit was on his feet. Stone aimed the gun at his head. "I'm not going to tell you again to lie down! Spread-eagle, now!"

The man obeyed.

Stone frisked him, found a knife, threw it into the kitchen. There was a roll of duct tape on the kitchen counter; he went to the man and taped his hands behind his back. "You just relax," he said. "I'm going to get you some help."

He found the phone and dialed 911.

"Nine-one-one," a woman's voice said. "Which emergency service do you require?"

"Police," he replied.

"Police," another woman's voice said. "What is the nature of your emergency?"

Stone looked around him, uncertain how to sum it up. "My name is Stone Barrington; I'm a retired police officer. There are four men shot at Ten-eleven Fifth Avenue, Apartment Nine-A, three dead, one wounded. I need an ambulance and the police." She started to ask him some other questions, but he hung up and called Dino at the 19th Precinct.

"He's on his way home," a clerk said.

"Thanks." Stone hung up and called Dino's portable phone.

"Bacchetti," Dino said.

"It's Stone. You'd better get over to Arrington's apartment; I've got a fine mess for you."

"Is Arrington all right?"

"Yeah, she's okay. The Bruce brothers are not, and I've got one dead wiseguy and one wounded."

"You call nine-one-one?"

"Yeah."

"I'll be right there." Dino punched off.

Stone took a moment to look around the apartment. A laptop computer sat on Arrington's desk, connected to her printer. A single sheet of paper lay in the out tray; he picked it up and read it. Next to the computer was a stack of three Federal Express packets, one addressed to the NYPD, one to the *New York Times,* and one to the Commissioner of Internal Revenue. After reading the final issue of *DIRT,* it was not hard to figure out what was in them. He picked up two of the packets, went to Arrington's large handbag on the floor beside the sofa, and tucked them into the bag. Then, starting to feel shaky, he sat down on the sofa and took a few deep breaths. His face and his hands were sweaty; he tucked the pistol into its holster, got a handkerchief from his pocket, and began to mop his face. Then he began to feel nauseous. He bolted for the bathroom.

Chapter 59

The bicyclist pulled up a couple of doors down from the address he had been given and got off the machine. It was a ten-speed racing bike, and he was dressed to use it—tight cycling pants, a nylon jacket, a helmet, and very large yellow-tinted goggles. He leaned against a tree and waited, consulting his watch. Half an hour passed, then the woman emerged from the building, just as he had been told she would, dressed in a ball gown and a fur jacket. The chauffeur braced at the rear door of the Mercedes S600; she got into the rear seat, and the car pulled away from the curb.

"We're going to the Plaza Hotel, Paul," Amanda said. "I expect to be there until about eleven. We'll go to the front door."

"Yes, ma'am," Paul said. "Mrs. Dart, would you mind if I stop at a drugstore and pick up some aspirin? I'm getting a headache."

"Of course, Paul; we have time." Amanda pressed the switch that raised the rear sunshade, giving her some privacy, then leaned back, her neck against the headrest, and took some deep breaths. Amanda could sleep in seconds, and she often took advantage of slow automobile trips in Manhattan, where the average speed of traffic was four miles per hour, to rest. "I'm going to take a quick nap, Paul," she said. "Please don't disturb me until we're arriving at the Plaza."

"Yes, ma'am," Paul replied.

Amanda liked to think of something pleasant

as she fell asleep. She thought about her lunch date with Dick Hickock the following day, and it made her smile.

The cyclist followed the car down Lexington Avenue; traffic was heavy. The car stopped for two lights, but the cyclist wasn't happy with the lay-out of traffic. Then something good happened. The chauffeur double-parked in front of a drug-store, put his emergency blinkers on, got out of the car, and went into the store. Perfect.

The cyclist maneuvered to the right of the car, where the woman was sitting, her head against the headrest, her eyes closed, mouth slightly open. He checked the door lock button; it was up. He stepped off the bicycle, leaned it against a parked car, and reached under his jacket. His hand emerged holding an icepick. The chauffeur's ab-sence made his pistol unnecessary.

Quietly, he opened the rear door of the Mercedes. The woman seemed to be sleeping. He took a wad of Kleenex from his jacket pocket, then, holding her head back with his left hand on her forehead, he drove the icepick up her nose and into her brain. Her eyes opened wide, but she didn't have time to cry out, or even to move. He jerked the handle of the icepick back and forth, in order to do as much damage as possible. She slumped, and a trickle of blood ran from her nose. He stanched it with the Kleenex, and she stopped bleeding. Her heart was no longer pumping blood.

He closed her eyes, then noticed the diamond necklace. He gave it a short, sharp jerk, and it came away in his hand. Then he shut the car door, got onto the bicycle, and pedaled away down Lexington. At the next corner he turned east, stopped, and looked back. The Mercedes passed him; the driver did not look alarmed. The cyclist smiled to himself and moved off.

The big car rolled to a stop in front of the Plaza. It was a gala benefit evening, and limos crowded the front door area, depositing their gorgeously dressed passengers. The hotel's doorman stepped up to the Mercedes and opened the rear door.

Amanda Dart's body rolled slowly out of the car into the gutter, now nothing but dirt.

Chapter 60

Stone was lying on Arrington's living room sofa, a damp washcloth across his forehead, when Dino walked into the room.

"Am I disturbing you?" he asked.

Stone opened his eyes. "Do I really have to get up and talk to you?"

Dino looked around at the carnage. "I think maybe that would be a good idea," he said. The sound of approaching sirens came, muffled, through the walls.

The last of the bodies was wheeled out of the apartment. Stone and Dino stood in the kitchen. Stone reached into the printer tray and handed Dino the sheet. "I thought you might like to read the final edition of *DIRT*," he said.

Dino read the document twice, then Stone handed him a Federal Express packet. "This is addressed to your department," he said, "so I didn't open it, but I expect it contains some backup for the charges in the scandal sheet."

Dino opened the packet and leafed through a dozen sheets. "Well," he said, "Mr. Richard Hickock has been a bad boy, but there's nothing in here for me. Federal income tax evasion isn't against the laws of New York State. I'll forward it to the FBI. Eventually it'll find its way to the proper law enforcement agency, I'm sure."

"Hickock could grow old while that happens," Stone said.

"Oh, they'll get around to it."

"You think you'll be able to get anything out of the wiseguy I wounded?"

"Who knows? We'll see what's on his yellow sheet, see what we have to bargain with. Maybe he'll hand me somebody."

"My bet is that a bullet from the nickel-plated twenty-five with the silencer killed Arnie Millman."

"I wouldn't be surprised. We'll see."

They made ready to leave. "Arrington!" Stone called out.

"Coming," she called back from the bedroom.

"How's the new apartment?" Stone asked.

"We're moving in in a couple of weeks," Dino replied. "Mary Ann is going nuts, buying stuff. Did you know Ralph Lauren makes wallpaper? I didn't."

Arrington appeared with a suitcase, walked over

to Stone, set down the case, and leaned against him. "I don't want to live here anymore," she said.

"You don't," he replied.

They made their way slowly downtown in a taxi.

"Pull over here for a minute, will you, driver?" Stone said. The cab pulled over to the curb. Stone reached into Arrington's bag, retrieved the two packets, got out of the car, and dropped them into a Federal Express bin.

"What was that?" Arrington asked when he was back in the cab.

"Oh, just jump-starting the wheels of justice," he replied.

"So it's over?" Arrington asked.

"It is," Stone said.

"No loose ends?"

"Well, yes. There's the murder of Martha McMahon, Amanda's secretary."

"*Murder?* You think Amanda pushed her?"

"That's my best guess, but nobody will ever be able to prove it. Amanda will get away with it."

She took her hand in his. "Stone, my darling," she said, "if I've learned anything in my life, it's that nobody gets away with anything. Ever."

He turned and kissed her lightly. "I hope you're right," he said.

IF YOU HAVE ENJOYED READING THIS
LARGE PRINT BOOK AND YOU WOULD
LIKE MORE INFORMATION ON HOW TO
ORDER A WHEELER LARGE PRINT
BOOK, PLEASE WRITE TO:

WHEELER PUBLISHING, INC.
P. O. BOX 531
ACCORD, MA 02018-0531